THE
FUGITIVES

ROBERT GRIFFITHS

Grosvenor House
Publishing Limited

This book is published by
Grosvenor House Publishing Ltd
Link House
140 The Broadway, Tolworth, Surrey, KT6 7HT.
www.grosvenorhousepublishing.co.uk

This book is a work of fiction. Any resemblance to
people or events, past or present, is purely coincidental.

A CIP record for this book
is available from the British Library

ISBN 978-1-83615-201-9

Dedicated to Kathy

1

A man with a lot on his mind had been trying hard to chill out but it was proving to be a difficult task. He'd spent the afternoon on a sun lounger reflecting on the vicissitudes of life, thinking of its ups and downs, successes and failures, happy and sad moments. He'd also been contemplating his current situation. While mulling over both the past and the present he felt concerned for his future, something that was now so much more uncertain and unpredictable than it had once been.

Sins of the past, misdemeanours he'd tried so hard to cover up and forget, had resurfaced to alter the course of his existence, probably forever. For reasons known only to himself he'd hurried off to the other side of the world desperately hoping to seek help from an old friend who turned out to be invaluable when he was in Argentina. Tomás sheltered him and assisted in his crossing the border into neighbouring Chile. Eventually the man on the run found himself in Mexico City. It was here where fate brought him into contact with two people from a very different world to his own. His first encounter was with an ex-military man who'd become a professional bodyguard. The second person he met had disparate roles. Ostensibly, he was a successful businessman with interests in construction and farming but, behind this respectable façade, he was one of the most powerful drug lords in South America. Recent weeks had been a whirlwind of upheaval and incredible danger.

As the man soaked up the last rays of the afternoon sunshine he had much to ponder. He had a new job and a different identity. He started thinking back to a month ago and pictured himself with his wife clearing autumn leaves off their garden in England, both contented and happy, but his home, his former workplace and the country of his birth were now history. Deserting Lucy pained him the most, she didn't deserve what he'd done to her but he couldn't have stayed.

Today, holed up in America, he had no woman in his life and no family or close friends nearby. California was different but it seemed as good a place as any to start out on a second life. Lying low and keeping his head down the man had been learning the wine industry but, before long, he hoped he could break free from the shackles of his current existence. *But what did his future hold?* The man was now a trainee wine manager, it was quite a fall in status. He reckoned he'd get used to it, but deep down he knew he'd messed up, screwed up big time. Loving wife, highly-paid job, comfortable lifestyle, all gone!

The man gazed wistfully towards the sky and the hills in the far distance. A setting, copper orange sun, half hidden below the horizon, created beams of streaky light over the sprawling lines of vines. Shadows cast by tall pine trees were becoming longer by the minute as the warmth of the day faded away. All was quiet and peaceful but that wasn't how the man felt inside. He kept on reminiscing about a place he'd rather be. He yearned for those happy days when clouds of differing shapes, sizes, colours and textures would scurry across the open skies of East Anglia, blown by the wind towards the cold waters of the North Sea. He was more used to the showers and stormy blasts of autumn in a country thousands of miles away on the other side of a continent and an ocean. He longed for the changing sights, sounds and smells of his homeland at a time when much of the world of nature would be shutting down as winter beckoned. The everyday sunshine was all very well but it wasn't what he was used to, or where he felt calm and contented, in harmony and at peace with his surroundings.

But, before long, life for the man in hiding was to become turbulent once more. Today, and the last few weeks, had been a temporary reprieve because the winds of change were about to whip up and transport him into unchartered waters. He was soon to be cast into a world he never would have expected to experience, even in his wildest dreams.

2

MID-DECEMBER

CAMBRIDGESHIRE POLICE HEADQUARTERS

Outside Police HQ in Huntingdon it was dank, dark and distinctly uninviting. DCI George Watling, the force's Head of Homicide, stared out of his office window at the relentless rainfall that lashed down from a leaden sky. Raindrops bounced off the tarmac on the car park and ricocheted off the roofs of surrounding buildings. Sheets of silver sheened water rolled over the tiles into gutters that overflowed, unable to cope with the incessant downpour. It was one of those days to stay indoors if at all possible.

Watling had spent the last half hour perusing a crime dossier involving his most recent investigation. Seven weeks ago, a human skeleton had been unexpectantly unearthed close to a demolished farm cottage. The remains, discovered by builders clearing the site for redevelopment, belonged to a young woman who'd been on a 'MISPERS' list for a very long time. The unfortunate victim had eventually been identified as a Cambridge University drop-out who'd been part of a group of hippies during the late sixties. The case had been solved, at least in the eyes of the force's top brass, but Watling wasn't at all convinced. Today was his lucky day. Earlier he'd received an e-mail from police colleagues in London with information that confirmed his doubts. He glanced again at the non-stop rain beating on the window before reaching for his mobile, time to contact DS Lester, his chief assistant.

'Hi, Pen, I need to see you, ASAP, are you free?'

'Sure, no problem, be with you soon, boss,' she replied helpfully. 'I'm about to get a coffee. Bring you your usual, shall I? Flat white, no sugar?'

'Yes please.'

Ten minutes later the tall, imposing figure of Penny Lester appeared outside Watling's door with a cardboard tray containing hot drinks. As was her custom she knocked firmly before entering his office. Once inside she plonked herself in the seat positioned directly opposite her boss and waited for him to lead the conversation. Watling leaned back in his comfy leather chair, hands behind his head, a broad smile breaking out all over his face. Time to impart some good news to his colleague.

'Well, Pen, I received an e-mail this morning from the Met. After reading it I immediately rang the CPS.'

He went on to say the Crown Prosecution Service had informed him that the ex-hippy, drug addict and alcoholic, Benny Hayes, would be standing trial next year but that wasn't the best bit. He would now be facing more than the one charge. They too had been contacted by the Met. After the legal team had sifted through all the evidence accumulated by the police, Hayes was not only going to be charged with perverting the course of justice by assisting in the illegal burial of a body, thus contravening the Burial Act of 1857 but, on the basis of all the injuries sustained by the unfortunate victim, he was also to be accused of manslaughter, and maybe even murder. His lawyers would have to prove his innocence. According to the CPS, the Cambridgeshire police, working together with the Met, had built up a very strong case and a wealth of evidence had stacked up over recent weeks. They'd been extremely busy down in London. Watling's broad smile grew even wider.

'Hayes's appearance in court, it's being hurried up, it'll be in the first half of next year, April looks most likely. New witnesses have appeared apparently, after hearing or reading in the media about the Fen View incident. Some guy who used to know Hayes really well has come forward along with others who could provide useful testimonies for the prosecution. They've all been interviewed. Old associates of Hayes have come out of the woodwork. They've given lots of detail on life at Fen View. It seems that our man has quite a few more questions to answer about what he got up to.'

'So, you reckon we might yet be able to nail the bastard,' exclaimed Lester.

'You bet! He'll be given a rigorous examination in court and with the Met having come up with additional evidence, well, it sounds like the CPS will be able to go after him in a big way. One guy reckons Hayes was there, in the cottage, when it all kicked off. This bloke was told by some woman that Hayes was actually in the place and that he was involved in what happened that day,' said Watling jubilantly. 'They're trying to trace this lady ... but no luck so far.'

3

THE NEW YEAR

John Jones, despite all his misgivings and negative thoughts, had settled in well to a new life in California. Over the last few months he'd purposely kept a low profile in the secluded Napa Valley hideaway up in the sparsely populated country north of San Francisco. His only regular daily contact had been with Ramon Fernandes, the manager of Tomás's latest winery venture. He saw Ramon's wife, Maria, from time to time as well. Roughly about the same age and with a shared interest in viticulture all three soon built up a good working relationship. John had also met members of the estate's labour force, a mixture of farm workers, office and warehouse staff but his social network went no further than that. When introduced to anyone Mr Jones was always referred to as an English friend of Tomás Rodriguez and was learning the wine trade with a view to becoming a future member of the company's management team.

In November John started studying all aspects of the industry and had accumulated an impressive amount of knowledge regarding production methods and marketing strategies. In the pleasantly mild winter temperatures of northern California he'd spent the last week with Ramon walking around sprawling vineyards on the estate that stretched their way along the valley. He'd been instructing John on the different forms of irrigation used from traditional 'old school' furrows and canals to sprinkler systems, drips, and the latest methods of fertigation, a process whereby computer-controlled amounts of water and fertilisers are fed to the vines. Recently he'd also been informed of the many bacterial, parasitic and fly-borne diseases that attacked the plants. John was a willing and able pupil. He was in his element in many ways, it wasn't medical science but it was an interesting combination of chemistry and biology. It was like returning to school or college. John was a student again but, aged fifty-one, very much in the mature category. Life, after all the recent turmoil, was beginning to feel good in the confines of the winery.

It was shortly after midday and John was standing in the main bedroom of his annexe home ready to take a shower when he heard a knock on the door. Grabbing his dressing gown, he hurried downstairs, it was Maria. Things were to about change dramatically. She told him there'd been a phone call from his friend in Mendoza, Argentina's wine capital.

'Tomás, eh! What did he want, Maria?'

'He seemed excited and said that you should go online to check out your local and national newspapers in England. Here, I scribbled some details down for you.' She passed him a scrap of paper.

John was intrigued to know what Tomás was referring to. After thanking Maria, he hurriedly switched on his laptop, the shower could wait. John looked down at Maria's notes and typed the words 'Benny Hayes, Cambridge, England' into the search bar. Various links to press articles came up on the screen. He clicked on the first, and began reading details concerning an ex-hippy with that name who was awaiting trial, he'd been charged with the illegal disposal of a body. Human remains had been found next to a farm cottage that had been knocked down close to Cambridge. Open-mouthed and not quite believing what he was reading, the story focused on a now elderly man who had once been the head of a commune of hippies back in the sixties. The account was all about the body of a young woman being accidentally exhumed during the clearance and subsequent redevelopment of John's old home at Fen View. The dead female's name was Sara Barrington-Webb. Apparently, she'd died in a tragic accident, over fifty years ago back in 1969, and had been illegally buried by Hayes and someone else called Roger Tyson. John's immediate thought was: *Why had he rushed off in such a mad panic to Argentina at the end of last October?* The body that had been discovered dated back to the nineteen-sixties. It had nothing whatsoever to do with him. *Did this mean that he was in the clear? Could he maybe return to England? But how was he going to explain his decision to do a runner to both Lucy and the hospital as well as the police? More importantly than all that: Where was the body of Suzy Wong? Presumably still undisturbed and unfound?*

It didn't take long for John to realise that, incredibly, there must have been two bodies buried close to the cottage. Only one had been discovered by the builders and the police ... and it sure wasn't his dead Filipina ex-girlfriend, Suzy.

4

The Christmas and New Year celebrations had come and gone, the winter daylight hours in England were becoming that little bit longer, it was late January. At police headquarters Watling was deep in conversation at his customary morning briefing session with Penny Lester. Despite there being other crimes to discuss and solve, attention was once again drawn towards Fen View Cottage.

'Any news on Doctor Ripley?' asked Lester.

'Nothing whatsoever, it's been over three months since he did his disappearing act. I'm sure there's more to it than him just being stressed and fed up with his medical duties and wanting to carve out a new life on the other side of the world. He was a respected and highly-paid consultant who was good at his job by all accounts. Why would he want to give that up? According to his wife they had a happy marriage, why run out on her then? It doesn't stack up, does it, Pen?'

'I agree, so what you going to do about it, boss?' Lester knew that Watling could be like the proverbial dog with a bone when he really got stuck into a particular investigation and she reckoned he wasn't about to let go of this frustrating case any time soon, despite the wishes of superiors like ACC Hoskins.

'Don't you worry, Pen, I've been doing plenty of thinking over the last few weeks. Yesterday, I rang up that property developer guy, Charles Black. He's still having the Fen View site turned into his new home but building operations have stalled apparently, lack of materials from abroad, he sounded pretty hacked off.'

'So, you reckon on having another look around the area, during the delay, ... am I correct?'

'Too damn right, Pen. We need to do it before the builders move back in. I'm thinking of asking for a GPR survey.'

Watling went on to explain what GPR was. Lester, although now a seasoned detective with several years of experience, had never come across it before. He said it was a ground penetrating radar survey. High frequency radio waves pass into the soil to form a 3D image of what might be below. It would show if there was anything else under the Cambridgeshire clay that the police should know about.

'The other thing we could use is corpse-sniffing dogs.'

'Are you kidding me?' asked Lester. 'Are you seriously thinking ANOTHER body might be buried in that patch of land?'

'Exactly! What if Ripley buried someone twenty years after Hayes did?'

'Possible I suppose, if pretty unlikely. But, OK, if this is your hunch, well, let's bloody go for it then, nothing ventured nothing gained and all that,' said Lester enthusiastically.

'We'll try the cheapest option first, that's the dogs, but if they don't come up with anything we'll use GPR. Time to call someone, Pen.'

Watling picked up his desktop phone and rang the officer in charge of the dog teams, a long-serving Sergeant who got on better with animals than he did people, a quietly spoken man called Rory Dickson. He quickly explained what he wanted doing and filled him in on the important case details. Rory's team would be over there first thing in the morning. Watling agreed to meet him onsite, accompanied by Lester.

'See you tomorrow, sir,' said Dickson.

'We'll be ready and waiting.'

5

Tomás Rodriguez, looking dapper in a crisp three-piece suit and wearing an expensive designer pair of trendy sunglasses, stepped off the plane at San Francisco's International Airport. Once through customs he hailed one of the many bright yellow taxis parked outside the terminal block. He was off to visit the latest escapade of his burgeoning wine empire, the new estate he'd purchased six months ago in the Napa Valley, outside a small place called Oakville. According to the taxi driver it would be an hour and a half's drive to reach their destination so Tomás sat back to admire the views.

The busy airport is located in San Mateo County overlooking San Francisco Bay, thirteen miles south of the downtown area. It was mid-morning, the traffic was relatively light and Tomás, feeling relaxed but alert on the back seat, was soon passing over Oakland Bay Bridge into Berkeley. Richmond came into view after fifty minutes, it was then on across the Casquinez Bridge into Vallejo and American Canyon. Eventually, the roadside signposts pointed the way to the city of Napa and the straight-line route of the St Helena Highway Number 29 headed northwards into rural farmland and the small settlement that is Oakville.

Tomás hadn't told anyone other than his wife, Lucia, and eldest son, Juan, about his trip to California. He wanted to turn up unannounced, he had three objectives in mind. First of all, he wanted to see Ramon Fernandes to discuss how things were progressing on his new estate. Secondly, he was looking forward to an overdue catch-up with his friend, John, and most importantly, he wanted to pass on some vital documentation to his English companion. Buried deep within Tomás's briefcase, safely tucked away, was a new passport and visa. His criminal friend, Federico Santos, had been busy in the underground depths of his office building in central Mendoza. Hopefully, the replacements would last considerably longer than the original illegal documentation had done. They'd been fundamental to John's escape out of Santiago but now that the authorities knew he might be travelling under the false name of Robert John Adamson in no way could they be used again. Doctor John Ripley was now plain Mr John Jones.

After paying the taxi driver the fare, plus a generous tip, Tomás walked up the dusty driveway to his estate and rang the bell of the manager's house, it was Ramon who answered.

'Señor Rodriguez, what a pleasant surprise! I wasn't expecting a visit, but do come in. Maria, put some coffee on please.'

'Ramon, Maria, it's so good to see you both. We have much to talk about.'

After an hour of drinking coffee and conversation Tomás asked where he could find his English friend.

'I left John in the annexe. He came around the bottling plant with me this morning, we can go and see him now if you like.'

Ramon led the way out of the house and through the garden towards John's home. It was Tomás who knocked on the door. After two taps John opened up and looked out in astonishment at his unexpected guest.

'Tomás! You cunning, old devil,' he gushed. 'Why didn't you let me know you were coming to California?'

'I wanted to surprise you,' responded Tomás with a smile, followed by his customary hearty laugh. 'We need to have a chat.'

'You'd better come in then.'

Ramon left them to it. Tomás reached into his briefcase and handed his friend a package.

'You'll be needing these I think.'

John opened up the sealed envelope and saw immediately it was his new passport and visa.

'Your good friend, Señor Santos, produced them I suppose?'

'He has his uses does Federico. Now that you have the necessary documents, Mr Jones, you can move about a bit. You are no longer Dr Ripley.' He was smiling and making light of the situation as usual. 'You must come and visit me in Mendoza, John. It's harvest time for our grapes before long, you can watch the picking and the treatment of them, see how they are turned into excellent wines. It will be a learning experience and a holiday all in one. I will show you Mendoza and the Andes properly, we'll visit the old colonial city of Cordoba and I'll take you to Buenos Aires to watch some real football.'

'I'd love to return to your beautiful country, Tomás.'

John sounded keen but he had serious misgivings about such a bold move so soon after his Californian confinement. After a few more pleasantries they strolled out of the annexe and headed over to join Ramon and Maria but during the conversations his mind was elsewhere. *Should he risk travelling to Argentina? Perhaps he'd head home to England, see his wife, beg forgiveness, or maybe continue to lie low in California?* Lots of thoughts and ideas were churning around in his head. It was a dilemma, he'd like to visit the beguiling scenery of Argentina once more, but he also had a nagging desire to explain things to Lucy back in England. His head was telling him to continue lying low in California. It seemed by far the most sensible option, but John didn't always do sensible.

6

A bitterly cold winter's morning greeted Watling and Lester as they headed towards the flat, mist enveloped fenlands outside Cambridge. It was time to reacquaint themselves with Fen View after arranging an early meetup with Rory Dickson and his small team of dog handlers. Their purpose was straight forward: the highly trained animals were to survey roughly three hectares of land around where the old cottage had once stood until its recent destruction. Watling was hoping the cadaver dogs would lead them to something of interest deep in the earth where a few months ago the skeletal remains of Sara Barrington-Webb had been discovered.

During the previous autumn's investigations, the police had compiled a long list of past residents going back to the 1950s. The catalogue of names eventually included a young man in his early twenties, John Ripley, a medical student at Cambridge University who'd lived at the place from the summer of 1990 into the early months of 1991. Watling still couldn't quite fathom why Ripley, thirty years later, had decided to rush off to Argentina. It was not the action of any sane, rational man. Something must have rattled him badly. *What had caused his sudden disappearance?* He reckoned it was connected in some way to the now demolished Victorian farm house, a place that might well have hidden a good many secrets accumulated during its long history.

Lester as usual did the driving, it was a short, fast journey along the A14 followed by much more sedate progress on the narrower backroads. On approaching their destination, she slowed the police car down to a crawl before parking up on a frozen grass verge. The detectives had come well prepared, both were suitably dressed in warm clothing ideal for a bleak countryside setting in the depths of winter. From inside the relative warmth of the car they surveyed the uninviting scene outside before slowly opening the doors and reluctantly clambering out.

'Bloody hell,' moaned Lester. 'It's fucking freezing!'

The temporarily abandoned site had the beginnings of a partially completed house in the middle of it. The outer shell of an impressively large property, constructed with a mixture of flint cobblestones and pale grey bricks, had been finished, along with a sloping roof topped with real slate tiles but it looked as if little had been done to the interior of the property. On one side of the building the foundations of what would probably be a large double garage had been completed. No builder or tradesperson was around, the place was completely deserted and very quiet. The surrounding rural landscape lay dormant, locked in the icy grip of an unpleasantly chilly winter's day.

Watling and Lester ambled their way across the hard and rutted ground, treading a path through cold air decorated with wispy bands of early morning mist. Despite the weather they could see that the property's perimeter had been marked by a makeshift fence made from flimsy wooden posts and steel wiring. What would be the eventual garden was a flat expanse of land. No new trees or shrubs had been planted as yet, only a few hardy weeds poked their frosty heads out of the soil.

'We'll use the dogs to cover where the gardens are going to be, we'll also need the area outside the fence looking at. Remember Sara Barrington-Webb was found on what was a patch of waste ground,' remarked Watling.

He walked carefully towards the spot where the skeleton had been unearthed a few months earlier. It was a good fifty metres behind where the cottage had stood. Lester followed gingerly in his footsteps. They soon came across the rectangular pit they'd first seen last autumn, it was to be the future site of a swimming pool. The human remains had been found at its intended deep end. Watling had a hunch there might be something else of a sinister nature buried under the adjacent surroundings, it would be quite a coincidence but not beyond the realms of possibility.

Watling was one of those people who believed in ghosts and the supernatural based upon personal experience. During the investigation the previous autumn police conversations with the locals and interviews with some of the past residents of Fen View had mentioned the appearance of apparitions, both in and outside the cottage. The site certainly had a spooky feel about it. *Perhaps the place had been the scene of a tragedy? Maybe various grisly goings-on had happened at the house that had stood all by itself, bordered only by trees and an ancient wind pump, for one hundred and fifty years before its recent demolition? Many families and individuals must have come and gone with the passing of time since its construction in the 1880s. If only the walls of old buildings could talk* thought Watling. It would definitely make his job a whole lot easier, although it would now be too late for that particularly fanciful thing to happen as the cottage was no more.

He was still pondering the curious idea of walls talking and revealing secrets from the past when a couple of white police vehicles pulled up behind his own car. The detectives walked over to greet the dog handling team. Sergeant Dickson was accompanied by his assistants and in each van an Alsatian sat patiently in the back. Watling knew that the dogs were specifically trained to sniff out bodies at crime scenes or after disasters such as floods and earthquakes. The incredible sensory faculties of this breed enabled them to detect both the dead and persons buried underground, but still alive, after the collapse of buildings. Watling was the first to speak as Dickson climbed out of the leading van:

'Good morning, Rory, I hope your dogs like working in the freezing cold.'

'Bit of harsh weather won't bother 'em. You'd better show us where you want doing, sir.' A man of few words he seemed keen to get down to business.

Watling pointed out the zone to be surveyed. After a brief discussion Dickson announced that the plot would be systematically covered by moving in lines from the road end of the site to the one-time wasteland.

'Start at the back please,' ordered Watling politely. 'The four sides of the intended swimming pool and the zone beyond it is of special interest. That's where the skeleton was found last October. I have a feeling another body, or bodies even, might be buried somewhere in that vicinity,' he added.

'Righto, sir, if that's what you want, we'll concentrate on that first then,' answered Dickson. 'Dave, Eddie, cover the ground in and around where the pool's going to be, look inside the hole and then any land that's within fifty metres either side of it.'

The team proceeded to mark out the area suggested, their initial job would be to examine it thoroughly. The animals were released from the vans and taken on leads across to the frozen mud at the rear of the property. Watling and a shivering, cursing Lester watched on with interest as the cadaver dogs began their work.

The swimming pool was looked at, it didn't take long. For about five minutes they couldn't detect anything, but incredibly, one of the dogs started to bark at the spot where Sara Barrington-Webb had been found. Despite the removal by the forensics team a few months ago small traces of human tissue must still have been left in situ.

'I'm well impressed by them dogs,' said Penny Lester, 'Well, bloody impressed.'

'Me too, that's the exact location where the body was found.'

The handlers all smiled and modestly commented on the skills acquired by good training, it was what the dogs had been taught to do. Their sense of smell was highly developed, it was indeed incredible what they could sniff out. Microscopically small bits of bone, flesh or hair could be detected by their incredibly sensitive noses. According to Dickson they were even able to smell remains buried under concrete, he was happy to impart the fact that an Alsatian has two hundred and twenty-five million olfactory receptors in its nose compared to a human nose that only has approximately four hundred.

'Other than what you've already found the hole is empty,' concluded Rory Dickson. 'We'll move on and look at its four borders.'

The team continued with their task. Much to Watling's disappointment nothing was detected after three sides had been examined. Only one other, the eastern patch of land, was left. After a few minutes of sniffing the ground one of the dogs started to bark and it sat down about five metres away from what would eventually be the edge of the pool.

'What's all the fuss about?' asked Watling excitedly.

'She's found something! She don't bark like that for no reason,' shouted Rory Dickson.

'Bloody hell, boss, you might be right after all!' yelled an animated Lester.

The spot was marked by Dickson with a yellow post that, with difficulty, he hammered into the hard ground. Watling extracted his mobile from his pocket and from a long list of contacts he tapped in Helen Sharp's number. The Head of Forensics answered within five seconds.

'Hi, George, what can I do for you?'

'Helen, you'll not believe this but I think we've found another body, ... at Fen View Cottage!'

7

MARCH

A solitary middle-aged man gazed in awe at the impressive façade of San Francisco International Airport. Sporting a new look: shoulder length hair combed back off his forehead, designer stubble, Ray-Ban aviator sunglasses, smartly attired in a light brown suit, open-necked white shirt and highly polished tan brogues he looked every inch a businessman who'd temporarily jettisoned his tie, or maybe even an off-duty rock star who'd abandoned his denims and leathers. Mr John Jones was about to return to his recent past and he felt, understandably, rather nervous about it all.

If the airport had been constructed to impress the many thousands of travellers who pass through it each year the architects and city authorities had succeeded big time. Made up of shiny white steel and glass panels with a rolling wave-like roof the building is a fine piece of modern architecture, enhanced even further by the futuristic control tower. After checking his flight ticket and latest passport John walked with a sense of trepidation into the equally stunning concourse. The day had finally come to take up Tomás's offer to visit Argentina again. Second time around, he hoped it would be mostly as a tourist instead of a fugitive on the run from the law. It was now four months since he'd been illegally sneaked into California under the cover of darkness by Federico Santos, Brazilian businessman, drugs lord and good friend of Tomás Rodriguez.

It seemed quite a while ago but back in the fall Santos, together with his grateful passenger, had flown into North America with a shipment of cocaine destined for the lucrative markets of California and coastal areas further north, mainly Seattle and Vancouver. Back then no modern state-of-the-art airport had been used. Santos's private jet had touched down on an isolated landing strip cut out of scrubland high up in the Coast Ranges to the west of Sacramento and since last November John had been a man in hiding. Although he'd taken to learning the industry with alacrity, under the tutelage of Ramon Fernandes, he was eagerly looking forward to visiting Tomás's Mendoza operations in western Argentina. He wanted to see the grapes being harvested and observe how they are then turned into wine but he was also desperate to break free from his confinement. It was time to test out the new documentation tucked away safely in his small backpack.

Understandably anxious, John walked over to the check-in desk for Copa Airlines. Having no American bank account or credit cards his ticket had been bought online by Ramon, John refunding him with cash. The stunning news concerning events in Cambridgeshire had been a huge surprise but also a massive relief to him. He felt he might be in the clear over in his homeland but reckoned on proceeding with caution during the transition from hiding in the Napa Valley to venturing out into the wider world. *After all the British authorities could still be on the hunt for him.* He realised that the police weren't fools, they might want to ask him questions about his departure from England. *Why did he leave both his wife and job so suddenly without any explanation for his actions?* It would be construed as a bizarre decision by all those who knew him well. During the last few days he'd been having thoughts about returning to England. *But what did he hope to gain from it? Forgiveness from Lucy perhaps? Highly unlikely!* His workplace might value his expertise but no-one was indispensable and he'd also left them in the lurch, a new consultant would no doubt have been appointed by Addenbrooke's Hospital. After a good deal of thought he'd come to the grim conclusion that begging forgiveness from Lucy and asking for his old job back were not good ideas. They would be the dumbest of dumb ideas. Returning to Cambridge was not an option.

Ramon had only bought a one-way ticket to Argentina because John didn't know exactly when he'd be returning.

Unfortunately, getting there was going to be a long journey with a lengthy stop-over along the way at Panama City's Tocumen airport. The initial flight from San Francisco would take about seven hours, he then had a delay before catching a connection to Mendoza. The onward travel would eat up another six to seven hours. As his plane was leaving San Francisco at around one o'clock in the morning, it would be well into the day by the time John arrived in Mendoza. Tomás had promised to meet him at the airport to then whisk him off to his impressive mansion in the district of Vistalba, south of the city. He'd suggested that John spend at least a fortnight in Argentina but possibly longer if needs be. Despite his nerves at stepping out into the wider world again, John was really looking forward to regaining his freedom and some independence.

Much to his relief going through the usual security checks and gaining entry to the departure lounge proved a breeze. The fake passport worked well even if the photograph showed a different looking John. Gone was the short-cropped hairstyle and the clean-cut look. In California he'd let his dark hair grow long compared to the more conventional and tidier style he'd previously favoured but, if passport control could be believed, it seemed that the old Dr Ripley had morphed seamlessly into the new Mr Jones.

The plane left San Francisco on schedule and landed in Panama by breakfast time. John decided to visit one of Tocumen's cafes and spent his time sipping coffee and reading a book about wines from different regions of Argentina and neighbouring Chile. Thankfully, the connecting flight was also punctual and by the end of the day he was in Mendoza, the long journey ending with the Boeing 737 touching down at El Plumerillo International Airport on its northern outskirts. Once again travelling through customs was easy, Tomás soon spotted his English companion coming out of the arrivals area.

'John, over here, over here!' he shouted while waving at the same time.

The recently titled Mr Jones recognised his friend and rushed over to greet him.

'Tomás, good to see you again, and in Argentina too,' he replied with a broad smile.

'Follow me, my car's not far away, did you have a good trip?'

'Damn sight easier than getting out of Argentina last autumn.'

Remembering the hair-raising journey through the mountains a few months ago both men grinned as they headed swiftly to the car park, soon the Rodriguez family's bright red Porsche 911 was travelling along the main road south away from the airport.

'Have you eaten, John?'

'Not since a large breakfast. I had lots of coffee in Panama, to keep me awake.'

'I'm hungry, you must be too, we'll go to my favourite restaurant in the city centre.'

'Sounds good to me!' was John's eager reply. 'Now you mention it, I'm starving. I'm looking forward to visiting your city and vineyards.'

'You will learn a great deal but you'll also see what a wonderful country I live in. I plan to take you to many places,' replied Tomás with his familiar hearty laughter.

'Hey, isn't that the industrial estate where we dumped my hire car last year?'

'Yes, you're right, I hope it's still there, but I haven't been to find out!' joked Tomás. 'Do you want perhaps to pick it up and return it maybe?' he added laughing.

'Yeah, very funny, Tomás. Let's hope it hasn't been found and the police don't know that I stopped for a while in Mendoza.'

Both men were smiling and laughing, good friends reunited.

'The police round here are few in number, crime goes on but is not a major problem, the car should remain hidden until someone decides to buy or rent that old warehouse,' said Tomás.

The Porsche turned off from the main highway that cuts a swathe through Mendoza. Eventually it came to a halt in a wide and leafy tree-lined street called the Avenida Sarmiento where Tomás parked up close to his favourite downtown restaurant.

'We are going to *Azafrán*, the best place to eat in Mendoza. The chef is a magician when it comes to food and its cellars are stocked with Argentina's finest wines,' enthused Tomás. 'Some of them are mine of course!'

'I can hardly wait,' replied John. He felt both hungry and thirsty after his journey.

Initially, at least from the outside, the restaurant looked quite modest with its understated sage green walls and accompanying solitary front window in the same dull green colour, but its rather ornate entrance door, also painted in sage green but with tasteful wrought iron details in front of the tall glass panels conveyed the opposite impression as did the small and arty looking name plaque attached to the wall close by. The friends entered the building and were immediately greeted by the head waiter. Tomás, being a regular customer, was well known and both he and his guest were politely shown to his favourite table in a secluded and private location at the back of the dining area. According to Tomás the building had been tastefully converted from a warehouse for imported delicatessen goods many years ago. Today it has the ambiance of a fine dining establishment, the inside walls being adorned by rack after rack of quality wines and paintings.

'I can recommend everything but I shall ask for the steak wrapped in pastry, beef wellington I think you call it in England, and the crème brûlée is truly fantastic,' enthused Tomás.

'I'll take your advice on the dessert course Tomás but I'm not keen on meats covered by pastries.'

After taking the order, the waiter called for the sommelier to advise on their choice of wine. Tomás knew the sommeliers that worked in *Azafrán*. It was a young lady of smart and attractive appearance who appeared at their table, Tomás had known her for the past six months, ever since she'd started working at the place.

'Ah, Lola, it's always so good to see you again, you're as beautiful as ever, meet my English friend, he's here on holiday and is learning all about our industry.'

Lola was introduced to John. There was an instant mutual attraction, a spark, between them. It had not gone unnoticed by the observant Tomás. After Lola had disappeared to find a bottle of the finest Malbec, he leaned across the table towards John and tapped him on the shoulder as well as gently kicking his foot.

'You like Lola, eh? I see it in your eyes. She is a lovely woman and recently separated from her partner. It is perhaps time for you to find a new lady in your life, as you will surely not be stupid enough to go back to England.'

'You really are a crafty old devil, Tomás. You're right, Lola is gorgeous. When I was reading all the news from Cambridge I did think about returning but, like you say, it would be madness. I now have a new life thanks to you,' replied a smiling John as he looked over in the direction where Lola had departed.

She returned with a vintage bottle of *vino tinto* from the restaurant's cellar. As all three of them had jokingly agreed earlier, it was not to be from one of Tomás's Maipu or Lujan de Cuyo estates. Instead she brought a bottle of Domaine Bousquet Malbec Gran Reserva, a 2018 vintage.

'You'll like this,' said a smiling Lola. 'It will complement your steaks perfectly.'

'Where is the wine from?' asked John as he gazed into her bright blue eyes.

'It's from the Uco Valley, south of Mendoza. Some of the best Argentinian reds come from around a place called Tupungato. The Bosquet family were originally from Carcassonne in the south of France but they moved to Argentina many years ago bringing their skills with them,' she answered knowledgably.

'John is here to see the harvest, he is going to be one of my managers working in Mendoza and California.'

It was the sort of news that Lola was hoping she might hear and she developed the conversation further.

'I'm travelling to the Bousquet estate on Tuesday, perhaps you'd both like to come with me and visit one of the best vineyards in the whole of Argentina?' Lola ventured. 'You can see what you're up against Tomás, and you too John,' she joked.

'I'm busy, I have meetings with my managers and a couple of buyers, but John can do what he likes.' He turned to his friend with a knowing smile all over his face. It didn't take John long to make up his mind on his plans.

'I'd love to join you, Lola, if that's OK with you?'

'Why of course it is! Great, meet me here, at nine, we'll go in my car,' she enthused.

'We have a date, see you on Tuesday. I'll look forward to it.'

Lola smiled and then left them to enjoy their food and the fine bottle of Bousquet. John's love life, which had been non-existent over the last four months, looked to be heading in the right direction. Two hours later he left the restaurant feeling happier and more positive about things. He'd enjoyed a fantastic meal and superb bottle of vintage Malbec with his good friend. To top it all he'd met a beautiful young woman with whom he had an instant physical attraction and their joint interest in the wine business was an added bonus. As Tomás and John walked out of the restaurant after midnight Tomás joked:

'The things I do for you!'

'I'm forever grateful. You are indeed a wonderful friend!'

'I know,' replied Tomás still laughing.

From an upstairs window Lola watched them drive off into the night. She too felt happy. From first impressions she liked the Englishman, she liked him a lot, and she felt sure that the feeling was reciprocated.

8

In England things weren't progressing quite so well for John. His situation with the law was about to get rather tricky. Helen Sharp's forensics team were meeting up with Watling and Lester at the Fen View Cottage site. Standing next to a bright yellow marker post they were staring down at the ground that surrounded it. A bitingly cold wind blew in from the north-east, its source region somewhere in the Arctic.

'This is the spot, Helen, where I believe there might be a second body. Sergeant Dickson's dogs are fantastic,' Watling enthused. 'For forensic reasons, we haven't disturbed anything. We'll leave you to it. Back soon, bye for now.'

'OK, see you before long George, damn good job I brought my winter jacket and a flask of tea with me, it's perishing out here.'

The detectives drove off and found a warm coffee shop in the nearby village of Cottenham. Meanwhile, Helen Sharp together with her deputy, Peter Hamilton-Maxwell, and the more junior members of her team methodically excavated the land under where the post had been planted. It was soon after midday when Watling and Lester returned. On seeing their approach Helen eagerly waved them over.

'George, there's definitely another body here! Maybe this place was once a burial ground?' she questioned.

'But not an official one,' was his brief and rather sardonic response.

Both he and Lester gazed down into a gaping hole that had been dug by a couple of burly police officers. At the bottom skeletal remains of the human kind poked out of the soil. It was an unpleasant sight made only worse by the bitterly cold day that had already chilled everyone.

'Early indication seems to point to this being a woman, somewhere around five to five feet six tall from what I've measured up so far, small to average height,' remarked Helen.

'This is fucking incredible,' blurted Lester, her penchant for using expletives showing no sign of abating. 'Two corpses, both women, and both close together at this God-forsaken place.'

'Do the usual Helen, soon as possible please, give me as much information as you can like you did with Sara Barrington-Webb. I'll let Charles Black know we've found another body on his land ... he'll be delighted, I think not!'

While the detectives returned to headquarters, the forensics team examined the site taking the usual photographs before carefully removing the remains to the laboratory in Cambridge. A few days later they contacted Watling with some information. When his mobile buzzed, he was holding court with his regular team of Detective Constables Jack Cooley and Alice Carmichael, together with Penny Lester.

'Hi, George, I've some interesting details for you.'

'OK, go ahead please. Let me know what you've found, Helen.'

'As we surmised the body is that of a woman, a young woman, aged around twenty we reckon. She's been underground for at least thirty years so that would take us back to the early nineties. Incredibly, wait for it, ... this bit's amazing, George, ... the DNA analysis of bone and skin fragments points to this girl being of South East Asian origin, ... just like the last one! Can you believe it?'

'In my job you have to be prepared for anything, Helen!' exclaimed Watling. 'A woman, young and Asian you say. What an incredible coincidence.'

'Indeed, it is incredible, as you say, George, but that's what it is!'

'Right, many thanks. We now have to track down this woman's name and find out who buried her there. This latest find puts our Dr Ripley right back in the frame big time.'

'It certainly looks that way, George. Keep in touch. By the way, any more news on his whereabouts?'

'We presume he's still in the Americas, but God knows where. He hasn't been seen since he left the airport in Chile under a false name. He must have abandoned the car he hired on his arrival in Buenos Aires but the police haven't found it. We're aware that he caught a plane from Santiago heading for San Francisco but it had to land in Mexico City on the way. He'd managed to change his name to Adamson on a new passport and visa. As we've mentioned before, he must have friends in either Argentina or Chile with criminal connections. Forging official documents is one hell of a skilled job.'

'OK, best of luck with your search. Sounds like he could be in a lot of places. Bye for now.'

'Goodbye to you too, Helen. Oh, one other thing, have you been able to check the dental details?'

'We're working on it, they'll be with you later today, if not it'll be tomorrow, we'll be in touch, leave it to us, George.'

'Great, I'll look forward to hearing from you. Speak again soon.'

He flicked off his phone and conveyed the news to his colleagues. They'd be asking more questions to locals on the Fens and researching any missing young ladies of South East Asian origin. Watling decided to focus on the period around 1990 when Ripley was at Fen View Cottage.

'Get over to the council offices please Jack, you too Alice. Go through the electoral rolls for the Cottenham area in the early nineties. Were there any families with Far East Asian origins? Also, check past records of students with Cambridge University, plus schools and colleges with girls from seventeen to twenty-five with a South East Asian background,' ordered Watling. 'Pen, you're coming with me. We need to visit Bob Hemingway's farm once more. We'll also call in at Addenbrooke's, let's see if anyone can recollect more information on Ripley. Before we go I've a phone call to make to my police friend in Buenos Aires. They need to be looking for the doctor and prioritise it as much as they possibly can.'

'What do you think, boss?' asked Cooley. 'Does this mean that Ripley is a major suspect again? I presume it must do?'

'Too right it does, Jack. It's looking as if Ripley did have a good reason to run off to Argentina in such a rush last October. The clearing of the land must have spooked him. I don't know for sure, of course, but it's looking like he may have buried the body of another unfortunate girl who met her end in that damn cottage,' answered Watling.

'Fucking hell!' Lester spat the expletive out. 'Two bodies, both young women with Far East connections, found in almost the same spot but buried about twenty years apart. What is it with that place? I'm beginning to think the cottage must have had a curse on it. It's weird, … really strange or what?'

Alice Carmichael, embarrassed as usual by any vulgar language, looked distinctly unimpressed by Penny's liking for using the "f-word" far too often. Following in the footsteps of Jack Cooley she gladly headed for the office door. Whilst respecting Lester as a dedicated and highly competent detective she was not one of her favourite colleagues. Watling turned to his sergeant:

'Pen, we need to find Ripley urgently, it's not going to be easy. He's changed his identity, he must have a contact or several in Argentina. If I get the green light to go there again I'd like you to come with me.'

9

The start of the working week saw John visit one of the many *fincas* (farm estates) on the outskirts of Lujan de Cuyo, a few miles from Tomás's home. As it was March the grape harvest was in full swing, it would continue into April. Accompanied by Tomás, John walked around the estate first thing on Monday morning. Long lines of vines, heavy with ripened, juicy grapes, stretched into the distance as far as the eye could see.

Despite the early hour the winery was a hive of activity. The fruit was being harvested by the age-old, tried and trusted method, the use of human labour. About fifty workers, mostly young men, were busily picking clusters of grapes off the vines. Tomás explained that this method caused less damage compared to using machinery and they could be more carefully selected for levels of ripeness. Once chosen the thick-skinned Malbec grapes were put into wooden cases before being loaded onto a truck that took them to the processing plant where they'd be stored and eventually squeezed to extract the juice. According to Tomás a worker would normally pick about five hundred kilograms each working day during the busiest period of harvesting. It had been an early start for the pickers, they'd begun after sunrise at seven-thirty. The best time to harvest is during the cooler temperatures of early to mid-morning. It was ideal for the workers, by the afternoon the temperature is often in the low thirties and the sun's strength is powerful at high altitude.

The Cuyo wine region around Mendoza stands at seven to eight hundred metres above sea level, it's one of the many reasons why Malbec grapes grow so well in the area. Lack of cloud cover and resultant low rainfall are amply compensated for by copious amounts of irrigation water from the numerous streams that flow east off the mountains. Some are permanent courses like the Rio Mendoza but many are only ephemeral, their channels dry for large parts of the year, particularly in winter. Ever since the pioneering days of wine production, started by Jesuit priests in the mid-sixteenth century, the region has developed into a premium location for growing vines.

After lunch the friends headed into a storage area. Tomás was keen to continue John's education:

'Inside this building the grapes are put on conveyor belts where the best ones are selected, they are then crushed and the must, as it is called, is sent to casks where the fermentation process occurs using only native rather than cultured or manufactured yeasts.'

'This is fascinating to watch, Tomás. We should go through all the chemistry, I'll need a flow diagram to help me I think.'

'At first it all seems a bit of a mystery but you'll get your head around everything from learning about the importance of cold maceration for up to twenty-four hours to something we call délestages.'

While John was enjoying his tour and learning a great deal from the highly knowledgeable Tomás his mind was flitting elsewhere. He was thinking about the following day and his meetup with the lovely Lola. He was feeling both nervous and excited as he hadn't dated a woman for what seemed like ages. He was half a century old, he'd been married for a decade but his 'second life', as he viewed it, had begun, and he had to re-invent himself whilst still maintaining some of the old Doctor Ripley. A different name, occupation and home had helped oil the wheels of change. A new woman would be a bonus despite the nagging guilt he still felt for abandoning Lucy. He was worried about what he should tell Lola. *Should he be upfront and honest?* After all, he had a terrible tale to tell if the truth was told. He decided to ask Tomás for his opinion.

'Tomás, you know I'm meeting up with Lola tomorrow. It's going to be a bit tricky, she's bound to ask leading questions. What do you think? Should I be telling her delicate details about my past?'

'It could be difficult. You'd better see how things go my friend. Perhaps you do not tell her too much at first. Anyway, you might end up hating one another after tomorrow! But I think you'll get on well together.'

'You can laugh all you like, you don't have my situation to deal with,' John sighed, rather forlornly.

'Everyone has to deal with their past and what they did that was right and what was wrong. Each one of us makes mistakes, no-one is perfect, John. Only God is supposed to be that and I don't believe in God so there is no-one anywhere in this crazy, crazy, mixed-up world who can honestly say that they have done everything right and never hurt or affronted anyone. We all wish we'd done some things differently. Hindsight is a wonderful thing. Hopefully, if you're a wise man, you learn from the past and are better prepared for the present and the future,' were Tomás's sage words in reply.

John thanked his friend for his thoughts, they returned to Tomás's lesson on wine production.

Later, at the Rodriguez household, John spent a convivial evening with Tomás and Lucia, sitting by the poolside. On the few occasions when the conversation stopped the magnificent snow-capped mountains of the Andes provided a perfect backdrop for moments of reflection. Midnight had come and gone, it was around one in the morning by the time they retired to bed.

Daylight arrived all too quickly. John was up early, he had an important meeting of the romantic kind and, at eleven, Tomás would be welcoming European wine importers. Under a bright blue sky, a light breakfast of *café con leche* (coffee with milk) and *medialunas* (croissants) was served on the balcony at the rear of the house. A little while later, Tomás dropped his friend off at the junction of the busy Avenida Belgrano where it meets the quieter Avenida Sarmiento in central Mendoza. It was five to nine. It would be a short walk down the street to the *Azafrán* restaurant where, on the hour, John was due to meet up with his new lady friend.

'Goodbye, I'll see you later. Enjoy the day out with Lola, you're a lucky man.'

'Thanks, Tomás. I feel like I'm young again, yes, see you later.'

He walked the short distance to the front of the restaurant on the opposite side of the street. As there was no sign of Lola, John decided to sit on the edge of one of large plant pots positioned outside the restaurant and watch the world go by. Pedestrians strolled past, one with a map open, another carried a Spanish phrase book. *Tourists!* Other more formally dressed individuals were walking quickly, some were running. *Residents, workers, not wanting to be late, heading for the many offices in the centre.* Cyclists and motorists also passed by but soon after nine o'clock a white Toyota Hilux pickup truck appeared and sitting in the driver's seat, with the front window wide open, was Lola, a beaming smile across her attractive face. She called out to her companion.

'Hi, John, do you always go around looking so smartly dressed in a suit?'

Her light brown hair with its blonde highlights, her clear blue eyes and bright white teeth all sparkled in the morning sunshine. The temperature was already in the low twenties, it was going to be a hot day. John's own temperature began to rise on seeing Lola.

'I always try to look smart, I have to for my job. Tomás does not employ untidy looking layabouts as his managers you know!' he replied with a laugh.

'Climb in,' said Lola as she opened up the passenger door of the Toyota.

'It seems like pickup trucks are all the rage in these parts. Tomás has one too, he took me up into the mountains in his last year.'

'Such a vehicle is vital for both our jobs, I travel throughout Argentina's North-west, on different sorts of roads, in all weathers, and I need the space to carry boxes of wine to the many places I work for.'

'So, you don't only work at *Azafrán* then?'

'I do much more than that. It pays well but not enough to survive on. I work for different producers and dealers, including your friend Tomás. I also work as a sommelier in other fine restaurants and at the top hotel in the city. My job is interesting and varied.'

Lola drove south out of Mendoza's business and commercial district heading for the Uco Valley and the Jean Bousquet estate, it would take about half an hour. Continuing on the mutually shared theme of the wine industry that had led to their introduction John asked:

'How did you become a sommelier, Lola?'

'After university, I went on several courses and became qualified. I am still learning but I hope to become a Master Sommelier. It is a reasonably well-paid job, it's one I'm interested in and enjoy very much, I'd hate to be stuck in an office or factory. In this part of Argentina there are plenty of opportunities. Wine is THE industry around here. But what about you, John? Tell me why an Englishman is in Argentina.'

This was the part John had dreaded. *What should he say? How much should he tell her? Should he tell her the truth and nothing but the whole truth or maybe modify and embroider it?* He decided that caution would be best, at least for now, he'd only just met Lola and going into detail as to the real reason for him being in Argentina might not be a wise move.

'Tomás, he's an old friend of mine, we met in Cambridge.'

'The place with the famous university, right?'

'That's correct. I studied there and became a doctor. Tomás used to be one too, that's how we met. He came over to England, from Buenos Aires, to learn more about paediatrics. That's what I specialised in.'

'Why change from that to the wine business?'

'I enjoyed being a doctor, it was valuable work, helping children and saving their lives but the hours were long and often stressful. I suppose I'd had enough, I fancied something different and asked Tomás if I could be trained up and possibly work for him.' Part of what he said to Lola was true but it had been twisted to suit the moment.

'Tomás has kept quiet about once being a medic, but he's a private and modest man. How interesting! My father, he too was a doctor, he retired a year ago. He used to work in the centre of

Cordoba, that's a city in the neighbouring state, it's where I was brought up, we lived in the so-called doctor's district, a place called Alberdi. My mother is an academic at the Catholic University in Cordoba, nothing to do with medicine though. She lectures on Italian and English Studies. Her family are all descended from Italians. There are many Italians in Cordoba. My father's family originally came from Spain in the 1700s. It is the same for many Argentinians,' Lola said.

'My mother was Welsh, my father too, both are now dead though.'

'I'm sorry to hear that, John. Have you any brothers or sisters?'

'Sadly no, but I have friends in England and some relatives in Wales. One of my best friends is Tomás. Apart from our medical backgrounds we both love football and I've always been interested in wine, ... drinking it mainly.'

Lola turned towards John and flashed him a smile. She liked a man with a sense of humour, she also liked sport in general, she'd always been an outdoorsy sort of girl. Her beauty had captivated John right from the start especially her radiant, golden brown tan. But most of all it was her lively cobalt blue eyes that he'd immediately fallen in love with when he first saw her standing over him and Tomás at their table in the restaurant. Her eyes were one of her best features but there were also many others, her friendly, bubbly personality matched her good looks.

'We need to turn off here and follow the road into the Uco Valley,' said Lola.

The satnav on the vehicle's dashboard pointed them along minor roads and John, gazing at the sun-bleached landscape outside his side window, noticed signposts pointing towards a settlement called Tupungato. It turned out to be a small town and after passing through its streets another sign indicated that the Bodega Jean Bousquet was a few kilometres down the road. As she liked to drive fast Lola soon turned into the entrance to the vineyard.

'Right, let me show you this place. I'll have to check in at reception first, let them know I'm here, I'm picking up various wines for a hotel and also one of the restaurants I work in.'

'OK, I'll follow you, tell me off if I do anything wrong.' John was feeling happy and relaxed. He liked this lady and unless he was very wrong she appeared to like him in return.

'Do you speak any Spanish?' asked Lola.

'Unfortunately, no I don't, it wasn't on the time-table at my school, something called Latin was but no Spanish, I learnt a bit of French but what use is that to me here,' joked John.

'I will act as translator then. The Bousquet family speak French by the way, they emigrated to Argentina because Malbec grapes perform better here than in the south of France it seems.'

'My French isn't that good, it's pretty useless actually,' added John. He found it amusing and Lola smiled at him.

They walked into the reception area and a young secretary met them.

'*Hola, Mariana. Éste es John, es un amigo*' ('Hello, Mariana. This is John, he's a friend'). Lola went on to ask if she could show her companion around the estate. She'd pick up the cases of wine later. Mariana replied that it was no problem. John then turned towards Lola and asked:

'How many languages do you speak, Lola?'

'Three: Spanish, English and Italian.'

'I speak English and a bit of Welsh ... but only swear words in Welsh! Languages are not my strong point, now science that's a different matter,' responded John with a broad smile.

'Follow me!'

A suitably amused Lola led the way out of the office building and they headed for the vines. Some of the fields had grape pickers busy at work. It was like Tomás's estate the day before but on a smaller scale with around twenty labourers at the most.

For the next hour Lola showed John around the Bousquet winery. She talked about how some of the finest Argentinian Malbec comes from the Uco Valley. She enthused on how the environment was so ideal. Highly fertile alluvial soils, deposited by the Rio Tunuyán and its tributaries over the centuries, and the long growing season were mentioned. Lola extolled the benefits of the bright sunshine that helped to ripen the grapes and concentrate their sugars. Interestingly, the wide temperature range between the heat of the day and the cool of the night suited the grapes and the high altitude of around one thousand metres and above meant that the relatively thin air helped focus the sun's rays on the ground and therefore the grapes. She added that insect pests in the area were very few. John asked about rainfall. Lola replied by saying it rarely happened, but added that the main danger to the grapes was the occasional summer hail storm hitting the normally hot and arid plains of Western Argentina and that's why netting had been installed next to the lines of vines. If needed, it could be pulled over the ripening fruit to protect it from any potential damage.

John was highly impressed with Lola's level of knowledge regarding the vineyard but there was more to come on its history. She said that the estate had only been established thirty years ago. Before that the area was unproductive semi-desert scrubland but Jean Bousquet, a third generation viticulturalist from southern France, had fallen in love with the place after holidaying in the region. He decided that the Uco Valley would be the perfect spot for wine production. He was later joined in his venture by his daughter and her husband. Today the Domaine Bousquet brand produces four million litres each year from all sorts of grape varieties: Sauvignon Blanc, Chardonnay, Pinot Noir, Merlot, Syrah and Malbec. Their impressive *finca* at the foot of the Andes covers two hundred and forty hectares and ninety-five per cent of the wines are exported to fifty different countries.

Later, over coffee in the estate's visitor centre, the pair discussed their interests, particularly sport. Lola regularly went horse riding, she played tennis at a local club and went running with a group of fellow sommeliers. Her life was lived mainly outdoors in the sunshine.

'Do you like horses, John?'

'Well, err, I suppose I don't dislike them,' was his rather understated and ambivalent reply.

'Good, we shall go horse-riding.'

'OK, that's fine Lola, but I haven't ridden a horse for years, the last time was on a Welsh farm, … and I fell off! I also remember riding donkeys on the beach as a child, that was great and a lot safer, you landed on soft sand,' said John with a smile.

Lola laughed and grabbed John's hands.

'Come on, I'll pick up the boxes from reception, we'll drive back into Mendoza, deliver them, then I've the rest of the day off. Riding lessons for you, Señor John, this afternoon,' she gushed.

'Sounds fantastic, lead the way.'

After dropping off the wine Lola told John that he'd need some different clothes to go riding in, he couldn't use his suit and good shoes. She suggested they pay a visit to a certain clothing store not far from her home close to the city centre. John agreed with her, he didn't think his light brown jacket and trousers were suitable but he announced, with a degree of embarrassment, that he didn't have enough money on him.

'Don't you have a credit or debit card?' Lola enquired innocently.

'I don't use them, I prefer cash.' *This could be tricky* he thought.

'You're living in the past, who uses cash in stores these days?'

'You're right, but I stopped using credit cards when I had one stolen,' lied John.

'I'll pay, you can pay me back later.'

'That's really kind of you, most of my money is at Tomás's place.'

By the early afternoon John had swopped his smart work clothes and shoes for a checked cotton shirt coupled with denim jeans, cowboy boots and a *gaucho sombrero* (cowboy hat). Lola too had changed from her summery dress into a casual white shirt, denim jeans, riding shoes and a faded red baseball hat. They headed north out of the city in the pickup truck with the front windows down and refreshing blasts of air blowing into the vehicle's interior. Before long they'd gone from busy streets into wild and untamed countryside that had altered little over the centuries. There were no irrigation canals or sprinkler systems and therefore no vines anywhere, the greening of the desert hadn't reached this particular area. Lola drove along a road that cut a path across a flat, dusty plain where clumps of grass clung onto life in an unforgiving, sun blasted landscape devoid of moisture. There were no trees, it was far too dry for that. In the distance, in the direction of the Andean foothills, deep, steep-sided gullies had been cut into the hillsides. It was as if the rocks had been lanced by a surgeon's razor-sharp scalpel and then pushed apart to create valleys and canyons where rivers sometimes flowed. John marvelled at the scenery, he'd never seen anything like it before.

Lola had a friend who lived in a little village, a miniature oasis. She kept horses and they often went riding at weekends. That's where they were now heading for an adventure that would take them into the wide-open expanses of a landscape sculpted by the wind, sun, meltwaters from the Andes and very occasional rainfall. John was eagerly looking forward to riding out in the wilds alongside the beautiful Lola. He felt happier than he'd been in a long time.

10

'I'd like to talk to Police Chief Diego Mendes please, can you put me through to him?' Watling waited patiently for his international call to be connected to the Policia Federal Argentina (PFA) headquarters in Buenos Aires.

'Señor George, what I do for you? I thought you finish murder case before Christmas.'

'We solved that one, Diego, but unbelievably we've found another body, this one was buried when Dr Ripley lived at the house. I reckon he's responsible.'

'You believe doctor in Argentina? He was, but now be anywhere. We try stop him in Santiago but he go Mexico, the police, they no find him. He then go America. What happen there?'

'The simple answer is that I don't know for sure but I believe he's either in Argentina or California. I think he's back in your country.'

'But nobody have clue where he be, or what his new name, that big problem, Señor George.'

'OK, Diego, you're right, but I'm re-opening our investigations into Dr Ripley. I wanted to inform you, please keep looking for him in Argentina. I'm asking the Californian police to do the same.'

'I have little manpower, Mendoza long way from Buenos Aires, we big country, many, many times bigger than you. No wonder you want keep Malvinas! You no evidence that Ripley doctor kill anyone I suppose?' Mendes was still laughing about his Falkland Islands joke when Watling replied:

'Not as yet.'

'OK, OK, we try but it not top priority you understand. Now is March, you here four month ago. Ripley change name and look, I think. It small chance we find him. I not promise miracle, Señor George.'

'I understand what you're saying, Diego, just do what you can please. I may see you in Argentina before long. Goodbye for now.'

'Ádios, Señor George, it be pleasure work with you again.'

Watling disconnected and, uncharacteristically, slammed his fist on the table. He wasn't so much frustrated by Diego Mendes but by the fact that he didn't know more about Ripley's whereabouts. He made the same call to a police chief in San Francisco. While listening and showing understanding the case would also be low down on their list of priorities. There were far too many other higher profile and more serious issues to consider in California involving their own American citizens. The disappearance of an English doctor, who may or may not have committed murder, did not figure high on their list of 'things to do.'

Half an hour later, Watling, accompanied by Lester, was on his way to Bob Hemingway's farm out on the Cambridgeshire flatlands close to the site of Fen View Cottage. As usual he made the police most welcome and was happy to talk to them.

'I thought all this had been sorted and that silly bugger Hayes was responsible for burying the girl, maybe even helping to kill her. Lucky sod seems to have got away with it too by the sound of things,' said Hemingway. 'Unbelievable it is. I watched the news coverage on TV,' he added for good measure.

Although he hadn't done it intentionally, Hemingway had hit upon a raw nerve but Watling refused to enter into a conversation about last autumn's Fen View case or the forthcoming court appearance for Benny Hayes. He'd come to visit the elderly farmer to announce that another body, also of a young Asian girl, had been found close to where the first had been discovered. Hemingway was understandably shocked by this latest revelation. Watling told him she'd been buried at about the same time when the medical student, John Ripley, had lived in the old cottage.

Hemingway couldn't add anything of note to what he'd already told the police. He'd never seen any Asian girl at the cottage in the six months that Ripley was there.

'Come on, Pen, let's try Addenbrooke's, we might have more luck there, let's hunt down that nurse, Mary Waring.'

They drove away from the rural expanses surrounding Cottenham and headed to the hospital on the other side of Cambridge. Fortunately, Sister Waring was on duty and she could spare them ten minutes. The elderly nurse was approaching retirement, she'd been working at Addenbrooke's since the eighties. She was 'part of the furniture' was how a junior colleague had described her to Watling and Lester when they arrived at the paediatric ward.

Mary Waring proved to be a jovial and obliging character. She was carrying far too many pounds in weight for the good of her own health but she was one of those many nurses who seem to put the interests of their patient's health before their own. She'd scurried down one corridor, up a flight of stairs, and along another before meeting the detectives and was out of breath when she greeted them in a small office adjoining the ward.

'I'm told, ... you'd like to, ... see, ... me,' the nurse panted as she blustered her way into the room. 'I'm Sister Waring by the way, ... please call me Mary,' she gasped between gulping in breaths of air.

'It's good to see you, Mary. I'm DCI Watling and this is DS Lester, we won't keep you long, we appreciate you're a busy lady.'

'Police again, eh! Is it about Dr Ripley?'

'Yes, it is, I fully understand that you spoke to my colleagues about him last October but I was hoping you might be able to tell us a little bit more.'

'What do you want to know exactly? I told your young detectives that John was an excellent doctor, he was well respected by all the staff and patients. When he left so suddenly, well, it was such a shock to everyone. It was so unlike him.'

'We know he went off to Argentina. I believe he had an Argentinian doctor friend who worked in this hospital for a while and that you knew him. Is this correct?'

'It was a long time ago, the doctor from Argentina was with us for less than a year. I checked the hospital records for your officers. I couldn't find anything, there were no details of him ever being here.'

'So, you remember this doctor but not his name or anything much about him, is that right Mary?'

'That's true, I wish I could be more useful, I'm so, so sorry,' answered a worried looking Sister Waring. She was a lady who liked to please people rather than disappoint them. It was in her nature to try to make people happy, it was her job to comfort her patients, to improve their lot and hopefully make them better. Like her Watling was also good at his job, he was a man who didn't give up easily and he persisted with his questioning.

'I realise that we're going back a while, Mary, but aren't there any people in the hospital that worked with John Ripley, and the Argentinian doctor also? Maybe they still work here? If they've moved on where did they go to? Are some now retired but still living in or around Cambridge? It must be possible to contact them? Any information, no matter how small, might help in our inquiries,' pleaded Watling. 'Please, think hard, Mary.'

'Well, in those days, it was a Dr Heslop who ran things, he retired and sadly died, poor man. The other doctors on the ward were Dr Shah, he returned to India, and Dr Alazawi who moved up north. I can only remember the first names of the nurses. Many have either retired, left the profession or moved on to other hospitals, a few had babies and didn't return to work.'

'This Dr Alazawi, he sounds an interesting possibility. Is there any way you can find out where he went to?' asked Watling.

'Give me five minutes, I'll ring our admin block and see if they have anything.' She rushed out and returned in a breathless state about ten minutes later. 'You're in luck. His full name is Amir Alazawi, he left us in 2007. Our records say he transferred to the Royal Children's Hospital in Manchester, it was a promotion.'

'You've been most helpful, Sister Waring, Mary, I mean. We'll take up no more of your valuable time, but we may want to speak to you again. Many thanks.' Watling and Lester, pleased to have a lead at last, left the hospital feeling more positive about the Ripley case. They headed swiftly back to police headquarters.

Watling immediately rang up the Manchester force, he explained who he was and the reason for contacting them. He asked if an officer could go to the children's hospital in order to see Dr Alazawi and inform him to expect a call from a DCI George Watling of Cambridgeshire CID. They needed to reassure the doctor it was nothing to do with him personally but an ongoing investigation connected to the period when he was at Addenbrooke's. They were to make it a top priority please. The doctor had to be made aware this was legitimate police business, it wasn't a hoax or indeed someone being nosy trying to find out confidential information. He asked Penny to check online to find the medic's contact details. Sure enough, she soon found an e-mail address and a telephone number for his department. He was now Professor Alazawi with an impressive string of medical qualifications. Watling told Lester that he'd ring him later after their meeting with Jack Cooley and Alice Carmichael. It would give Manchester police the chance to get in touch with him, he'd then be expecting a call from Cambridgeshire knowing it was genuine.

* * * *

By early afternoon both Jack and Alice had returned after checking electoral rolls from the late eighties and early nineties for the Cottenham area. They'd also contacted the university's administrative offices and all the local schools and colleges that had sixth forms. Unfortunately, they'd found very little from the electoral rolls but their university and secondary education investigation had thrown up plenty of names of Asian female students in the age range from sixteen to twenty-five. It would be a mammoth task trawling through that amount of information. They'd pursue other avenues first. Watling decided to ring Helen Sharp in forensics.

'Hi, Helen, have you any news for me yet?' he asked hopefully.

'We've done a fair bit, George. The girl had similar injuries to the last victim but far less in number. This one had a few broken bones in her neck but not the extensive injuries suffered by the unfortunate Miss Barrington-Webb. As you already know the DNA analysis points to her being from the Far East, either China or maybe the Philippines, that sort of area.'

'If she was from the Far East she might well have been at the university but we've only found records for one missing Chinese girl and she was found alive, thank goodness. Filipina and Thai girls, they've been brought into the UK over many years by traffickers for sex work and cheap labour. Have you found anything from dental records?'

'A complete blank unfortunately. We've built up a picture of her teeth but there's no match-up with any UK dentistry records. All the available dental data has been checked thoroughly, it points to this girl having come from abroad.'

'OK, thanks for that, Helen. Please keep me posted.' He finished the conversation and turned his attention towards his team.

'Helen has nothing of any real use as yet regarding the girl's identity but Pen and I visited Addenbrooke's earlier today. We spoke to Mary Waring, the ward sister, and we have a lead to follow up,' said Watling with a broad smile.

'What's that then, boss?' asked a keenly interested Cooley.

'A Doctor Amir Alazawi. He might be able to tell us something about Ripley and his Argentinian friend. He now works in Manchester but was at Cambridge when the Argentinian doctor was there,' Watling replied. 'I'm going to ring him, you can listen in to the conversation.'

Watling punched a number into his mobile, his call was answered swiftly.

'Hello, Ward 15. How can I help you?'

'I'd like to speak to a Professor Amir Alazawi please. I'm Detective Chief Inspector George Watling from Cambridgeshire CID. He should be expecting to hear from me.'

'OK, hold the line, I'll put you through,' said the ward clerk.

Watling waited a few seconds before he heard the Professor's voice.

'Amir Alazawi here.'

'Hello, I'm DCI George Watling, Cambridgeshire CID.'

'Ah yes, I was told to expect a call, how might I be of assistance to you?'

'It goes back to your time at Addenbrooke's, Professor, you knew a Doctor John Ripley I believe?'

'Yes, Ripley you say, that's right, he worked in the paediatrics team with me. He was extremely competent, always professional and liked by all. I believe he's still in Cambridge, a consultant these days?'

'He was until recently but he left in rather a hurry and went off to Argentina. It happened at the end of last year, he abandoned both his job and his wife.'

'Wow, I didn't know, I'm so sorry to hear that.' He sounded genuinely surprised and upset.

'When you worked with Dr Ripley, I believe he struck up a friendship with an Argentinian doctor who was working at Addenbrooke's.'

'Yes, they were big friends.'

'What I'm trying to find out is the name of the Argentinian doctor. You could help with our inquiries if you could tell me anything about him.'

'Well, he looked and sounded typically Argentinian I suppose, that much I remember. He was a good doctor too, he spoke English as if he'd lived here all his life, he was excellent with the patients and their families but he was only with us for about six months. We knew him as Dr Tomás, spelt without a letter 'h', that was his first name.'

'That's useful, many thanks for that, but we need his surname ideally, unfortunately the hospital doesn't have any records.

Look, maybe this'll help you. I've been checking out common Argentinian second names. Do any of these sound possible to you? How about Gonzalez or Gomez, ... Rodriguez also, ... Fernandes, Lopez and Dias are all very common, ... as is Martinez. Ring any bells with you?' Under the table he had his fingers crossed hoping that he might get lucky. The line went silent, Watling thought he'd been disconnected, but Alazawi's voice broke the momentary quiet.

'Now that you mention it, you've jogged my memory. I seem to recall seeing a letter, it was on the top of an in-tray at the children's ward office. I can picture it clearly. From the list that you've reeled off I've a strong feeling that the envelope was addressed to a Dr Tomás Rodriguez. The first thing I noticed was the strange stamp and postmark. I'm confident that it was sent from somewhere beginning with the letter M, only possible place I can think of is Mendoza. It's amazing what you can remember if you try hard enough, well done DCI Watling for nudging my brain in the right direction!'

'So, you're saying it's a Dr Tomás Rodriguez from possibly Mendoza. That's fantastic! You don't realise how helpful you've been, Professor.'

'Please call me Amir, I'm happy to assist in any way I can. I hope neither of them are in any trouble?'

'I can't tell you the details, police confidentiality I'm afraid, but it's nothing to do with their skills or professionalism as doctors.'

'OK, well if you need to talk again you know where to contact me. I have an important meeting in five minutes, I must go or I'll be late.'

'We'll get in touch if we have to.' Watling ended the call and looked around the table at his colleagues.

'Dr Tomás Rodriguez is the man we need to find, looks like he's based in the city I visited last autumn, we're getting somewhere at long last. I feel another trip to Argentina coming on.'

11

While things were going badly for John back in England the opposite was true in Argentina. He was about to enjoy a riding lesson with Lola out in the wastes of the semi-desert not far from Mendoza. Her sommelier friend, who lived in the small village of Capdevila, owned a paddock where she kept horses, all three were geldings. Lola chose the chestnut and picked the black one for John. From previous experience she knew that *Negro* had the most placid temperament out of all the horses, he would be ideal for a novice rider. John, not being familiar with equine terms, asked Lola what a gelding was.

'You don't want to know!' She smiled before adding, ... 'it's a castrated male by the way.'

'Ouch! The thought of it brings tears to my eyes!'

They both laughed. John had quite a dirty sense of humour that he hid well. He suspected Lola did too but he couldn't be sure of that just yet, he thought he'd better behave himself for now. After leaving the pleasant shade provided by the trees encircling the paddock they headed off in the direction of the Andes. The area north of Mendoza is mainly an arid plain dissected by stream beds that remain dry for much of the year. As it was late summer, the wettest season, the occasional river course had water trickling along it.

Lola led the way across a desolate landscape. Grassy tussocks broke the monotony of loose sand and baked dry mud. They plodded on into more thickly covered scrubland vegetation. Clouds of dust, kicked up by the hooves of the horses, filtered through the still air. They continued along a narrow track that snaked its way between large areas of creosote bush, a hardy drought tolerant shrub. Lola decided to head towards the entrance of a ravine.

'We'll follow this river course up into the hills. It's normally dry but there's always a bit of water flowing along it in March from all the snowmelt in the mountains. The horses will need a drink in this heat.'

'Us too!' added John, wiping his brow.

They journeyed across yet more barren tracts of land and gazed in wonder at the valley sides of the canyon. Impressively large fans of sediment, accumulated over many centuries, formed aprons of debris along the base of the hills. After following the valley route steadily upwards for about an hour Lola decided it was time to rest the horses. They drank from the stream but there was very little grass worth grazing. Lola sat on the river bank next to John, both of them staring down at the shallow dribble of water below their feet. John lifted his head and looked up river, he noticed a signpost pointing to a place called El Relincho Cabagatas.

'Who lives out here in the wilderness?' asked John as he looked into the distance at a small group of buildings that resembled an isolated farmstead.

'It's a riding centre. We could have hired horses there but why bother when I have someone who lends them to me for free.'

'That makes sense,' he replied with a smile.

Earlier, on the journey out of Mendoza, Lola had decided to ask some important questions, she reckoned now would be a good time.

'John, I have something to ask. If we're going to see each other I need to know more about you. You have an air of mystery I think. Tell me, … why have you come all this way to Argentina? What makes a highly educated, well paid doctor switch jobs and become a deputy manager of a wine estate thousands of miles from home?' She smiled and waited for an answer.

John hadn't planned on telling her anything about his past, at least not yet. He preferred to live in the present and think only about the future. But Lola was not only a highly attractive woman, she was intelligent too. He quickly reasoned that if he wanted to keep seeing her it would be better to be honest. He couldn't continue to live a lie for the rest of his life, especially with those who he hoped would be close to him. He decided to tell her the truth, well, most of it. A few white lies about his age and where he was born wouldn't hurt her. He'd already said that he was forty-five when in reality he was fifty-one but he looked good for his age. He'd kept himself slim and fit and he still had most of his hair, it was dark brown with a few flecks of grey and he wore glasses only for reading. He'd mentioned that he was born in Hong Kong, well before the UK ceded it to China in 1997. Detection work by Lola or any other interested parties such as the Argentinian police would be difficult if not impossible. He'd also lied to her by saying his name was John Jones.

'I do have a story to tell you, Lola, you will be shocked no doubt. I hope you will still want to see me after hearing what I have to say.' He'd been looking into her eyes but his gaze switched to the twinkling rivulet of water flowing a few feet below them.

'A few months ago, I had to leave England in a hurry. Tomás has been brilliant, a wonderful friend to me.'

John told her all about the fateful night at Fen View Cottage when he was a Cambridge medical student. Lola never interrupted his story, she just stared at him with increasing concern and disbelief written all over her face. John eventually finished, there was no more to say. It was Lola's turn to speak.

'Wow! I've only known you a short time, but I can't believe that you're a man capable of all that. What an awful mess you were in.' She hugged John. 'Thank you so much for telling me the truth, even if it is so horrible.' Tears began to well up in Lola's eyes.

'Where does all this leave us?' asked John.

'You say you had to give up your job as a doctor but what about your personal life? Did you have a partner, a wife maybe?'

'I do have a wife, we've been married a little over ten years. She knew nothing, she would have been horrified. It was a real shock to me when I saw what was happening at the cottage. The tragedy that happened there was a dreadful incident from my past, one that I've hidden at the back of my mind hoping that someday it would fade away.'

'I can see why you didn't say anything to the police, even to your wife. You had to keep everything quiet, untold. You are now well away from your past. It is difficult for me to take all this in, but I appreciate why you need to move on and start a new chapter.'

'Thank you so much for your understanding, Lola, I'm so grateful. Tomás, he had the same reaction as you when I told him last October. Look, I hope we can still be friends. I'd like you to be a part of my life here in Argentina, maybe also in California. We get along so well.'

'I want that too,' she replied.

They hugged one another, tightly this time, both felt contented in each other's embrace. John decided he should ask some questions of his own.

'Lola, what happened with your ex-partner?'

'We split up and went our separate ways, it was last September, we'd been together for seven years. He's an actor and was always away, usually in Buenos Aires. I thought he was wonderful at first but eventually I discovered he was cheating on me, he had several lovers that he kept quiet about. I became fed up hearing all his lies. Apart from that he was often out of work, money became a problem but that wasn't the main issue. Lies lead to more lies John, life becomes a never-ending stream of deception. Lies destroy people, they destroy relationships.'

'Where's he now?'

'He moved from Mendoza to Buenos Aires to be closer to work and his various women. I haven't heard from him since we split, it's best that way.'

'We both have had our problems, very different ones maybe! I want us to be together. I love being with you, you've made me feel happy again.'

They looked each other in the eyes and kissed, a passionate kiss that lasted until one of the horses suddenly snorted. Laughing, they both looked up at the bright blue sky. It was time to move on, the horses had drunk from the stream and eaten what little there was that was worth consuming of the surrounding grass. After making their way back downriver they returned to the paddock in Capdevila before driving to Mendoza. Lola was working in a restaurant that evening, before then she returned John to Vistalba. They made a date for dinner on Friday. It had been a lovely day but, driving back to the city centre, Lola had a lot on her mind. She liked John, she liked him a lot, but could she really trust him?

12

Watling had spent his morning visiting the scene of an unexplained death. The body of a young man had been discovered in an alleyway in the centre of Cambridge. It looked like yet another drugs-related case but the police couldn't assume that, the incident had to be properly investigated. However, Watling had decided to distance himself from this inquiry, he'd pass it on to DI Pete Rigsby. The Head of Homicide had other fish to fry, an important meeting had been arranged with ACC Hoskins. Watling was itching to visit Argentina once more, he had a good lead to follow and was keen to meet up with the doctor, or ex-doctor, called Tomás Rodriguez. Before discussing his plans with his boss he'd spoken again to Diego Mendes in Buenos Aires. The senior PFA officer had agreed to help his English colleague as much as possible. All men, aged forty to sixty, with the name of Tomás Rodriguez in the province of Mendoza were to be identified by the Argentinian police. Watling felt confident that one of them would lead him to the elusive Dr Ripley. At the meeting he asked Hoskins for the thumbs-up to travel to South America adding that he'd like to take along Lester, having her support could come in useful. He knew he was pushing his luck.

'Well, George, I can see why you want to go there again now that this, this second body has turned up, but the expense, it's not cheap you know, I have budgets to think of,' said Hoskins grumpily.

'I'm confident we'll find Ripley and return him to England. He's got a lot of explaining to do,' implored Watling.

'How long do you think you'll need?' Hoskins still sounded irritable and tetchy about the thought of two of the force's senior detectives travelling to the other side of the world using up some of the county's limited financial resources.

'Can you give me a fortnight, sir?' asked Watling, more in hope than expectation.

'You can have a week, especially if you're taking Lester with you. You'd better make it worthwhile, George. Your last visit turned out to be both a waste of time and money,' replied Hoskins sternly. He wasn't convinced, but a second body and the important lead from Professor Alazawi had tipped the balance in Watling's favour.

'Rigsby will be in charge while I'm away. We'll be back as soon as possible. Many thanks, sir.'

A couple of days later, on Wednesday, Watling and Lester were in the sprawling metropolis that is Buenos Aires. The March weather was hot and muggy, it was still summer in the capital, but they weren't there for long. Within a few hours of their arrival they were travelling to Mendoza on an internal Aerolineas Argentinas flight that took off from the Jorge Newberry Airport, named after an early Argentinian aviator. The second journey, high above the plains of the *pampas* grasslands, didn't take long. Once in the country's wine capital they hired one of the many yellow and black taxis to take them from the airport to the main police station along the busy Avenida Belgrano where they were met by Provincial police boss, Andrés Dias.

'Welcome to our beautiful city,' said Dias cheerily.

'Beats England in March,' replied Watling as he looked around at the wall to wall sunshine.

'Ah yes, your famous English weather, not good, no?' Dias sounded sympathetic.

Dias was a tall man, well over six foot, with broad shoulders, completely bald head, boxer's squashed nose and deep set, piercing, blue-grey eyes. Watling reckoned he was aged somewhere between forty and fifty, slightly younger than himself maybe. Despite his tough guy exterior Dias seemed amiable enough and keen to help the visiting police officers.

'Andrés, you know we're looking for an English doctor, John Ripley, who we believe could be responsible for a murder. He now lives under a different name and was seen at the end of

October travelling to Mendoza from Buenos Aires in a white Ford. That has gone missing, he eventually caught a plane from Santiago. Ripley bought a one-way ticket to San Francisco but the flight had to be diverted to Mexico City due to an engine problem. Unfortunately, the police there couldn't find him. He could still be in that city, or have made it to California, or be here in Mendoza. I think your city is the most likely place otherwise we wouldn't be here. This doctor has a friend, maybe several, in Argentina. He definitely knows someone who is capable of producing a new British passport for him.'

'And you now look for a Dr Tomás Rodriguez,' replied Dias. 'We have men in Mendoza province with that name who forty to sixty, Señor George.'

'Thank you, what you've done already has been most helpful.'

'Three live in Mendoza. Others live countryside on *estancias* or *pueblos*, that ranches or villages,' added Dias.

'Who are the three who live here?'

'One in cement industry, one business and one doctor in hospital. He who you look for I think, Señor George.'

'The doctor, we need to see him urgently.'

'I plan take you hospital now. We see this Dr Rodriguez.'

Watling, Lester and their helpful Argentinian companion headed out of the building towards a parking lot full of police vehicles. Dias confirmed they were going to the Hospital Central de Mendoza not too far away from police headquarters. Sure enough, within ten minutes, they were at reception asking to see a Dr Tomás Rodriguez. They were in luck, he was on duty but had finished seeing his patients for the day. There was one problem however, they'd been directed to the geriatric ward, it sounded rather ominous, it was disappointing news, unless Dr Rodriguez had switched his specialism from the young to the elderly since his time in England. On meeting the doctor Watling soon realised they'd come to see the wrong man. This doctor was too young, he looked forty at the most, he'd never worked on a paediatric ward, either in Argentina or the UK. He'd hadn't heard of a John Ripley. Watling thanked him before they all walked disconsolately through reception and outside back to the parked police car.

'Shit! ... I thought we were onto something. Turned out to be bit of a bum steer,' Lester said with her typical bluntness and taste for colourful language.

'Too damn right, Pen, it's very disappointing, I thought we'd be in luck, but perhaps our Dr Rodriguez has changed professions, we must keep on trying.'

'Who you want see next?' asked Andrés Dias in his not quite perfect English. 'We not far from cement place.' So that's what they did, they headed north out of the city to a limestone quarry about five miles away.

'Bit of a change from hospital work, if this is where he is these days,' said Lester after she'd climbed out of the police car to survey the surroundings. She gazed around at the quarry and was not expecting any better luck. Her doubts were soon proved correct. This Tomás Rodriguez was driving a dust covered digger and had never been to England. He was an uneducated man who appeared flustered and bewildered by the unexpected presence of three police officers at his place of work. He couldn't speak a word of English and Dias acted as translator. He was never a doctor, now or in the past. Dias reassured the man he was not in any trouble before they left and turned onto the main road to return to civilisation in the city.

'The third Tomás Rodriguez, he live other side of Mendoza. It over hour away, traffic busy now, not good,' said Dias.

As they entered Mendoza, after passing the international airport of El Plumerillo, the evening rush hour was in full swing. Streets were clogged up with vehicles pouring out of industrial estates and office complexes. Car horns sounded and frustrated motorists, keen to head home, gesticulated at other drivers, same as any other busy city the world over at this time. Watling and Lester, irritated by their lack of success, were also exhausted. Watling yawned as he sat in the front passenger seat while Lester, stretched out in the back, looked shattered and struggled to stay awake.

'We can see this other Tomás Rodriguez in the morning, Andrés, we're tired, we'd better go to our hotel, freshen up, have some food and much needed sleep.' It had been a lengthy period with little in the way of rest. The previous day they'd caught the long-haul flight from Heathrow and managed only intermittent sleep onboard. The high temperatures in Argentina hadn't helped, neither of them had acclimatised as yet. 'Go to our hotel please, Andrés. Can you pick us up in the morning, half past nine, is that OK?'

'No problem, Señor George, see tomorrow.' After dropping them off he headed away into a steady stream of noisy traffic.

On the other side of the city, in a quiet, up-market suburb, Lucia Rodriguez had been trying to contact her husband, Tomás, for several hours. He wasn't in his office and, much to her frustration, not answering his mobile. In desperation she decided to leave a voicemail message:

'*Tomás, ¿dónde estás? La policía ha estado aquí.*' ('Tomás, where are you? The police have been here.')

Tomás had received the message alright. He was driving home a worried man. This could be serious. *What was going on? Had his tax forms been filled in incorrectly?* He employed an expensive accountant to look after the firm's finances. *Had he fouled up? Or was it to do with John?* If it did concern his friend he was supposed to be in Mendoza looking at the tourist sites. John needed to be warned that the police had been to Tomás's house. *Where the hell was he?* An anxious Tomás put his foot down hard on the accelerator of his pickup truck, returning home as fast as he could through the busy evening rush hour traffic.

By six o'clock he was back. Lucia, Juan and John were all seated around a large table in the kitchen-diner when they heard Tomás's vehicle screech to a halt in the driveway outside. After locking it he bounded up the steps and burst through the front door into the room.

'What's going on?'

'Juan picked John up in town earlier, they've only just returned. Where've you been? I've been trying to contact you all afternoon,' Lucia didn't try concealing her irritation even though their English guest was in the room.

'I was in a meeting at one of the estates. When I eventually saw your message, I rushed back home. What did the police want?'

'They didn't say much other than it was important that they speak to you as soon as possible. I mentioned you'd be in later. They said they'd call again at seven.'

Tomás glanced up at the clock on the kitchen wall, it was nearly six fifteen. The police would be arriving in less than an hour.

'Look, I haven't a clue what this is all about but it could be to do with you, John. That's the obvious conclusion. You will have to hide in the cellar. Take food and drink with you if you haven't eaten yet. The police must not find you here under any circumstances. If they question us we deny all knowledge of seeing, meeting or even knowing you. Go there immediately please, they could turn up before seven,' said an animated and worried Tomás.

'Look, I'm really sorry, Tomás. The Fen View Cottage case is supposed to have been closed. But, according to Lucia, they weren't English police earlier this afternoon. It was a couple of Argentinian officers.'

'It might not involve you but, just in case, you should hide. Juan, you keep well out of this, go to Maipu until I call you. Your mother and I will be here when the police arrive. Lucia, you let me do the talking please.'

'OK, I'll do that, Tomás, but if this doesn't concern John, what's it about?' asked Lucia.

'I don't know!' was his terse reply.

Juan left the house willingly. He was fully aware of John's past. Despite what he'd been told, Juan was happy to be pleasant to his father's great friend, he'd welcomed him into the Rodriguez household. However, he was not prepared to become involved in any lies and deceit with the police. He had a whole life ahead of him and didn't want it blighted by any record for harbouring a man who might be a criminal. Juan left the house and sped off in the family Porsche to the Maipu office, glad to be out of the way. He'd spend the night there.

John was hurriedly ushered into the cellar. Tomás switched on some strip lights that would have to be turned off before the police arrived. John was led to the far corner, it would be a good hiding place. The large subterranean space was full of wine bottles stored on wooden racks stretching from floor to ceiling, various bits of junk filled other areas. An old table and an armchair that had seen better days were at the back. At least John had something to sit on. He was politely told to remain silent and stay seated, no moving around. Any noises or movements might be detected by inquisitive detectives. Lucia, trying to calm her nerves, busied herself by cleaning up the kitchen area after pouring herself a large glass of wine. She filled the dishwasher with used plates, cups and cutlery, there must be no evidence of visitors left lying around the place.

Just before seven the front door bell rang. Tomás reminded Lucia that he'd do the talking, he knew his wife was a gregarious woman who normally liked to chat to people but now was not the time. Tomás, although forever warm and friendly, was a more guarded and secretive individual. He answered and was greeted by Argentinian police officers, both middle-aged men with serious looks on their faces. They entered into the kitchen and got straight to the point:

'*Señor Rodriguez, ¿Traficas con drogas?*' (Mr Rodriguez, do you deal in drugs?)

13

Andrés Dias parked his police car outside the Argentinos Hotel in the centre of Mendoza at exactly half past nine. He was a man who believed in punctuality, unlike many Argentinians who prefer to take a more relaxed attitude towards timekeeping. Watling and Lester were waiting in reception. He had some interesting information for them.

'We no go Vistalba to see next Tomás Rodriguez.'

'Why not?' asked Watling. 'We need to meet him as soon as possible, please.'

'He come to us … last night!' answered Dias, a broad smile plastered across his face. 'He arrested. We find cocaine, … in his warehouse, … so we interview him.'

'*Puto maldito infierno!*' shouted out Lester. 'A wine producer who deals in narcotics!' Her loud, very rude expletive and reference to drugs in the hotel's reception area and adjoining dining room turned many heads. Both staff and residents looked across in their direction.

'You learn Argentinian, señorita, naughty words first! That good, funny me think!' enthused Dias. He stopped speaking and for a while couldn't stop laughing. Once recovered he continued: 'Rodriguez, he at police station. You can see now, yes?'

The police chief drove Watling and Lester the short distance to his headquarters. Dias, in his fractured English, told them that Rodriguez was a well-known local wine merchant who'd been brought in for questioning after $250,000 worth of cocaine had been found hidden behind crates of wine. The police had received a tip off from an employee at a distribution centre in Maipu. The worker had been stunned to find illegal drugs stored at his boss's depot. Dias went on to explain that the police had called at Rodriguez's home the previous evening and arrested him on suspicion of drug trafficking. He'd denied all knowledge and vehemently protested his innocence. The man had no history of such crimes and didn't have a criminal record. Dias told his visitors that Rodriguez was a well-educated and respected member of the local community, a supporter of several local charities for the less well-off and those in hospitals needing medical care. The fact that the warehouse looked to have been broken into, the entrance gate padlock had been cut, helped give credence to Rodriguez's claim. The police had told him that he'd be free to go home eventually after more questioning. He'd been kept in a police cell overnight but no charges had been brought against him.

'We no tell Rodriguez about you. It big surprise. We insist he stay, we say Drugs Squad travel from Buenos Aires, interview in morning. We believe him, we think someone else use warehouse, emergency maybe, he say he know nothing. Drugs problem growing in Mendoza, like world all over.'

'OK, Andrés, let's go and meet this Tómas Rodriguez, he sounds an interesting character,' said Watling. 'I'm keen to talk to him.'

After checking in the visiting officers at reception, Dias led the way into an office followed by Lester and then Watling. Seated in front of them was a middle-aged man of smart appearance flanked by a young police officer. Tómas froze when he saw the tall figure of Watling enter the room. He recognised him immediately, it was the English detective he'd seen on the border with Chile and at Santiago airport last October. *Shit, this was going to be tricky!* Tómas knew he had to remain calm not only for his own sake but for John's as well. He could guess what was coming, he'd be fielding some awkward questions. *How the heck had they tracked him down to Mendoza? A person or persons must have recollected him from his short stay in England over twenty years ago. Both John and himself would be in big trouble if he didn't convince this Englishman that he'd never heard of a Dr John Ripley.*

'*Policia Inglés* have questions, this Detective Chief Inspector Watling and Detective Sergeant Lester,' said Dias. He looked across at Watling and Lester. 'It OK, Señor Watling ... Señor

Rodriguez here, he speak English perfect, better even than me,' he joked.

Watling looked hard at Rodriguez. He felt sure he remembered him from somewhere but he couldn't place when and where. *Must have been on his previous trip to Argentina.* Rodriguez calmly gazed up at the English detective as if trying to give the impression that he'd never seen him before and was happy to answer any questions that might come his way.

'What can I do for you, Señor Watling?' asked Tomás helpfully in perfect English.

There were no opening pleasantries, Watling got straight down to business:

'Señor Rodriguez, tell me now, did you ever work as a doctor?' Tomás remained calm and unruffled.

'I've been a wine producer and merchant ever since I took over my father's firm.'

The truth had been twisted to suit the situation but he didn't want to say anything about his medical training and subsequent hospital work in both Buenos Aires and Cambridge. He was banking on the fact there were no records, at least in England, that would catch him out. Tomás had hoped to throw the detective off course by his answer but Watling was a wily customer when it came to asking questions and finding the truth. He persevered.

'We are looking for an Argentinian man, Tomás Rodriguez. For a while he worked at a Cambridge hospital.'

'I am Tomás Rodriguez, that much is true, but I'm a wine producer only. It is a very common name in my country, there must be many men called Tomás Rodriguez, probably hundreds, if not thousands, in Argentina and also neighbouring countries in South America. Sorry I can't help you more.' He sounded convincing enough.

'OK, Señor Rodriguez, let me ask you something else.' Watling was persistent in his questioning as usual.

'Please do,' replied Tomás calmly.

'Do you know or have you ever known an Englishman called Dr John Ripley?'

Tomás knew that this question was coming at some stage and he was fully prepared for it.

'I know no English doctors, Señor Watling,' lied Tomás.

Watling went on to explain why he was looking for him. All three police officers watched Tomás's facial expressions and body movements intently as Watling recounted some of the case history that included his own unsuccessful trip to Argentina a few months ago. Tomás was determined to divulge as little as possible about his past. He sat impassively and listened politely to Watling. Inside he was a bag of nerves but, whenever he said anything, Tomás spoke clearly, keen not to display any shred of anxiety.

'That's a sad story, Señor Watling, I can understand why you have come all the way to Argentina. I hope you catch this, er, Dr Ridley or Ripley but, I repeat, I know nothing that might help you. Good luck with your inquiries.' He turned towards Dias and added 'Am I free to go now, señor? I have important meetings today, my business, it does not run by itself you know.'

'You can leave, señor, we see you again about drugs.'

But as he stood up Watling had another question for Tomás.

'Oh! ... before you go, one other thing, Señor Rodriguez, could you please tell me who is your doctor, here in Mendoza?' Tomás looked at Dias and an awkward moment followed. It was Watling who broke the silence. 'It'll help us with our inquiries and maybe lead to your elimination from our list of men aged forty to sixty with the name of Tomás Rodriguez.'

Tomás was hesitant to answer but he had no other option if he wanted to remain above suspicion. The unexpected question had thrown him completely. *This could be a major problem!*

'OK, Mr Watling, if you really must know, but I don't see why you need such personal details, it's a Dr Martinez,'

'Where is his surgery?'

'At Lujan de Cuyo.'

Tomás gave the information reluctantly but he realised he couldn't avoid the question. If he had nothing to hide it would not be a problem, but Señor Rodriguez had a lot to conceal. He left the police station a free man but one with plenty to worry about and he soon stopped his Ford pickup truck at the first service station he came across. Tomás hurriedly leant over the passenger seat and opened up the glove box. He took out one of the burner phones that he specifically kept for awkward situations related to his business and some of the company he kept. It could be easily trashed and disposed of after he'd made a few emergency calls.

14

Lucia Rodriguez had spent a restless night in the family home. As instructed by her husband she'd kept quiet when the police had called the previous evening to accuse Tomás of being a drugs dealer. Lucia, a highly respectable, middle-class, part-time teacher, wife of a wealthy wine merchant and local benefactor, had been shocked to the core by the events of the last twenty-four hours. Her immediate and understandable thought was that this was all a terrible mistake. In her opinion Tomás was an honest wine producer and before that he'd been a good and conscientious doctor. He was a hard-working, honourable pillar of the local community.

Shortly after the detectives arrived Tomás had been taken to Mendoza's main police station for questioning. Dutiful husband that he was, Tomás had rung Lucia to soothe her anxiety by saying the police had reached the conclusion that he wasn't dealing in illegal substances and not personally responsible for hiding drugs. It was a huge relief to Lucia to hear the news but it didn't help her sleep. Tomás had to stay overnight in police custody because other detectives wanted to question him first thing in the morning. He told his wife he wasn't sure why he was being detained, the police hadn't elaborated on the matter. It could be about the discovery of the hessian sack in his warehouse that contained plastic packets of cocaine or possibly something else. Tomás carefully hadn't mentioned what that might be over the phone, she would be able to figure that out for herself.

John had spent an equally troubled night in the Rodriguez household. After an uncomfortable and worrying half hour hiding in the darkness of the cellar he was informed by Lucia that the police had left, taking Tomás with them for further questioning. John expressed his remorse for what had happened but felt confident that Tomás wasn't a secret dealer and had not been knowingly responsible for storing any narcotics. He did his best to reassure Lucia, he knew Tomás had criminal friends but wasn't about to say anything about her husband's dubious connection to a drugs lord. Lucia told John that he must continue to lie low until the troubles blew over. He was not to leave the property, he had to stay hidden and well out of view.

After having let Tomás Rodriguez leave the confines of the police station Andrés Dias discussed matters with his English visitors:

'So, Señor Watling, what you think? Is this wine dealer connect to your investigation?'

'He was a cool customer that's for sure. He gave little if anything away but he was disturbed by me asking for his doctor's name. We must visit this Dr Martinez as soon as possible, he's bound to know if his patient was a medic in the past. I can't imagine them not discussing such things.'

'What about putting a watch on Rodriguez's property, boss?' suggested Penny Lester.

'Good idea, Pen. Andrés, is that OK with you?'

'I spare man for you. He watch Rodriguez house, it not far away.'

'Thanks Andrés, that would be very helpful. Dr Ripley might be hiding there. We need to keep an eye on who comes in and who goes out. As well as us finding Ripley you might learn more as to why Rodriguez was storing drugs.'

'We on this, Señor George, let get coffee.'

After his release from police custody Tomás's first call was to his surgery in Lujan de Cuyo to speak with Dr Martinez, saying it was a matter of the utmost urgency. Fortunately, he was on duty and between seeing patients so Tomás was put straight through.

He mentioned the police would be visiting his surgery, he wanted Carlos Martinez to do him a favour and lie for him by saying that, as far as he was aware, Tomás had never been a doctor, he'd tell him the reason why later. Unsurprisingly, Dr Martinez wasn't happy about being untruthful, he was an honest man and didn't want to find himself in trouble with the authorities. Tomás implored him as he was in danger and Carlos reluctantly agreed to abide with his strange request, but he wanted an explanation, the sooner the better.

After ringing off, another number was hurriedly dialled.

'*Federico, ¿qué diablos está pasando?*' yelled Tomás angrily. ('Federico, what the hell's going on?')

'*Tomás, tenemos que encontrarnos,*' replied a calm voice. ('Tomás, we need to meet')

Federico Santos went on to explain all about the drugs find. Tomás was understandably angry but he knew that antagonising one of the most powerful men in the trade was not a wise move for anyone to make even though their friendship went back many years. For the first time ever, they arranged a meeting at Tomás's house for later in the day.

Tomás now had three problems to deal with. Firstly, the cocaine stash, secondly, the need for John to stay in hiding at his home because the English detectives were looking for him and thirdly, perhaps most importantly, he was extremely anxious about what the police might find out from a visit to his doctor. After agreeing to the evening meeting with Santos, Tomás ended the conversation and lifted himself out of his Ford pickup truck. He hurried across the service station's forecourt in order to discard the burner phone. After looking around to reassure himself that no-one was watching he pushed it down into the bottom of a trash bin before driving home to see Lucia and John. Tomás was not his usual happy self, he felt ill at ease due to the predicament he was tangled up in. *He was in a very messy situation and knew he had only himself to blame.*

15

When Tomás arrived back home he talked about his time in police custody with both Lucia and John. Today his business would be run by his eldest son, Juan, he would not be going to any offices, meetings, or to his wine estates. He had too much thinking to do and problems to sort out. To make matters even worse, Lucia was not in a good mood, she was angry with Tomás. In the privacy of her kitchen, without John being present, she spoke to her husband in a firm voice as if she was talking to a recalcitrant child in one of her classes:

'What have you been up to Tomás? An honest answer please!'

'Lucia, I swear to you that I haven't hidden any drugs. How many more times do I have to tell you?'

It was partly the truth but definitely not the whole truth. His wife didn't know of his close friendship with an international dealer in narcotics. She'd heard Tomás talk about Federico and was well aware that they met up for football matches in Buenos Aires as well as other parts of the country. Tomás had told his wife that Federico was a wealthy businessman, in the agricultural and construction industries, but that was all. Again, this was true but Lucia was led to believe that Federico's wealth had been accrued lawfully from his farm in the Amazon region and his building industry based in both Mendoza and Rio de Janeiro. She had no idea about his part in major drug smuggling activities that involved a complicated web of criminality stretching throughout not only South and Central America but northwards into California and Florida.

'OK, Tomás, but please tell me how have these drugs found their way into one of your warehouses?' Lucia asked accusingly.

'Look, Lucia, I know nothing about it. The place was broken into. Powerful cutters were used on the padlocks to the gates. They must have thought it a good place to hide cocaine.

The police are looking into it. They're not blaming me, I'm in the clear. I'll also be making my own investigations, it could be one of my employees is responsible,' he added for good measure, knowing damn well that it wasn't.

'What are we going to do with John?' Lucia didn't want Tomás and herself to be implicated as accomplices to someone running away from the law.

'John must stay with us for now. He cannot afford to wander around Mendoza but we'll have to get him out of here. Don't worry, I'll find a solution to the problem, give me time to think what would be best.'

Later in the day John joined them for dinner, as did Juan, they sat at the large table inside the kitchen-diner with the window blinds fully down and all curtains closed. Afterwards Tomás and John retired to the hideaway hut in the garden with a bottle of light and fruity Chilean Merlot. They walked quietly along a garden path that was one long pergola smothered in semi-tropical climbing plants in full leaf and bloom. There was plenty of cover but Tomás had reassured John many times that the rear garden with its patios, swimming pool, tennis court and balconies was extremely private anyway, he was confident they wouldn't be seen by any prying eyes. He joked that the only way to spy on the back of the property was by an overhead drone or by an individual stationed high up in the Andean foothills with an incredibly powerful pair of binoculars. As far as Tomás knew no such looking glasses existed and he'd never seen or heard a drone over his property. On their stroll to the summer house he told John that someone else would be joining them, they had much to discuss and important plans to make.

Bang on eight o'clock, Federico Santos, dressed all in black, was dropped off by taxi in a dimly lit side street about a hundred metres from the secret entrance to Tomás's home. It was Thursday evening and the darkness of the Mendoza sky matched the colour of his baseball hat, coat, shirt, trousers and trainers. Santos liked working at night, he was accustomed to sleeping in the day especially at siesta time on hot summer afternoons. He'd always functioned better during the dark hours. It was quieter, there were fewer police on duty and he had learnt from experience that illicit, clandestine activities are best completed after dusk and well before dawn.

Santos had been a criminal ever since his childhood. However, much to his credit given his impoverished formative years of scraping a living in miserable shanty towns, he eventually began to run legitimate businesses in both Rio de Janeiro where he was born and in his adopted city of Mendoza. He'd learnt the building trade from his father, as well as several uncles and an older brother. As a teenager he assimilated knowledge of electrical skills and was particularly proud of the day that he illegally tapped into the city's electricity supply. It enabled his section of Alemão, a ramshackle *favela* (shanty town) in the northern parts of Rio, to enjoy free energy. He became a recognised and respected leader of his little part of the world. His influence had spread by the time he reached his early twenties. He'd built up his own firm and an air of respectability but, underneath that front, he was also happy to deal in drugs throughout Rio and other Brazilian cities such as Sao Paulo and Belo Horizonte. Both enterprises brought him great wealth and when he turned thirty he bought a condominium in a fashionable part of Rio's South side facing onto Copacabana beach and the Atlantic. He lived there with his wife and son whenever possible. During his thirties the illegal narcotics trade increasingly took over from the legal construction business and he became a major player in transferring drugs throughout South America especially in his native Brazil but his activities spread southwards into neighbouring Uruguay and Argentina. This brought him into conflict with rival gangs throughout the continent and beyond into Central America and the United States. Federico Santos, one-time street urchin, met Tomás Rodriguez, established member of the Argentine socio-economic elite, by chance at a football match at the giant El Monumental Stadium in the Belgrano district of northern Buenos Aires, it was a time when he was expanding his business empire into Argentina. Tomás persuaded him to move his legitimate business headquarters into Mendoza and he now had an office block in the centre of the city and a builder's yard on its outskirts.

Now well into his forties, Santos still had his luxury apartment in Rio as well as a much smaller one in Buenos Aires. He'd bought a house in the hill country outside Mexico City as a fortieth birthday present to himself and for the last five years he'd owned a sprawling cattle ranch in the Brazilian state of Rondônia, on the southern fringes of the Amazon region. Federico Santos was a highly complex man with many facets to his personality. His practical skills had made him an expert builder but above all he was an astute businessman. Apart from his native Portuguese he also spoke both Spanish and English proficiently. His multifarious talents had made him extremely wealthy and powerful. Above all else he was a ruthless and dangerous man who stopped at nothing to obtain what he wanted and people stood in his way at their peril.

During the past two decades Tomás had established a close friendship with Federico. Right from their first meeting they'd formed a bond, a togetherness that had grown and flourished based initially on their shared passion for football. However, despite the bonhomie that existed between them, Tomás had always felt rather intimidated by Federico. Unsurprisingly, he was wary of a man who could flit between very different worlds with apparent ease. He'd never invited Santos to his home or introduced him to Lucia. They were poles apart in so many ways, it was their love of Club Atlético River Plate in Buenos Aires that had brought them together. Tomás had grown up a highly privileged and extremely well-educated member of the upper echelons of Argentinian society but his friend had dragged himself out of the squalor of living in Rio's notorious shanty towns. One born into wealth, the other to poverty, but today both were extremely wealthy and powerful men.

As darkness fell, Tomás, sitting in his secluded summer house with John by his side, waited nervously for Federico to make a first ever appearance at his home. After exiting the taxi Santos turned around and looked carefully in all directions. He'd travelled alone, it was a risk he didn't normally take, he'd none of his bodyguards with him. He too felt anxious, it was strange for him because he wasn't a man who normally worried about things but he had to be sure that no-one had followed him out of Mendoza's city centre. He was fully aware that some of his rivals were keen to find him after recent happenings, he couldn't be too careful. Many reckless men he'd once known were now dead, victims of often violent killings in cars, aeroplanes, on the street or, worst of all, at home in front of loved ones. Happy in the knowledge that he hadn't been followed, the shadowy figure of Santos walked the short distance along the alleyway to the back of Tomás's property and surveyed the high barrier in front of him.

The five metres high, white-washed, brick-built wall was cocooned by a colourful and thick climbing plant, Chilean jasmine, in full bloom. It was late summer and much of the high walling was densely covered in dark green foliage and bright white flowers. Santos had been tipped off by Tomás to look out for the trellising and find the place where there wasn't any. He located the correct spot and carefully pushed aside the loose plant cover. A re-enforced steel entrance to the extensive grounds, also coloured white to help camouflage it, appeared before him. He tapped the number code into the Digi-lock whereupon the door's locking mechanism was released. He opened it gently while constantly looking behind. Still no sign of anyone, that was good. He slipped into Tomás's garden making sure to quietly close the door behind him. All was done expertly with minimum fuss and no noise. Santos had been a creature of the dark for as long as he could remember, everything about the evening was second nature to a man like him.

16

Watling, Lester and Dias had been busy. Their first mission after leaving police headquarters was to visit Tomás Rodriguez's doctor. They'd not bothered to ring the surgery to give any warning, better to turn up unexpectedly but Tomás was no fool. The urgent call an hour or two earlier had done the necessary. Martinez was prepared rather than surprised, but he feigned shock all the same at the sudden arrival of police officers. For the benefit of his guests Dias spoke in his not quite perfect but still impressive English. He guessed the doctor would understand him and, sure enough, Dr Martinez, like most well-educated Argentinians, turned out to be fluent in not only his native tongue.

'We wonder if you help us?' asked Dias. 'My police friends, they look for criminal, he hide in our country. I let them speak.'

Dias's comments about 'police friends' and 'criminal' were still ringing in the doctor's ears and echoing in his thoughts as Watling got down to business.

'I'm looking for an Englishman who is in Mendoza, he is suspected of murder,' were Watling's opening and somewhat dramatized words.

Lester looked across at her boss. *He's over-egging it.* John Ripley was a suspect and nothing more and they weren't certain where he was, but she could understand Watling's strategy. Dr Martinez looked alarmed.

'Señor, what have I got to do with an Englishman suspected of murder?'

'We believe that you have a Tomás Rodriguez as one of your patients,' continued Watling. 'He told us this earlier today when we interviewed him at police headquarters. We think Rodriguez might know where this Englishman is.'

Each passing sentence was a bombshell surprise to Martinez. *What did the police want?* He was going to have to be very careful and non-committal with his answers.

'Yes, I've been Tomás's doctor for many years, he has a wine business.'

'We're aware of that, but was Tomás Rodriguez a doctor himself before he became a wine grower and merchant?' asked Watling.

Carlos Martinez knew what the right and honest answer to the question was. Both he and Tomás were the same age and had trained together as doctors in Buenos Aires.

'Not that I'm aware of,' lied Martinez. 'He's a businessman, a highly successful one.'

'So, let's get this clear, doctor, you're saying that Tomás Rodriguez has always worked in the wine trade, is that true?'

Watling persevered with the insinuation that he either knew or thought that Rodriguez had once been a doctor. He stared hard at an uncomfortable looking Martinez.

'As I've already told you, as far as I know, he's just a businessman.'

'You say you've been Señor Rodriguez's doctor for some time. Has he ever mentioned to you about working in England?' asked Watling.

Martinez well remembered Tomás telling him that he'd spent a few months there when he was a young doctor but he couldn't divulge this fact to the nosy detective. He'd promised not to incriminate Tomás, he was his companion as well as doctor. He knew all of the Rodriguez family and occasionally socialised with them.

'Tomás travels all over the world, I expect he's visited England,' was Martinez's evasive and non-committal reply.

'We think Rodriguez knows a doctor called John Ripley. Did he ever mention having any English friends?' asked Watling.

'He's never talked of England or having friends there. We always stick mainly to medical matters to do with himself.'

Martinez started to break out into a sweat and become increasingly fidgety despite an efficient air conditioning system operating in his office.

'OK, doctor, you've been very helpful, sorry we've interrupted the day, we'll let you get on with seeing your patients,' said Watling.

After leaving Martinez they walked out of the surgery into the Argentinian sunshine. Lester asked the key question:

'What do you think, boss? Was he telling the truth?'

'Was he hell as like! He knows Tomás Rodriguez a lot better than he's letting on.'

'I listen, watch him sweat much, make me think you right. He not man used telling lies,' added Dias.

'I didn't believe him either,' concluded Lester.

'Rodriguez obviously got to him before we did,' added Watling. 'He was covering for him.'

Their next job was to meet up with the Argentinian detective who'd earlier been assigned by Dias to keep watch on the Rodriguez home. Detective Dominic Benitez had positioned himself in a street that looked onto Tomás's large property. He could see the front but, much to his frustration, the rear of the house was totally private.

'You see anything, Beni?' asked Dias, speaking in English again for the benefit of both Watling and Lester.

'*No, jefe!* (No, boss!),' was Benitez's reply. 'Lady, … leave, … back, … *hombre joven* (young man), … leave, … no return. *No veo* (I don't see) Rodriguez, … *y nadie más* (and no-one else).'

Benitez's English was far more stilted and limited than his boss. He'd seen only two people leaving the house, it sounded like it was Rodriguez's wife and son. Dias had found out from colleagues that Tomás Rodriguez had a wife called Lucia and that they had three children in their twenties. Dias asked Watling what he wanted to do as he had to get back to his office.

'You go, we'll stay here for now and travel back into Mendoza with Beni later.'

Watling and Lester decided to go for a wander around the block leaving Benitez to continue his watch. Watling wanted to acquaint himself with the surroundings, to see all sides of the house and familiarise himself with the local district. He was now convinced that Señor Rodriguez, the wine dealer, would lead him to John Ripley. Watling was warming to his task.

17

Federico Santos made a sudden but not unexpected appearance in front of Tomás's back garden hideaway. He peered in through the window and saw Tomás and his English friend talking, their faces illuminated by the flickering light of a white pillar candle. Tomás waved for Santos to come inside, it was summit meeting time for them.

'Welcome, Federico, my friend, it's good to see you,' said Tomás before adding, 'but please tell me, what the fuck's going on?' His tone had changed mid-sentence from being welcoming to sounding well hacked off with his gangster companion.

'Don't worry, Tomás, everything's under control.'

He stared hard at both Tomás and John and proceeded to place a Glock pistol on the table in front of him. Both men felt unnerved by the unexpected appearance of a powerful hand gun but Tomás knew that Santos liked to frighten and intimidate. The drugs lord sensed the alarm that the gun had caused. It amused him but, initially, he showed no sign of emotion. Then he broke into hysterical laughter.

'You are my friends! You have nothing to worry about.' He calmed down before continuing, 'but I have many enemies. You know the risks of my trade, Tomás.'

'The drugs, found in my warehouse, I presume they belonged to you?'

'You're right, I apologise, but we had to put them somewhere in a hurry where we thought they'd be safe. I didn't want to store them at home or at any of my business premises in the city, it would be too much of a risk. My enemies have both watched.'

John sat quietly in the background, he didn't feel qualified to enter into any conversation on illegal narcotics. He stayed an interested but worried listener as Santos continued the conversation.

'We stole the cocaine from some people based in Cordoba. You have maybe heard of the Andretti family, Tomás? They are American Italians, not very nice ones, they have links to the Mafia in New York as well as Sicily. They are major players in the drugs trade. We are rivals, big rivals. Anyway, without my knowledge, some of my men raided an isolated farmhouse used by the Andrettis as a depot in the hills outside Cordoba. The idiots then brought the stolen goods to my city centre office instead of our secret location. One was wounded in the shooting at the farm. He was left behind, my men had to escape in a hurry. He was no doubt tortured before they killed him. He must have told them where I live. Members of their gang have been seen in Mendoza over the last few days. The organisation is led by one of three brothers, he's based in New York. They no doubt want their cocaine back. They are not happy, they are looking out for me, I am in a difficult situation, so, I need to lie low for a few weeks. I've decided to leave Mendoza for a while.'

There was a brief pause in the conversation, Tomás didn't quite know what to say in reply, John was stunned by what he was listening to. Santos continued by asking Tomás a question:

'The police, what did they say to you?'

'I'm in the clear, thank God! Lucia has been giving me a hard time, she thinks maybe I'm a drug dealer. The police questioned me, but don't worry, Federico, your name wasn't mentioned.'

'That is good, Tomás, that is good (he smiled), but they do know about me and, how shall I say, my different interests, but they ignore what I get up to. I have friends in high places, senior officers, I pay them well to leave me alone. As far as they're concerned I am an honest man with a building business.' He smiled again, pleased at the power he exerted. Some guardians of the law were almost as corrupt as he was, they were happy to accept bribes from a drugs smuggler. It supplemented their income and helped pay for life's extra luxuries.

'You say you need to go away for a while. What are you planning? Where are you going to?' asked Tomás.

'I don't know for certain just yet, I have many different homes. I am always a man on the move, to stay in one place too long is dangerous in my business. My wife, Helena, she and my son, Gabriel, they live in Rio, as you know, I try to see them as often as I can, but it is difficult.' A feeling of great sadness was evident in Santos's voice. He knew he had to keep them hidden away for their safety, he didn't see them often enough and realised he wouldn't be sharing their company for a while given his current situation.

'So, now you need to hide away somewhere.' Tomás turned and looked towards his English friend. 'John, he too needs to disappear.'

'Señor John, you are back in Argentina, it is a big surprise after I deliver you safely to California. Why is that?' Santos enquired.

John went on to fill him in with the details as to why he was sitting in Tomás's back garden hideaway. He told Santos that a couple of English detectives had unexpectedly turned up in Mendoza looking for him and together with the local police they were probably watching Tomás's property for any sightings. At the moment he was trapped, he couldn't risk being seen for both their sakes.

'What do you plan to do, Señor John?' asked Santos. 'Once more you are in a tricky situation.'

'I could try to get back to California but the airports would be dangerous, the police will be looking for me,' replied John. 'I too need to find a hiding place, in this country preferably.'

'My good friend here has met an Argentinian woman, she is now the new lady in his life,' said Tomás. He laughed as he spoke the words, spilling some of his drink in the process. He then poured more wine for Santos as well as topping up John's glass and his own.

'I'm supposed to be seeing her tomorrow night in Mendoza,' exclaimed John, a little embarrassed by Tomás revealing this personal information to Santos.

'So, you now have a good reason for staying here, Señor John, the things we do for love, eh?' said Santos. He joined in the laughter at the thought of John looking desperately for sanctuary but still managing to strike up a romantic attachment with a local lady.

The men talked for the following two hours during which time they steadily drank their way through the red wine and several bottles of *Quilmes*, a popular Argentinian lager. Tomás was no longer in trouble, unless his doctor spilt the beans, but it was very different for both Santos and John. A rival drugs cartel was busily searching for Santos and there'd be no mercy if they found him. He went on about hiding out until the heat on him had died down, he reckoned on going off to parts of Argentina that the Andrettis wouldn't think of looking for him. John, meanwhile, desperately needed to get well away from the police who, once again, were hot on his heels but he had a dilemma. He also wanted to pursue his budding romance with the lovely Lola. Tomás, on the other hand, yearned for a quieter life with his wife and family and to be able to concentrate fully on his wine business. Santos mentioned the possibility of going south into the isolated expanses of Patagonia, he had the ideal hideout down there.

At the end of the evening Santos suggested that John come back into Mendoza with him. Leaving under the cover of darkness would get him away from Tomás's house and he'd be able to then see Lola the next day. It was an offer gratefully accepted although John wondered what he might be letting himself in for, but was eager to keep Tomás out of any trouble with the police. Santos and John could exit through the back entrance. If the place was being watched it was highly unlikely that the rear of the grounds would be covered so late at night. As Andretti's men seemed to have found out where he lived, Santos, wanting to keep his movements and location a secret, had ruled out returning to his house. Instead, they'd head for the Park Hyatt Hotel in the heart of the city. Santos had booked one of the luxury penthouse apartments for three nights through to Sunday morning. He had an ongoing arrangement with the management to pay double the normal price for the suite whenever he needed it suddenly. Santos had contacted the hotel earlier to say he'd be arriving later. On Sunday he was planning to fly off in his private jet. John could stay with him until then if necessary, he could see Lola tomorrow evening. They'd arranged a romantic meal together at *Cachè Bistro*, a fine restaurant with a quiet outdoor space.

The men from completely different worlds travelled together by taxi into the city centre. They didn't speak a word to one another all the way back to the impressive Park Hyatt with its magnificent Spanish colonial façade overlooking the Plaza Independencia. Best to keep quiet, any idle chit-chat would be overheard by the driver. Both men were fugitives, both were on the run and needed to hide, one due to serious criminal activities, the other from the sins of his past.

18

After their preliminary walk around Tomás Rodriguez's neighbourhood both Watling and Lester had returned with Benitez to police headquarters late on Thursday afternoon, well before Santos's nocturnal arrival at the rear entrance to the property. Once back in their hotel plans were made for the following morning. Together with Benitez they'd keep tabs on Rodriguez's place observing all who came in and out. They'd reassess the situation at midday, Watling was mindful of the fact that they only had a week in Argentina, time was limited, and it was passing by all too quickly.

When Friday dawned, it was another sunny day in Mendoza. Watling and Lester made an early start and were strolling around the up-market area where Rodriguez lived. The large, detached properties were all well maintained with extensive gardens to front and rear, sprinkler systems aplenty sprayed fountains of water to keep the lawns emerald green and flowered borders lush and verdant despite the dry climate. Rodriguez's colonial style home with its balconies was surrounded by other properties, no access existed along the sides but at the back it was different. This was something that Watling had noticed the previous day. He'd spotted the alleyway separating the rear of the property from the back wall of its neighbour with enough room to walk along the ginnel. Watling led the way down the passageway, Lester followed. The Rodriguez household had a wall that was far too high to be scaled unless one came equipped with a long ladder. What made it even harder for any would-be intruders were the plants, attached to an old and weathered wooden trellising system. Watling started to brush aside some of the vegetation as he searched for any possible entrance. He was not to be disappointed. In an area where the climbers hung loose, due to an absence of trellising, he found the secret back doorway into the property. It was an expensive construction made of steel and coloured white to blend in with the wall, a high security system, certainly no old-fashioned affair.

'Well, well, look what I've found, Pen,' Watling whispered to Lester. 'I wonder why Señor Rodriguez needs all this?'

'Security must be important to him, boss. Maybe there's a lot more to Rodriguez than meets the eye. Perhaps he does deal in drugs as well as wine.'

'Maybe, ... but wealthy men like to feel secure. They feel vulnerable in their castles, especially in countries with plenty of poverty.'

'Not much of that around here!'

'Agreed, but I bet there is in other parts of Mendoza. We need to keep a watch on this back entrance as well as the front of the house.'

Watling decided to go back to Benitez to tell him, as best he could, what they'd found. Penny was to stay close to the alleyway. Unfortunately for them a vigil the previous evening would have proved far more useful. They'd have seen the shadowy figure of Santos arrive and, a few hours later, observe him leave with the doctor they were so eagerly looking for. The horse had bolted, they'd arrived several hours too late because, when Friday dawned, the English doctor was ensconced in a luxury penthouse suite at the Park Hyatt Hotel looking forward to his evening date with Lola. Sat opposite him was the brooding presence of Santos planning his escape from Mendoza on the Sunday morning. He was busy, as usual, making important calls to his many accomplices.

The only people in the Vistalba property on Friday morning were Tomás and Lucia, they had no idea their home was being spied upon at both the front and back. Tomás had taken the day off but, like Santos, he too was thinking and planning ahead. *What would be best for his friends?* John, on the run again from the English law, and the disreputable and ruthless Federico. He wanted to help them both but he desperately needed to untangle himself from the mess they'd brought down upon him. Tomás owed that to Lucia and his family, they were innocents who'd been dragged into the difficult situation that now confronted him. In some ways he wished he'd not been so forgiving when he'd listened to John's story, he should have told him to return to England and confess to his sins of thirty years ago. He also regretted ever getting involved with the likes of Santos. Wine was Tomás's business, it had made him rich, but he'd crossed onto the wrong side of the law by harbouring and assisting people who were essentially criminals. Tomás reached the conclusion that he'd have to meet up, as soon as possible, with these friends on neutral territory somewhere in Mendoza. A quiet café, outside the city centre, would be best, he knew the ideal place. He contacted Santos. After a few failed attempts he finally got through, another meeting was arranged for the next morning. It would include both John and Lola, they had much to discuss.

19

John woke up on Saturday morning in Lola's comfortable king size bed. He hadn't had much sleep and felt tired, his state resulting not only from sleep deprivation. The pair had enjoyed a great evening and an even better night together. The alarm clock read 09.54. John heard the shower being turned off and waited impatiently for his lover's return, they had an important meeting later that morning at eleven. During the previous evening, over dinner, John had discussed his plans with Lola. He told her that English police officers were looking for him and they were in the city. This was a surprise after thinking he was in the clear. He'd read the English press reports online. He could only presume that further building work at Fen View Cottage had uncovered another body and the police were once again searching for him. John told Lola that he'd have to go into temporary hiding, maybe in the south of the country. He doubted that Tomás would be with him but he'd be accompanied by a friend of his, a Brazilian businessman called Federico Santos. John had asked Lola if she'd like to join him.

Lola was hopeful that she could take some weeks off as it had been a while since her last holiday, but she'd have to make suitable arrangements with her work places first. She was excited at the thought of keeping John company on an adventure into Patagonia. There were plenty of horses in the region and many wilderness areas to go riding in. Lola wasn't put off the trip even after John felt compelled to tell her all about Santos and why he too had to leave Mendoza in a hurry, but for a very different reason.

Lola, dressed only in a red towel wrapped around her wet hair, walked through into the bedroom.

'I hate saying it, Lola, but please put some clothes on, we need to hurry up, we're meeting with Tomás and Santos soon.'

'Where we going?'

'A place called *Essenza*. It's a café near the, ... er, ... Parque San Martín, ... on a street called, ... the, ... erm, Avenida, ... Arístides, ... Villanueva, ... does that sound right?' replied John as he carefully read his scribbled notes on a crumpled piece of paper.

'I know the place, it's ideal for breakfast, come on we'll get there early, I'm hungry.'

John showered and dressed in less than ten minutes. They then rushed out of the apartment and headed towards their destination. *Essenza* wasn't too far away, it was just down the road on the way to the park. Soon they were busy eating croissants that they coated with *dulce de leche* (caramelised milk jam) and drinking coffee at a quiet corner table. Before long Tomás was dropped off by taxi. Santos, also in a taxi, arrived shortly after, both men ordered coffees only. It was Tomás who kicked off the conversation, he was keen to sort things out and get his life back on an even keel.

'Right, my friends, we have important plans to make. As you know, we have to decide how to get certain people (he glanced in turn at Federico and John) into hiding for a while, I have my ideas. How about you, Federico?'

It was John who spoke next, not Santos.

'Before we go any further can I say that Lola knows all about Federico and why he needs to lie low and she is also aware of my situation. She wants to come with me, wherever I go, she goes too, we're both happy with that.'

'Do you think that's wise, John? There could be lots of dangers.' Tomás sounded alarmed.

'Don't worry about me, I'll be OK,' said Lola, full of bravado. 'I can look after myself. I'm a big girl.'

It was Santos's turn to speak:

'That's fine, Lola, but please don't blame me if we run into trouble. I need somewhere well away from Mendoza, I certainly can't use Buenos Aires. The Andretti family have many men in the capital, they'll have been tipped off to look out for me, it'll be unsafe. A few people in the city know where my apartment is, they could be persuaded to tell one of the Andrettis. Lola, if you're coming with John that's up to you but I can't promise you total safety. I shall have my bodyguard with me but it is perhaps best if eventually you and John go on somewhere else well away from me. We can travel together at first, we'll use my private jet and fly to Patagonia. I've arranged for it to be waiting on the runway tomorrow morning at the local airport. I plan on leaving around midday.'

'If you're going to Patagonia, John and Lola could go to my farm outside Trelew. I'll let my manager, Dai Davies, know that you're coming,' said Tomás helpfully.

'That sounds great,' replied John. 'You've talked before about Trelew. Surely the English detectives won't know about it and, from what you've told me, there won't be too many Argentinian police around.'

'My secret hiding place in Patagonia is tucked away in the middle of nowhere beside the coast,' said Santos. 'I've only used it once before, but first of all we need to take John and Lola to your farm, Tomás.'

'So, we are decided then, you three meet up at the airport tomorrow. Federico will be there with his pilot and plane. I presume you're still staying at the Hyatt tonight, Federico? What are your plans, John?' asked Tomás.

'Lola and I have discussed things. I shall spend today and tonight with her. The detectives will be looking for a man by himself, not one accompanied by a woman. We'll meet Federico tomorrow at the airport.'

'As for me, I shall look forward to getting back to my work. I'll keep in touch with you, John, via the Davies family in Trelew. Adieu, my friends, good luck to you all. Oh, and please remember, if asked, you don't know me and never have!'

Tomás drank up his coffee, paid the bill for everyone and walked out of the café to find the nearest taxi. As he looked up and down the street he was oblivious to the unmarked police car parked about fifty metres away. Inside it, observing the goings-on, were Dias, Watling and Lester. Tomás's house was now under watch 24/7, he'd been seen leaving earlier that morning and was followed into the centre of Mendoza.

Tomás soon came across an empty taxi. After jumping in, the vehicle was followed by Dias's police car. Before it pulled away Watling and Lester climbed out from the back seats. They were eager to keep tabs on the three individuals Rodriguez had met in the café. They'd walked past the place several times in the last half hour and knew who Tomás was with after casually looking in through the large windows. There was a small, muscularly built man dressed all in black and what looked to be a couple, a middle-aged man with long hair, designer beard and sunglasses accompanied by an attractive, younger woman.

Five minutes after Rodriguez had left the café it was the turn of the man dressed in black to make his departure. Watling told Lester to track him and keep in touch. He needed to know where this man was going but he also wanted to be assured that Penny was safe even though she was well capable of looking after herself and was carrying a firearm.

Watling meanwhile, pretended to read a newspaper while leaning on a wall opposite the café, but he didn't have to wait long for the couple to leave. Once outside they headed towards the busy city centre. Watling followed at a discrete distance, far enough away not to be suspected but close enough to keep watch on them. Eventually the couple stopped outside a low-rise residential complex made up of luxury flats. After the blonde woman had pressed the required code the couple disappeared inside out of view. Watling ambled slowly up to the building and observed its title engraved on a wall plaque, he memorised it. A little further down the road he stopped again and jotted this information in his notebook, along with the name of the street. He'd no idea who the lady was but he felt damn certain that the man, despite his changed appearance, was Dr John Ripley.

20

Dias tailed Tomás's taxi back to his home in the southern outskirts of the city. Lester, meanwhile, tracked Santos to a swanky hotel in the centre while Watling decided to observe the block of luxury flats from a short distance further along the street. He rang his colleague, she answered immediately:

'Hi, boss, what's happening? Our man in black has gone into a fancy looking hotel called the Park Hyatt. I'm in the square next to it full of gardens and fountains, just down the road from where we're staying.'

'OK, keep where you are, Pen. I'm outside some apartment block. The couple went inside a few minutes ago. I'm going to observe this area for a while.'

'Have you heard anything from Dias?' asked Lester.

'No, nothing yet, speak again soon.'

It was roughly half an hour later when Dias called Watling to say that he'd followed Rodriguez back to his home. Benitez would continue to keep surveillance, Dias had to return to headquarters. Watling told him that both Lester and himself were in the central area tracking the three others.

For a while nothing happened but just before one o'clock the couple left the block of flats, Watling, trailing about fifty metres behind, walked after them. He contacted Lester and asked her to forget about the man in black, they knew where to find him, she was to join up with her boss. The detectives, together and sometimes independently, would pursue the couple.

On leaving the apartment complex, John and Lola headed for the Plaza Independencia. It was where Lester was already stationed so she was soon reunited with her boss when he arrived in the square. The plaza is a leafy place pleasantly shaded from the heat of the midday sun by an array of attractive sycamore and acacia trees. The detectives kept their eyes fixed on the couple, wherever they went, they followed. It was no easy task as the plaza was a busy place thronging with a mixture of locals and tourists. A crafts fair was in full swing and live music from buskers filled the air. Other squares in the city centre, the Plazas San Martin, Espana, Italia and Chile were later visited as the couple, hand in hand, flitted from shops to bars, to museums and back to shops. Later in the afternoon they ended up in the large Parque San Martin on the western edge of the city's business district. Now arm in arm, they walked around the perimeter of an elongated boating lake and took in the sweet smells of a fragrant rose garden before stopping to sit on a bench. Watling and Lester had kept them in sight at all times, both convinced that the man was the elusive character they were after. At about four in the afternoon they decided to apprehend their suspect. Watling approached the couple by himself, Lester stayed in the background.

'Excuse me,' said Watling. 'I'd like a word please.' He stared down at the man. 'I have reason to believe you are someone I've been looking for. I suspect that you're an English doctor called John Ripley?'

John glanced up at the tall man who'd unexpectantly interrupted his conversation with Lola. He realised immediately that his cover had been blown, the past had caught up with him at last. For a second or two he wondered whether to run but that would be a stupid move, a totally futile gesture. *Time to come clean. No point in running any more. Where could he go to anyway? He had Lola with him. An honest chat and a long overdue confession were now necessary.*

'We should talk, I can explain everything to you. Let's find a coffee bar somewhere,' said John calmly.

Watling was joined by the bulky figure of Lester, a worried looking Lola stayed quietly by John's side. They headed for one of several cafés distributed throughout the impressive park, a place designed in the late nineteenth century by the French architect, Charles Thays. Watling bought coffees for everyone. For roughly half an hour John Ripley held centre stage and proceeded to tell the detectives and Lola all that had happened many years ago in Fen View Cottage.

'So, Dr Ripley, you tell me it was an awful tragedy and, if what you say is really true, I can maybe agree with that conclusion, but you should still have gone to the police at the time and told them the truth. You've had lots of people searching for you since you ran away. A great deal of valuable police time and resources have been used up. I can sympathise but I cannot condone what you did either back in 1991 or more recently. You broke the law and deserted your wife and job. You have a lot of explaining to do, in a courtroom, to Lucy, and to your hospital,' said Watling.

'So, you want to take me back to Cambridge I suppose? I don't think that's a good idea. I have a new life in Argentina and America. I've suffered enough for the sins of my past,' pleaded John. 'Now you want me to suffer some more.'

'I'm a policeman, John. I've come all this way to Argentina to find you, to question you and bring you back. I have to uphold the law, that's my job.'

Unbeknown to all four of them someone else had been tracking not only John and Lola but also Watling and Lester as they'd been traipsing their way around the central areas of Mendoza. He'd been told where Lola lived and been asked to keep watch over both John and his girlfriend. He'd pursued them through the city centre and soon noticed that they were being tailed by a man and a woman who looked as if they could well be the English police. He'd followed them into the park and for the last half hour he'd been sitting quietly reading a magazine and drinking coffee in the café pretending to be minding his own business when, in reality, he'd been trying hard to eavesdrop the conversation at the corner table about five metres away to his left. He'd heard enough.

The man decided to take off his fake glasses but he tilted his old and faded blue hat further down over his broad forehead before ambling across towards the table. Suddenly, with no prior warning, he took a pistol fixed with silencer from his pocket and shoved it hard into the middle of Watling's back. He then whispered menacingly into the detective's left ear:

'Leave it alone Inglés, ... fuck off back to England, ... take your lady friend with you.'

John glanced up at the man and recognised the tall, imposing figure immediately. Underneath the old baseball cap it was Ángel, Santos's chief bodyguard. He'd turned up in the nick of time as usual. John well remembered his dramatic evening in Mexico City a few months earlier, this guy had the happy knack of appearing in the right place at the right time. Ángel continued with his instructions:

'John, go now, take your lady with you, you know where, my boss, he is expecting you both. Get out of here, fast.'

The customers and staff looked petrified by what was happening, some had spotted the powerful looking hand pistol stuck into the back of a stranger, and those that hadn't soon got the message as the bad news that they were in the wrong place at the wrong time was quickly passed from table to table. Customers were ordered by Ángel to put all their phones away otherwise they'd be shot. No calls, no photos, no sudden movements and hands up in the air please were the orders of the day.

Hand in hand with Lola, John sped from the café and headed swiftly out of the park. They walked hurriedly, and sometimes ran, along the street all the way to the Hyatt to link up with Santos in his penthouse suite. Soon after they'd left, Ángel noticed that Lester was carrying a gun under her thin jacket. He asked her to hand it over by slowly putting it on the table top with the barrel pointing towards her. She meekly obliged, she didn't have much choice in the matter. After apologising to the stunned café owner, frightened waitresses and dumb struck patrons for the sudden disturbance and distress caused by him pulling a gun on one of the customers, Ángel marched Watling and Lester outside into the bright afternoon sunshine. No-one inside the café dared to move a muscle or say a word, the place was gripped by nervous tension, fear was everywhere, you could have heard a pin drop it was that quiet. They realised that the customer from their worst nightmare had his cold eyes fixed on them all. His look and general demeanour screamed out to all that this man was an evil bastard who meant business and one false move would bring the perpetrator an early death and no-one wanted a red, round hole in their head. After ushering Watling and Lester outside, Ángel spoke quietly but firmly to them:

'Do as I say and you'll live but if you ever come looking for my friends again you go home to England in coffins, I guarantee you that. Now walk slowly away from me, as far as those trees in the distance and don't look back or I will have to shoot you both and I am a very good shot, probably the best in the whole of South America. I never miss.'

Watling and Lester wisely did as they were told, it took them about a couple of minutes to stroll along the pathway as far as the trees. They then stopped … time to turn around which they did, slowly. They stared back in the direction of the café, the big man had disappeared. Over in the distance the wailing noise of police sirens could be heard. Maybe the café owner, or one of his customers, had plucked up enough courage to ring the police but the brute with the gun was well away from the scene of the incident.

'What do we do now?' asked Lester.

'Do as we've been told I suppose,' replied a deflated looking Watling. 'It's far too dangerous for us here. We've found what we came for, even if we can't take Ripley back with us, we now know what he did all those years ago. We've had a confession from him.'

They left the park hurriedly not wanting to be detained by the local police. It had been a fraught last hour. After a quick stop at their hotel they walked to police headquarters where they met Dias to thank him for his assistance and explain all that had happened in the park. They'd be staying Saturday night in their hotel but next morning it would be a flight to Buenos Aires. It was then back off home to a safer life.

21

Watling rang up Cambridgeshire police headquarters from the hotel room and was put through to his boss who was attending a social event, it was late Saturday night. Eventually, a concerned ACC Hoskins barked out an order to his Detective Chief Inspector:

'I want both you and Lester back here, George. Ripley's been found, you've discovered what happened thirty years ago. The investigation into the doctor's whereabouts is now closed, I repeat, closed! The case is over ... apart from Hayes's trial of course. I don't want any more time and money spent on it. Most importantly, I don't want either of you getting killed over all this. It sounds like Ripley's mixing with hardened criminals. Get back here safely, George, soon as possible.'

'I fully understand, sir. We'll travel to Buenos Aires tomorrow and catch the first flight home.'

'Both of you take Monday off, come back into work fresh on Tuesday morning. There's plenty to keep you busy. A body was found outside Peterborough yesterday and, as I'm sure you're well aware, Benny Hayes's trial is coming up soon.'

'OK, sir, see you before long.'

The ACC ended the call and Watling went off to join Penny in the hotel bar. She was onto her second double gin and tonic. He too needed a stiff drink after meeting Ripley and his gun-toting rescuer. He ordered a double whisky.

John and Lola had returned to the Park Hyatt after their hasty exit from the park. Santos had been expecting his guests and welcomed them into his palatial suite. It was early evening, the sun was still shining, but it wasn't long before the bright light of the day started to dim and fade. As darkness enveloped the city the lights of Mendoza were a spectacular sight when viewed from the top floor apartment.

'You're welcome to stay here for the night,' said Santos kindly. 'It'll be safe, unlike Lola's flat. I expect the police will have found where she lives, they're bound to visit it hoping to capture you, John. Best stop here I think. Ángel will have done enough to scare off the English officers but I instructed him not to harm anyone, that would have been unnecessary. He's meeting us at the airport in the morning. As you know, I've agreed with Tomás that we shall fly to Trelew. We'll drive to his farm where you'll be dropped off, I'll then move on to my Atlantic coast hideaway.'

'Thank you once more, Federico. You and Ángel have saved me yet again.'

'You don't need to thank me, John. Any friend of Tomás is mine too. Take a holiday with Lola down in Patagonia but tonight you must remain in hiding here with me. I'll order room service and insist on paying.'

John and Lola wisely agreed to stay in the penthouse suite. They talked with Santos long into the night, mainly about each other's very different lives. John decided to ask a delicate question regarding Federico's connection with Tomás, he'd been wondering for a while whether his great friend was also involved in drug dealing. His suggestion was soon dismissed.

'Don't worry, John, your friend Tomás, he is an honest man and has made his money from only the wine trade ... at least as far as I'm aware,' he added as an afterthought with a wry smile. 'He's refused to launder money or act as a cover for my business dealings in any way whatsoever. Since our first meeting we've always got on well, he is great company for a man like me who is forever on the lookout for enemies, he cheers me up with his laughter and I trust him completely. I'm envious of Tomás, I wish I could be like him and live a normal life but, you know something (he laughed), I think I frighten Tomás. That is sad, but I find it funny also!' He laughed again, after a few glasses of wine Santos had started to relax and was beginning to display a softer side to his multi-faceted personality.

'Maybe I shouldn't ask you this, Federico, but don't you ever feel guilty about dealing in drugs?' probed Lola bravely.

'A good question, Lola. I should do, I know, but my simple answer is no, I don't feel guilty, I don't feel guilty at all. I started carrying drugs around from one shanty town to another when I was a child. It became a way of life for me but, as I grew up, I began learning about the construction industry and built up a successful business in my home city.'

'Why not stick to that then?' asked John hoping not to offend Santos.

'Because making money makes some men want to earn even more money, you become always greedy for more, you become obsessed, you are never satisfied with what you've got. I continued to deal in drugs. Cocaine, marijuana, ecstasy, you name it, I could deliver it. My friends and I became the leading suppliers in Rio and neighbouring areas, we eventually moved into Sao Paulo and battled with the cartels there. I've been wounded twice.'

Santos rolled up his left trouser leg and showed the scarring left by a bullet wound in his calf muscle. He then proceeded to lift up his shirt to reveal skin damage caused by a knife on the right side of his chest. He seemed proud of the wounds inflicted by the dangers of his trade.

'Both my industries prospered, but the drugs money, it was unbelievable. I grew rich quickly. My drug is money. When you go from no money to plenty of money it is the best drug in the world.'

He poured himself a beer from the well-stocked fridge and offered one to John that was readily accepted. Lola declined, she hadn't finished her wine.

'But what about all the human misery?' she asked, still in courageous mode after being fortified by several glasses of Malbec.

'If I think about it too much it would worry me, but I don't have any sympathy with those who use drugs. If the rich want to buy my cocaine so be it, I'm happy to take their money. Thank you very much I say. Someone has to meet the demand, so why not me? As for the poor ... well for most of them drugs are an escape from a world that offers them only suffering and more suffering. You talk about human misery, you know nothing of the misery caused by poverty, you have never experienced it, been amongst it or been touched by it in any way. A long time ago I lived in squalor day after day, year after year. The world is a place full of unhappiness, for both the rich and poor, with or without illegal drugs. I don't have a conscience about what I do but (he chuckled), if hell exists I shall be sitting alongside the devil when I die!' Santos swallowed back his drink, laughed once more, before continuing: 'But for now I shall enjoy life to the full, until that time comes.'

After learning a great deal about Santos's pathway through life, the two different worlds he lived in and the somewhat blasé attitude he had towards his criminal activities the hour was late and tomorrow would be a busy day for all. Santos made a few calls before retiring while Lola and John went off to their bedroom. It would be a night only for sleeping, they were both tired and Sunday was going to be a busy day.

Tomás had spent his Saturday afternoon and evening quietly at home. Irritatingly, Lucia continued to ask questions about the drugs find in one of his warehouses but the fact that her husband was in no trouble with the law had improved her mood. They enjoyed the late summer sunshine on one of the terraces at the back of the house. Like most parents they discussed their children, even though all three were now adults they were still their responsibility, Tomás and Lucia took parenthood seriously. They moved on to talking about having a week's holiday together in July, the height of winter, at Las Leñas, a ski resort high up in the Andes. They'd also try to fit in a trip to their little beach house on the Atlantic coast, outside Necochea, before the end of the autumn in either April or May.

Over dinner, Tomás sprang a surprise. He told Lucia he'd decided to travel to Trelew the next day, it was very short notice for his wife but he'd been meaning to have a few days down there to catch up with Dai Davies to discuss business plans. He also felt duty bound to make certain that John and Lola arrived safely before leaving them to enjoy their holiday together in the Patagonian countryside. He'd take the opportunity to travel in luxury, at no cost, courtesy of Federico's private jet.

Juan, their eldest son, arrived home late soon after midnight, earlier he'd been playing floodlit tennis and then visiting a night club with friends. Before retiring to bed he agreed to drop his father off at the airport in the morning. He'd be happy to manage the family business while Tomás was away, Juan knew that one day he'd inherit the wine empire and was always eager, when the opportunity arose, to prove he'd be up to the task.

Ángel had rushed from his rescue mission in the park to Santos's heavily guarded property located only a short walk away from Mendoza's central area. It took around ten minutes from the Parque San Martin, security guards had seen his approach and opened the entrance gates for him. The house, in a quiet residential district, was the most protected home in the city. After high perimeter walls there was a network of electric fences and tripwires and behind these outer defences three extremely large and potentially aggressive dogs, held firmly on leashes by their handler, regularly roamed the grounds. Inside the house, in a ground floor office, one security guard had a bank of TV screens in front of him, CCTV cameras were strategically placed around the property keeping a wary eye out for any unwelcome intruders. A guard with an automatic rifle protected the ground floor and another one patrolled upstairs, similarly armed. Ángel had his own rooms on the first floor. There was an open-plan living area with separate bedroom and bathroom. A pistol and high-powered rifle were always stationed near his bed, the wardrobe contained more boxes of ammunition than it did clothes. The top floor was Santos's domain, all the windows were bullet proof. The home was sealed off to outsiders but, judging by the strange faces seen milling around it in recent days, the Andrettis were onto where Santos lived when in the city.

Both Ángel and Santos had their main homes in Rio de Janeiro facing onto the Atlantic. It was where Ángel's lover, Luciana, resided as well as Santos's wife and teenage son.

Ángel was spending this particular night, as he so often did, in the Mendoza fortress, ready to link up with his boss in the morning at the airport. He'd have preferred to be with the curvaceous Luciana, a high maintenance lady with expensive tastes in clothes, jewellery, restaurants and holidays. Fortunately, Santos paid him handsomely, far better than the Brazilian Army where he'd previously been an elite member of their Special Forces. His bank balance had grown significantly since coming into Santos's employ three years ago, but he wasn't interested only in the money. Ángel was a man who enjoyed his job. If there was any protecting or killing to do, he was just the right man for it.

22

Federico Santos was not usually an early riser but today, Sunday, would be different. He was showered and dressed by six o'clock, ready to make several calls before breakfast. The first was to Ricky, he was told to meet his boss at Mendoza's small regional airport at eleven, ready to fly the seven hundred and fifty miles south to Trelew. The flight wouldn't take long, they'd be there by lunchtime. A couple of Santos's part-time employees would meet them.

Being fabulously rich, Santos was a man who could afford the finer things in life including expensive cars. He owned several and had recently taken delivery of a specially designed, custom built Land Rover Discovery. It was an eight valve, 6,200 bhp model built like a tank, a tough vehicle and also fast. Fuel consumption was alarmingly high but that didn't worry a man who was exceedingly wealthy and didn't give a damn about the environment. His new car had armour plating on the doors, bonnet, roof and boot and all the windows were bullet-proofed. He'd instructed his men to make sure it was full of guns and ammunition as well as fuel, ready and waiting for him on arrival in Trelew. The plan was to drop John and Lola off at the farmhouse not far outside the town. Tomás would be travelling with them too, he'd contacted Santos on Saturday afternoon and asked for a lift, it was not a problem, all three could be driven to the farm. Santos would then take refuge in an ingenuous property hidden from view on the remote Valdes peninsula, a piece of barren, salt-encrusted land that sticks out into the Atlantic Ocean, linked as it is by a narrow isthmus to the Argentinian mainland.

The drugs lord reckoned on lying low for a few days. It would give him an opportunity to make operational plans for the coming months. After recent events with rival organisations he had to figure out what would be the safest routes for moving coca paste and cannabis plants out of Bolivia and Paraguay into both Argentina and Brazil for processing and packaging and then how to transport the narcotics on to highly lucrative markets throughout the Americas. Drug shipments north into Central America, especially Nicaragua where Santos had a friend and business partner, and the U.S. needed discussing. There was also the ongoing feud with the Andretti mob to consider. Their South American base was Cordoba, a city that had become a major hub for the flow of drugs into Argentina from neighbouring countries. Santos had a lot to think about and several problems to solve. A gang of his men, acting without permission, had stolen a quarter of a million dollars' worth of cocaine, it was a stupid and unnecessary act of aggression against a rival gang. The three brothers who controlled the Andretti empire weren't going to let that pass quietly, pride had been dented, someone had to pay the price and that would be Santos if the Andretti boys ever got their hands on him. He couldn't return the drugs because they were now with the Drugs Enforcement Agency, a branch of the Argentinian police force. Santos was in big trouble with this rival cartel, they'd been sniffing around his Mendoza base for days. Shadowy figures had been seen circling at night outside his home and loitering near his city centre office.

Fortunately for Santos his rivals had no idea where he stored his supplies of illegal drugs. Wisely, he had warehouse facilities scattered throughout the Americas. The Andretti gang hadn't a clue that their particular package of stolen cocaine had ended up in a wine warehouse belonging to one of Santos's closest friends. This was very good news as far as Tomás Rodriguez was concerned because if the Andrettis had been aware of that fact they'd have come looking for him as well as Santos. After more calls over a working breakfast, Santos was joined by John and Lola. He politely told them to get a shift on before ordering a taxi to take them to the airport later.

Armed with his favourite pistols and a small bag of toiletries, Ángel left his boss's place. He intended walking to the airport, the exercise and fresh air would do him good before having to be cooped up in a plane. He too would be heading south to Patagonia. Surprisingly for a man with all his army training, Ángel didn't realise that he'd been spotted leaving the house. A man called Chico followed him all the way to the airport. This unsavoury looking character was the youngest of the three Andretti brothers and, by far, the most unhinged and unpleasant of them all. Other members of the Andretti mob had surrounded the airport, all were under orders to keep an eye out for Santos.

A few miles away, in the quiet, leafy suburb of Vistalba, Tomás had inadvertently slept in. He'd drank far too much wine late into the early hours despite Lucia telling him repeatedly to ease off bearing in mind his travel plans for the next morning. After a snatched breakfast, that included several cups of strong black coffee and a couple of paracetamol tablets, he would soon be stepping into the passenger seat of the family's sports car. Juan was ready to drive him to the airport to team up with the others, but things were about to change. Tomás's mobile pinged, it was Santos, his voice serious and full of concern.

'Our plans have altered, Tomás. The Andretti gang are at the airport, the place is swarming with them. I don't want any trouble or them knowing about my private plane.' He spoke in a commanding voice that stressed the urgency of the situation.

'I was just about to leave home to join you, Federico. What do you want me to do?' replied Tomás anxiously. His bad headache had just got a whole lot worse.

'Come and meet us, use your Range Rover, the one you keep hidden away. I've instructed my pilot to leave by himself and fly to San Raphael. It's the nearest airport in the direction we want to go. We'll meet him later today. Tomás, you'll have to drive us there, Ángel will sit with you in the front with John, Lola and me in the back.'

Tomás was not a happy man, he was expecting a fast trip south in a luxury jet, now he had been asked to ferry everyone on a long car journey and he felt in no fit state to drive.

'Fuck it, Federico, you've put me in the shit too many times lately,' he said angrily but in a quiet enough voice so that Lucia, next door in the kitchen, couldn't hear.

'Tomás, calm down! Look it's vital we shake off the Andrettis. They'd kill us given half a chance, but don't worry, I won't let that happen. You'll all be well looked after.'

Santos sounded calm and assured but Tomás felt the exact opposite. He was worried about what he'd once more got himself into, as well as feeling really bad about dragging both John and Lola into a whole pile of trouble but, half an hour later, a nerve-racked Tomás parked up his large Range Rover in a quiet street not far from the airport. Santos and the rest hurriedly scampered into his vehicle. Tomás had to head to San Raphael, one hundred and fifty miles away, it would take around three hours. They'd meet Ricky at the town's airport and continue their long journey south from there. It was imperative to be well clear of the Andrettis, they had to lose them before heading to the farm or anywhere else for that matter.

The Andretti gang had been skulking around the airport watching all the comings and goings since dawn. Chico's accomplices had ringed the place. They'd seen not only Ángel arrive but Santos also, accompanied by a long-haired man and a blonde-haired woman, in a taxi. Everything had been keenly observed. They too had a vehicle parked up in an adjacent street close to where Tomás's car was waiting and its driver had it all revved up and ready to follow Santos and his entourage to wherever they were planning on going. As it pulled away Chico sat in the passenger seat, a gun resting on his lap and an evil grin smeared across his ugly, pock-marked face. He was looking forward to ridding the world of Santos ... his travelling companions also if necessary.

23

The car journey from Mendoza to San Raphael heads along Ruta 40, one of the world's great highways, comparable in status to America's famous Route 66. The road runs parallel to the Andes for over three thousand miles linking the desolate semi-deserts of southern Patagonia, near Rio Gallegos, to the equally arid but much warmer lands around La Quiaca, a high-altitude town on the border between Argentina and Bolivia. For Tomás Rodriguez the drive south would cover less than a hundred miles on the road favoured by so many South American adventurers. Eventually he would have to turn off along the straight as a die RN143, a far more isolated road ideal for a possible hijack.

Tomás was familiar with the route from his home city down to San Raphael, a picturesque town that marks the southern limit of the Cuyo wine belt. He'd visited the place often enough. Normally he was by himself or with his wife and family, the usual reason for travel being either the wine business or seeing friends, sometimes both combined. But this was different. He was now heading there with one of the major figures in the world of international drug trafficking, together with his bodyguard, plus a friend on the run from the English police and, most worryingly of all, he had to transport a young lady sommelier who'd become caught up in an extremely tricky situation. Tomás felt especially guilty having Lola in tow because he'd been responsible for introducing her to John. He fervently hoped they'd all have a safe journey and be able to climb aboard Santos's plane at San Raphael's little airport without any hassle but he knew only too well that Santos was on the run from a ruthless American drugs cartel desperate to find him. Trouble had a habit of following Santos around.

Only the previous night Tomás thought he'd be spending a few days visiting one of his latest ventures, a sheep farm that was diversifying into growing strawberries, raspberries and blackcurrants with the help of irrigation water channelled from the River Chubut. His plans were for the fruit to be used in the production of preserves for sale all over South America. John and Lola were coming along for a holiday. Tomás had only himself to blame for rashly deciding to accept a lift in a private jet rather than opting for the safer alternative of travelling south on a scheduled internal flight. Now, due to suddenly changed circumstances, he'd been forced into driving Santos on a long road trip. To make matters worse, Tomás was nursing an annoyingly persistent hangover that didn't show signs of clearing any time soon. Realising that his wine merchant friend was both feeling unwell and looking harassed at the prospect of the drive to San Raphael, Santos did his best to reassure his old buddy.

'Don't worry, Tomás, you have Ángel and me to look after you all. Everything's going to be fine.'

As the smallest person in the group Santos positioned himself in the middle of the back seat lodged in between John to his left, the driver's side, and Lola to the right. The large, muscular frame of Ángel sat in the front passenger seat, Glock pistol at the ready in his right hand. He was constantly on the alert looking out at the passing scenery and vehicles for any sign of danger.

'Once in San Raphael we'll head to Trelew by plane and then go our separate ways. All you have to do, Tomás, is make sure you get us there,' added Santos.

'This is quite an exciting start to our little holiday, Lola,' joked John, as he tried to ease the tension that he sensed existed between Tomás and Santos.

'I can see that life is never going to be boring with you, John, or with the company you keep.' She too tried to make light of their situation.

Santos did most of the talking as they headed south out of Mendoza at a steady 60 mph on the RN40. Tomás concentrated hard on the driving, he had to with his dull headache and tired eyes. Ángel remained quiet and impassive in the front while John and Lola joined in the conversation. Talk was mostly about the contrasting views on the opposite sides of their vehicle. To the right, flat expanses of irrigated farmland, mostly full of vines, spread outwards and upwards into the foothills of the snow-capped mountain peaks of the Andes. John, recognising various landmarks and roadside advertising hoardings, remarked that he'd been this way only a few days ago with Lola. She agreed, they were travelling along the road they'd taken to the Bousquet winery at Tupungato. In stark contrast to the greenery of the well-watered fields, the land to their left, the east, was dominated by desiccated, serrated ridge tops, the Sierra de Tunuyán, an infertile range of hills cut into by hundreds of dried-up river courses, arroyos, that only carried water after the occasional summer downpours. Whilst his travelling companions marvelled at the impressive and contrasting landscapes, Santos, stuck in the middle on the back seat, kept on reassuring everyone that all was well. He felt sure no-one was tailing them. He'd been looking out of the back window regularly, there was nothing to worry about he kept on repeating … but the Andretti mob were following behind at a discreet distance.

Unfortunately, Santos had been seen earlier leaving the side street near Mendoza's airport. Chico and his men had trailed them out of the city in their filthy, dust covered SUV. Heavy traffic helped hide the fact that Tomás's Range Rover was being followed.

Chico ordered his driver to turn the radio down, he was trying to hear a call from his older brother seated in a helicopter high in the sky above them. It had taken off, from a patch of derelict land in suburban Mendoza, only a few minutes before Tomás and friends departed the airport area. From his vantage point Bruno was able to keep watch on where Santos was heading. After studying a road map on his cell phone, he advised his younger brother to overtake the Range Rover and head to Pareditas, a place where the road to San Raphael veered off from the RN40. Bruno reckoned that if Santos had decided not to use the airport in Mendoza he'd probably be hoping to elude his enemy by heading for the nearest airport instead. Bruno would keep careful watch on their quarry from the air, the Andrettis on the ground could maybe ambush Santos somewhere along the lonely road to San Raphael if and when the opportunity presented itself.

Following his brother's instructions, Chico's vehicle passed the Range Rover and accelerated off to the small settlement of Pareditas. They'd park up along the roadside and observe which way Santos headed once at the junction of the two different routes there. Chico and Bruno were full of optimism, things were looking good, a successful chase would be followed by a triumphant capture, big brother would be pleased. Neither of them had a clue who the driver was or for that matter the man with the long hair and the attractive female, but if they were collateral damage when they eventually intercepted Santos and his bodyguard, well that would be just too bad.

24

Luca Andretti stared out at the dark waters of the Hudson River from the comfort of his top floor apartment on West 72nd Street in the heart of New York City. For the past five years he'd been renting a luxury penthouse in an elegant seventeen storeys high condominium. The building, constructed in 1928, had undergone several reincarnations during its lifetime. The monthly rental was $4,000 which was OK for this part of Manhattan, the Andrettis could easily afford it. Luca and other male members of his family used the place as their operations centre. However, for much of the time it belonged to Luca, he was the head honcho after all, it was the office from where he directed the business operations as well as a residence for entertaining his mistress and high-class, if also high-cost, prostitutes whenever the fancy took him.

Luca, now aged forty-five but looking a good deal older with his beer gut and bald head, controlled a drugs empire stretching from Maine in New England all the way down the eastern seaboard through the Carolinas to Florida, on into Mexico and various Central American countries such as Guatemala and Nicaragua. It extended further south to cover most of South America. Due to family connections there were strong links with Italy and Europe. The Australian market was expanding as was the Far East with a distribution depot in Manila. Luca's other home was the city of Cordoba, his South American base in Argentina but he, like his younger brothers, had been born and brought up in New York City and that's where he spent most of his time. The Cordoba operations were run by a capable subordinate, his cousin, Carlo Pozzo.

Many Italians had migrated to Cordoba from the nineteenth century onwards, a few were corrupt and dealt in illegal practices, the Andretti family were a prime example. The current godfather of the clan was Ricardo Andretti. He'd relocated his criminal empire from Cordoba to New York City back in the 1970s in order to link up with family members there. Their ancestors, all connected to the Mafia, had emigrated to America as long ago as the early 1920s. Ricardo was now seventy-two, semi-retired, and happy to leave most of the business affairs to his sons. He lived with his wife just south of Central Park, not far from Carnegie Hall, the world-famous venue for concerts. Luca's and Bruno's families lived in the same apartment. Little brother, the unmarried Chico, made up the extended family set. To escape the uncomfortable summer heat of high-rise Manhattan, and as a weekend retreat, the wealthy Andrettis also owned a large detached, early twentieth century house out on Long Island, in the Hamptons, their palatial home and grounds fronted onto the Atlantic.

Luca, being the eldest and most ruthless of the three siblings, was now the undisputed boss of the organisation. Reliable middle brother, Bruno, did the donkey work under Luca's instructions whereas the younger Chico did most of the killings. That was his strong point, his only speciality in fact, because apart from being handy with a gun he was a bit of a dumbass who'd missed out badly in the brains department.

Luca didn't usually work Sundays, he preferred to spend the day with family, either strolling around Central Park or relaxing at their Long Island beachfront mansion but, on this particular day, he was directing an important and delicate operation. It was lunchtime in 'The Big Apple'. Luca, always greedy for food, was eating an extra-large cheese burger and French fries between making calls to his gang members. From high up in central Manhattan, Luca was supervising operations happening several thousands of miles away in South America. He was barking out instructions to his second in command. Bruno, with the help of powerful binoculars, was surveying the irrigated plains, arid hills and parched plateau lands of western Argentina.

'Bruno, keep a damn good look out on where that son of a bitch Santos goes!' snapped Luca aggressively. As he spat out the words bits of beef burger flew from his mouth and dollops of tomato ketchup and mustard dripped down the front of his white shirt. Expletives followed as he wiped the mess he'd created with a napkin, his action only made it look a whole lot worse.

'Don't worry bro, we're on his tail, he's heading south from Mendoza. We reckon he's going to a town called San Raphael to connect up with his fancy jet at the airport there,' replied Bruno reassuringly.

'I thought you said his plane was parked up on the runway in Mendoza. What the fuck happened?' asked Luca, choking on a mouthful of food.

'Yeah, that's right, it was earlier this morning. He turned up at the airport, with some cool looking dude in shades, a lady in toe also, before meeting up with Ángel, his bodyguard. We reckoned they were planning on going off somewhere in the jet, but then, all of a sudden, they left the airport and met another guy in a car parked up in a nearby side-street. Chico has followed it out of the city.'

'OK, OK, so you've got Santos in sight. Don't let that fuckwit brother of ours screw this up, Bruno! You know how stupid he can be. I want Santos taken alive. We get our cocaine back or the money he owes me, with interest,' ordered Luca.

Half his burger accidentally dropped on the floor, a string of expletives followed. Long streams of vulgar language flowed out of Luca's mouth most days of the week except at the times he turned all respectable when around his wife and family. He'd started swearing and cursing at a young age, well before he became a teenager. Back then his Italian-American 'mamma' threatened to wash his mouth out with soap and water but the warnings only increased Luca's fondness for using foul language. In the circles he moved it added to his street cred.

'We'll get Santos, don't you worry,' answered Bruno reassuringly. He'd spent his working life trying to placate his volatile and difficult to please older brother.

'Just follow them, don't do anything until I say so. Pass that on to Chico, I can't get him on his mobile for Christ's sake … dumb fucker's gone and got it switched off I expect. Keep me informed, I need to know what's going on, Bruno, and don't, I repeat don't, do anything until I say so. I don't want this fucked up! When you've got Santos let me know immediately, I'm then coming down, I want to deal with Santos, slice him up myself.'

25

It's seventy-seven miles by road from Mendoza to Pareditas. At the road junction, Tomás, as the Andrettis had anticipated, turned left onto the RN143 in the direction of San Raphael. The powerful Range Rover headed away from the vineyards of the Tunuyán and Uco Valley areas into far drier and dustier lands as it ventured into the sun scorched desert that separates the small settlement of Pareditas and the well-watered oasis town that is San Raphael. This part of the journey would take over an hour in the searing heat of a late summer's afternoon. For most people in this part of Argentina it would be siesta time, especially on a Sunday.

It was not long after crossing yet another dried-up river channel, the Rio Seca De Las Peñas, that Ángel suspected they were being followed. In the sky, to his right, he'd seen the hazy outline of something. At first, he thought it might be a giant bird of prey, possibly a condor gliding on a rising air current, but after hearing the faint buzz of an engine he quickly realised what it was.

'Could be bad news, boss. Someone's following us, in the sky to our right, there's a helicopter,' he said, while looking skywards out of the side window.

Santos had also noticed something. He'd been staring out of the back window roughly every five minutes to see if anyone was trailing them. He too had observed a possible problem. A dark coloured vehicle had been tailing them ever since they'd turned onto the RN143. It looked like an old and battered Jeep Cherokee. He, like his bodyguard, was becoming increasingly concerned that enemies were after him once more.

'OK, everyone, don't be alarmed but I think someone's following us. They've been careful to keep their distance. The gap has never changed, and that makes me real suspicious,' whispered Santos.

'You and me too, boss, you've seen the car, me the helicopter,' said Ángel.

'*Mierda!*' shouted Tomás in annoyance. 'What do we do now?' His headache had returned and he started fumbling about in the car's glove box looking for paracetamol tablets.

'Put your foot down, Tomás!' ordered Santos. 'Let's see what happens.'

After hurriedly swallowing a couple of pills, Tomás did as he was told and concentrated his attention fully on the road ahead. John and Lola were now looking up at the sky through the side windows and turning their heads to see out of the car's rear window. Santos told them to keep calm, he didn't want their pursuers thinking they'd been rumbled.

'This changes our plans. Head straight into the centre of town please, Tomás, don't stop at the airport,' ordered Santos.

In the distance, in front of them, the first signs of San Raphael were coming into view. The town is surrounded by vineyards fed by an intricate system of irrigation canals constructed during the early nineteenth century pioneer days. They developed where two major rivers flowing out of the Andes converge, the Rios Diamante and Atuel supply plenty of water to the area. Highly fertile alluvial soils have been deposited over thousands of years and the first settlers from Spain and Italy soon realised the agricultural potential of the area. *Fincas* sprouted up, flourished and swiftly grew in number. Throughout the town itself many of the major roads are lined with *acequias*, street side canals, as well as by rows of leafy sycamores and acacias that provide welcome shade on hot summer days. Without irrigation San Raphael would find it hard to exist.

Tomás, as instructed, passed alongside the airport on the way into the town's centre. Santos's Cessna could be seen parked up next to a row of aircraft hangars. Whereas it took Tomás almost three hours to cover the journey from Mendoza it had only taken Ricky twenty minutes to fly there. After passing the entrance to the Aeropuerto de San Raphael, Tomás headed towards the central square with its palm trees and fountains and found a parking spot along a nearby street. After leaving the car they walked towards a restaurant Santos knew well, the *Café del Mundo*, positioned in one corner of the Plaza San Martin. It was closed for now so they decided to spend some time wandering around the area, watch the world go by, and maybe take a look at the impressive cathedral. They were safe in the busy plaza. Santos, unsurprisingly, was keener on observing who might be walking about. He'd been thinking hard and later, apart from dinner in the café, he wanted to discuss necessary re-arrangements to their plans with his companions in peril.

Chico had also driven into San Raphael under strict orders to observe Santos from afar. Both Bruno and Luca didn't want a shoot-out in the centre of a busy town, a 'blood bath' with many casualties would look bad in the papers and on television. The police would be forced into an investigation. It was always best to carry out gangland feuds in the countryside well away from populated areas and preferably at night.

An hour spent strolling around had given Santos all the time he needed, his imaginative mind had formulated a crafty solution to the tricky situation they were in. He'd make clear to his companions what his plans for later would be, but that could wait for a while. They entered the café when it opened at five, after the afternoon siesta. Drinks were ordered, dinner would follow and then they'd get down to serious business. Most Argentinians eat late so the café was quiet between five and seven during which time they'd been served with a three-course meal. It was time for Santos to reveal his master plan.

'I think we have a busy and maybe difficult few hours ahead, Andretti's men have followed us here, of that I am sure. They've tracked us by car and helicopter, they too are in town as well as the sky. They probably know we are here in this cafe right now. I deliberately chose this table well away from the windows, they can't see so easily from outside. The place is getting busier, soon they won't see us at all.'

'Is that not bad?' asked Tomás, alarmed at the situation. 'We can't see them either!'

'I don't think they'd want to cause any trouble in here or in the town centre, too many customers around, too many possible casualties and witnesses. People taking photos, videos even, the power of social media. There is strength in numbers,' replied Santos.

'So, Federico, what do you reckon we should do?' asked John.

'We wait for dark and for this place to really fill up. Then we make our move. I've been thinking about our options.'

'What have you in mind?' asked Lola.

'We could go back to the car, drive on out of town, head south to Patagonia but Trelew is a long way off. We'd have to travel through the night. Tomás is tired, he couldn't drive all the way. We could share the driving, but we'd have to stop to change drivers and fill up with fuel. I'm sure we'd be followed.'

'Stopping anywhere that's quiet, even at a gas station, would be the perfect opportunity for Andretti's men to jump us!' exclaimed Ángel.

'Exactly!' responded Santos. 'That's why we won't be doing that. You'll have to leave your car here in San Raphael, Tomás, it'll be safe for a few days.'

'That's fine, one of my staff can pick it up,' replied Tomás. He was all ears waiting to hear his friend's plans.

'OK, so we ditch the car,' said John. 'Are we going to still use your plane?'

'We will, but we have to do it unexpectantly and quickly. We need a head start on the Andrettis, we have to get away from them, and I think I know how,' answered Santos. The little man from Brazil broke into a smile.

Santos was a clever and cunning operator. That's how he'd managed to stay at the top of his business and also keep himself and others safe for so long. Throughout many years of moving around the Americas he'd made loads of money as well as overcoming innumerable dangers and, despite many formidable foes, he'd always managed to find a way out of any difficult predicament still alive and kicking and ready to make more money. He was a slippery customer and an old hand at getting out of the troubles that regularly confronted him.

Santos reassured everyone that all was going to be OK. He told his friends they'd be moving out of the restaurant before long, but there must be no rush, nothing to attract any attention from prying eyes. Santos knew it was going to be a very dark night, visibility would be poor, especially once away from the glare of lights in the central plaza. Santos was buzzing, he felt good, he oozed confidence. He informed the others it was the time of the month when there'd be a new moon with no full or even half-moon to light up the night sky, Santos reckoned that darkness would help in their escape. His plans for the evening would eventually involve them flying to Trelew from the local airport. Santos reckoned that the enemy possessed only a helicopter and a car. He'd researched their capabilities and was happy to tell his companions that the helicopter's cruising speed was about 170 mph, its maximum wouldn't be much more, their car would struggle to average 50-60 mph in the black of the night across sometimes bumpy roads through seemingly never-ending stretches of desert. On the other hand, Santos's jet could easily do 400-500 mph and it had a range of well over one and a half thousand miles. The Andrettis's helicopter would have to stop to refuel, its range would be around six hundred miles. Trelew was about eight hundred miles away. A bit of simple arithmetic and anyone could work out that Santos and his friends, providing that they could get into their jet and take off safely without any hassle, would be in Trelew well before the Andrettis and anyway, once safely airborne, the enemy wouldn't have a clue where they were heading. The trickiest part of the evening would be leaving the café unnoticed, making their way to the airport and then climbing on the plane without being seen and intercepted.

'This all sounds fine, Federico, but how the hell do we get out of here without anyone connected with the Andretti mob seeing us? They watch us leave, then they follow us to the airport and then they attack us. What are we going to do?' asked Tomás in a rather exasperated voice.

'Don't worry, Señor Rodriguez,' said Ángel. 'My boss and I, we have discussed things, our plan is a good one, it will succeed.'

'When we get to Trelew we'll have several hours advantage over the Andrettis, that's if they ever realise we've gone there in the first place,' added Santos.

Tomorrow he'd be safe, well out of the clutches of the Andretti gang, and his three friends would also be out of harm's way on Dai Davies's sheep ranch. Tomás could discuss business ideas with his farm manager while John and Lola would be free to enjoy a holiday in the wide-open spaces of Patagonia. That was the plan but sometimes even the best laid schemes don't run smoothly.

26

'What the fuck's going on?' asked an irate Luca Andretti. He was still in his Upper West side apartment trying to direct operations happening over five thousand miles away on the other side of the Americas.

'I'm at the airport, Luca, refuelling the chopper,' replied Bruno. 'Chico's with the others, they've tracked Santos down. He's with his mates in some café, lucky devil. I'm starving and badly need a drink.'

'Remind Chico to keep watch only,' ordered Luca. 'I don't want no fucking shoot out in a town with the fuzz all around the goddam place. Go get yourself some eats and a cold beer, Bruno.'

While they were talking Chico and his four henchmen were stationed outside the *Café del Mundo*, all placed in strategic positions around the Plaza San Martin. Chico and his deputy, a big brute of a man named Sergio, shared a pair of binoculars as they tried hard to keep watch on their intended targets. They could see Santos and his party seated, talking and laughing, at the back of the café, but the gang's watching brief became increasingly more difficult as the light of the day gradually faded. The popular eating and watering hole filled up quickly with customers and it became harder and more challenging to see what was going on once the inside surfaces of windows started to steam up with condensation. As the evening wore on good visibility from the square into the café became impossible.

This frustrated Chico but, despite his reputation for recklessness, he wasn't completely dumb. Even he realised that he couldn't go barging in and causing an almighty row in such a crowded place. A shoot-out would be complete madness, confrontation would have to wait for later when a suitable opportunity presented itself. His eldest brother's implicit instructions had been passed on by Bruno several times: Luca wanted Santos alive. Best time to capture him would be somewhere quiet and rural during the long night ahead. He had to be patient, only keep watch for now.

Over three hours had been spent inside the café, it was nearly half past eight when Santos decided to explain how they were going to leave the café safely and make their way to the airport without being followed.

'OK, everyone, we need to start moving soon,' he said calmly. 'I've paid the bill and tipped the staff well, the manager knows my plans, he is fully aware of our predicament. He wants no trouble and expects us to leave without fuss. We leave quietly and secretly.'

'And how is that going to be achieved, Federico?' asked Tomás, concern written large across his face.

'Is there a way out around the back?' questioned John.

'Ángel and I, we have been here before. Just after the toilets area there is a door that opens into a yard that cannot be seen from the square, it leads outside onto a side street. That is our way out of here.'

'What happens when we are in the street? Won't we be noticed by the Andrettis?' asked Lola.

'It's well screened by all the surrounding buildings and trees, we can depart without being seen,' replied Santos.

'My boss is right!' added Ángel firmly. 'He will leave first, with Tomás, the rest of us will follow five minutes later. Two taxis will be waiting at the end of the street to take us to the airport, my boss booked them an hour ago. John, you, Lola and me will be in the second taxi.'

'We will meet up again at the airport, then catch my plane to Trelew where I have arranged for us to be met by my men,' said Santos.

'OK, suppose we manage to reach the airport, what about Andretti's men? Some we know are outside keeping watch on this place but what's happened to their guys in the helicopter?' asked Tomás.

'They're bound to be waiting for us at the airport!' exclaimed John.

'That may well be so, it is highly likely, that's why we are going into the kitchens here first before leaving. I've agreed it with the manager and my friends in the kitchen,' said Santos. He broke into one of his broad smiles. 'Tonight, my friends, we are travelling to the airport in disguise, we go there as chefs, waiters, and in your case Lola, a waitress!'

Ángel took over from his boss: 'If we are seen leaving here from the backyard, and that's unlikely to happen, we'll look like staff going off duty. Later, at the airport, we'll look like a team of everyday caterers delivering food and drinks onto the plane. We'll borrow some trolleys and packages containing food and drink items. I know where to find them.'

'Wow, I like it! The plan sounds ingenious. Let's hope it works. I reckon it will … if we remain calm and collected,' said John positively.

He smiled at Lola, she smiled back, but Tomás was less impressed.

'Well, I'm not so sure about all this,' he blurted out. Then, after looking at the others and a moment of reflection, he spoke again: 'But, OK, maybe it's crazy enough to work. I suppose it beats having to shoot our way out of here and onto the plane.' After another brief pause he added with a confidence he didn't really feel inside: 'Let's go for it then. What the hell are we waiting for?'

Tomás and Santos went first. After borrowing the requisite coats, trousers and head gear they ventured into the yard at the back of the café. After slowly and carefully opening a door built into the side wall of the courtyard they were out onto a quiet, dimly lit pavement. Like many Argentinian streets, its name is connected with one of their military heroes from the past, in this case a Colonel Ricardo Day. Without looking back towards the plaza outside the front of the café, the two men walked casually to the end of the road. Sure enough, a taxi was waiting for them, they jumped in and the driver sped off in the direction of the airport. Five minutes later, John, Lola and Ángel, dressed in similar catering attire, followed suit. There were no hitches, things went smoothly, all five of them were at the airport within a quarter of an hour after leaving the café. Things couldn't have gone any better.

Outside the *Café del Mundo*, Chico was becoming increasingly worried. For the last fifteen to twenty minutes both he and Sergio couldn't see any of the blurred figures that had recently been seated at the table where they knew Santos and his companions had positioned themselves. The misted-up windows were now impossible to see through. Chico decided he needed to find out what the hell was going on in there. After telling Sergio what he intended to do, he ventured inside the busy café.

A few minutes later he returned fuming. Santos, all of them, had disappeared. One of the waiters had told him that the bill had been settled half an hour ago and the group had left, he didn't know where they'd gone. Urgently, Chico rang his brother at the airport.

'Hi, Bruno, bad news! Santos, and the other fuckers, they've given us the slip, they've somehow left the café. Must be some other way in and out, we had the main entrance and the backdoor exit covered.'

'I bet they're on their way here,' responded an unruffled Bruno. 'I'm with the chopper, it's refuelled ready to go. Santos's plane is still parked up. Luca told me to just wait here, observe what was going on, have a meal and a beer in the meantime.'

While the brothers conversed on their mobiles Santos's two groups had already arrived at the airport. Cleverly disguised as catering staff making deliveries, they made their way onto the Cessna Citation. Bruno, meanwhile, stared out through the café's windows and noticed there was activity around the jet.

'Looks like they're taking deliveries on Santos's flash plane, Chico. Get over here ASAP, leave a couple of men to keep a watch on the café in case Santos makes a sudden appearance.'

'OK, be with you soon.'

The Cessna's powerful engines suddenly started up with a roar. Still disguised in catering uniforms Santos and his companions were sat back in their reclined seats feeling rather pleased with themselves. Ricky, the pilot, accelerated rapidly down the short runway. As they were about to take-off Bruno shouted down his phone:

'What the hell, I don't believe it! Get over here, Chico, real quick, all of you. Santos's plane has only just gone and taken off!'

A moment later Bruno's other cell phone rang, it was big brother, still seated in his lair in the centre of Manhattan. He now had the unenviable task of telling Luca what had happened. Upon hearing the bad news, he imploded and bawled down the phone, something about running an organisation staffed by morons. A stream of expletives blasted down the line.

'I'm coming down, run the fucking show for proper. How come that asshole brother of ours can lose five people when they're sitting in a goddam café for fuck's sake!?'

Once his rant was over, it was time for action. He intended catching the next flight out of New York. Destination Buenos Aires.

27

While John and his friends had been travelling by car to San Raphael, Watling and Lester were catching an afternoon flight out of the international airport on the outskirts of Buenos Aires, intending to be back in London on Monday morning and hoping to be in Cambridge by the afternoon. During the long flight they had much to discuss, it helped pass the hours. In some ways their Argentinian trip was mission accomplished but, unfortunately, Ripley wasn't travelling back with them to face the music in England. They were happy to have caught up with the elusive doctor at long last but it had been a Saturday with a difference, it was the first time in his long police career that Watling had experienced a gun stuck in his back. Before that scary incident they'd listened to an honest and plausible account from Ripley about what had happened three plus decades ago, back in 1991. Watling, quite rightly, had wanted to extradite Ripley back to the UK, but his gangster friend had put an abrupt stop to that.

'As far as Hoskins is concerned the Fen View Cottage case is now closed, Pen, apart from Hayes's trial of course.' Watling sounded disappointed and frustrated.

'If we can't do any more we ought to see Mrs Ripley out of courtesy and pay a visit to Addenbrooke's to put them in the picture.'

'I agree, we need to see her first, as soon as possible, and then visit the hospital. You want to know something else, Pen? The case might be officially closed but I'm not finished with it, even if Hoskins is.'

'Right, well, you'd better keep things low key, very hush-hush then, he won't be happy if you spend any more police time and resources on it and gets to find out. We've plenty of other stuff to keep us busy.'

Watling went on to explain that he'd be at work on Tuesday and Wednesday before taking some time off. He wanted to go with Jill for a holiday, but he'd definitely be doing some detective work in his own time over the next few weeks. Lester could help out if she'd nothing better to do when off-duty. Watling said he wanted to delve more deeply into the 'spooky' theme that kept cropping up whenever they'd been investigating the Fen View case.

'Do you know, Pen, I think I once told you that I didn't believe in ghosts. Well, that wasn't strictly true. Believe it or not, I have first-hand experience of the supernatural.'

'What! ... you're kidding me? Do you really believe in all that guff, sir? It's a load of bollocks! There's no such thing as ghosts, or an afterlife for that matter.' Lester had a way with words, always direct and to the point, no skirting around an issue.

'Don't dismiss the idea of ghosts quite so easily, Pen. Many would disagree with you, including me.'

Watling went on to describe his own paranormal experience, something that happened many years ago. At the time he and his wife were on holiday in Devon. The old building they'd rented for a week had been a railway station but, like so many others in rural districts across Britain, it had been closed down after the then Transport Minister, Richard Beeching, introduced sweeping cuts to the rail system during the 1960s. After lying empty the station became a private house but was later converted into a holiday home during the 1990s. Watling and his wife stayed there soon after the self-catering accommodation was opened. One night, after going to bed and before falling asleep, Watling heard strange noises. It sounded like furniture being thrown about. He realised that the racket was coming from the attic space above the bedroom. Watling woke Jill up, she too heard the din. It was a weird, worrying experience. Eventually what had sounded like the crashing together of chairs and tables died down but Watling and his wife, understandably, decided to keep the bedroom light on until dawn arrived. They mentioned the strange incident to the owner who apologised for what had happened and offered a hefty discount on the rental cost. After further discussion with the owner, more was revealed. Apparently, the owner's elderly parents, who'd used the house before moving into a care home, had also experienced strange happenings. The scariest of the lot was when the father of the owner saw a ghostly face peering around the bathroom door one night. Watling continued his story: on the morning after the event, he and his wife used a stepladder to help them open the hatch to the attic in order to peer inside with the help of a torch. What they saw was only a small, dark and dusty space, not enough room for an adult to stand up in, and it was empty apart from a few scraps of old but undamaged furniture.

'Bloody hell, boss, that would have freaked me out. I'd have left the bedroom and slept in the car.'

Watling went on to say that the owner, Mr Mason, told him the old railway station had a long history going back to the 1870s. From what he'd heard from elderly villagers a tragedy had occurred there during World War II. A soldier, on leave, had disembarked off a train and was walking along the platform in the dark. He'd been drinking heavily. No lamps were on because of 'black-out' regulations and, in his drunken state, the serviceman either forgot about or perhaps didn't realise that there was a long drop from the platform to the station car park and bus stop below. He didn't use the steps, he recklessly jumped off the platform and the long fall killed him. Mason was told it was the soldier's ghost that sometimes haunted the place and his father had described the face he'd seen momentarily as that of a young man. According to local hearsay the soldier was a lost soul, unable or unwilling to pass over to the other side was how Mason had put it.

'I don't know whether to believe all this shit but it sure makes for an interesting story, boss. So ever since then you've believed in ghosts, yeah?' asked Lester somewhat sarcastically.

'I know it seems illogical, especially to the uninitiated like you, Pen, but there's a lot we don't understand and things that modern science can't or hasn't as yet explained. God knows why we stayed on at the place.

'Don't suppose you returned for another holiday?' asked Lester somewhat sardonically.

'Absolutely no chance!'

Watling went on to say that he'd be visiting Bob Hemingway, at his farm on the fenlands, as soon as possible. He wanted another chat to find out more about the history of the now demolished cottage. He'd also love to visit Benny Hayes in London, but with his court case pending that wouldn't be possible. Watling reckoned that Hayes knew a lot more than what he'd told the police so far. Seances had been held there, even a full-scale black mass had been mentioned by Janey Harrison, his ex-girlfriend. He'd also told the police about seeing the ghost of a lady dressed in Victorian clothing. Watling had a contact, a good friend, who might be able to help.

'I know a Cambridge don at Christ's College. He's into paranormal stuff and is a member of the famous Ghost Club. Are you interested in doing a bit of spare time detective work, Pen? Can I count you in on this?'

'You bet, it sounds fascinating!'

28

Before leaving his Manhattan penthouse to catch the next flight from JFK to Buenos Aires Luca Andretti was in discussion once more with his brother.

'How many goddam airports are there in Argentina, Bruno? Do you have any idea where Santos has gone?'

'Must be well over thirty, Luca, it's a big country, but we've had one hell of a lucky break. Normally we wouldn't have had any idea where he's flown off to, and our chopper can't compete with his fancy jet for speed or range, but guess what? His pilot has been careless, he's only gone and left us a massive clue!'

'Yeah, and what's that then?' shouted Luca aggressively, eager for information.

'One of our men followed the guy into the airport café, before Santos showed up. When he took out his wallet at the cash till something fell from the pocket of his flying jacket. He didn't realise he'd dropped a scrap of paper. It stayed on the floor, our man picked it up ... and guess what?' replied an exultant sounding Bruno.

'What for Christ's sake? Get straight to the point!' shouted an impatient Luca.

'The paper had all sorts of stuff on it, how much overtime he was owed, how much fuel he'd put in the jet and, wait for it, this is the important bit, the distance, the co-ordinates and the compass bearing to an airport! I reckon we hit the goddam jackpot, Luca!' exclaimed Bruno.

'And where is this fucking airport?' snapped Luca.

'I checked it out, place called Trelew. It's some hick town down south, about seven hundred miles away, in Patagonia. That's where they're heading, Luca. That must be the place!'

'Right, listen to me Bruno, and you listen damn good. Get Chico and three of the men to travel to Trelew in the chopper, you go with them. The other guy can drive down, I suppose it'll take him most of the night but you'll then have the Jeep as well as the helicopter. You'll have to stop on the way to refuel, must be another airport between where you are and where you're going?'

'There is, I've already checked, place called Neuquén, it's around half way.'

'Good, you're not a dumbass like Chico. Now go there ASA fucking P, Bruno. We have two men down in that part of the world. I'll tell them to shift their asses to the airport and follow Santos when he arrives. When you get there, join them, keep an eye on Santos, watch where he goes. Does he meet up with anyone? See whether the group split or stay together. I hope this is a break and hasn't been done deliberately to throw us off the scent. Have you thought of that, Bruno? Perhaps Santos's pilot is a damn sight smarter than you think.'

'Gotcha! Instructions fully understood. It's possible the details might have been dropped deliberately in order to fool us. You could be right, but what else have we got to go on?' Unlike Luca he hadn't thought it might be a clever ruse. He was hoping they'd just got lucky.

'I'll travel by plane from Buenos Aires. Be with you as fast as I can. Leave Santos to me, and keep Chico in order, remember I don't want no goddam shootings or killings, not until I arrive!'

'OK, Luca. When can we expect you?'

'Tomorrow, buddy. The trip from here takes twelve hours, I've then got to find an internal flight. I can sleep on the plane, I'm off to the airport right now. Contact our men, all around Argentina, I want as many airports watched as possible, especially Mendoza, he might be heading back home. Hopefully Santos turns up in Trelew, but we can't count on it.'

'OK, Luca, leave it with me, I'll sort things out. See you soon. Keep in touch.'

'You can bet on it!'

Luca ended the call. He quickly packed his travel bag, remembering at the last minute to take out the small firearm and ammunition he kept in a side pocket. It wouldn't go down well with the security guys at the airport. He then hurried out of his apartment and headed for the lift to the ground floor. Once outside a yellow cab was hailed, Luca asked to be taken to JFK Airport, quick as possible. The driver was told it was urgent. The taxi weaved its way along the busy streets and avenues of Manhattan across the Queensboro Bridge into Brooklyn, and then through Queen's, on to the airport overlooking Jamaica Bay. Soon after the East River crossing Luca, rude as usual, ordered the driver to 'hurry the fuck up', he was driving 'too damn slow for God's sake'.

The boss of one of New York's leading criminal gangs had a plane to catch and an important meeting to attend with Federico Santos. As far as Luca was concerned that son of a bitch owed him $250,000, plus some interest to keep him sweet. If Santos couldn't oblige he'd happily kill him ... and his friends.

29

It was late Sunday night when Santos's plane touched down on the runway at Trelew's small airport. Fifty years earlier the place had gained worldwide notoriety after being the site of a shoot-out between escaped prisoners with left-wing political leanings and soldiers belonging to the far-right military junta. After their break-out the prisoners were hoping to catch a plane to neighbouring Chile before flying on to the Communist haven that was the island of Cuba. Only six out of one hundred and ten escapees made it across the border into Chile, a country led by the Marxist, Salvador Allende, at the time. The fortunate half dozen even made it to Cuba but many of the captured paid a heavy price, execution by firing squad. The Argentinian generals didn't take kindly to dissenters and acted with ruthless efficiency.

Unlike what happened half a century before, Santos wasn't expecting any gun battles or trouble of any kind on this particular evening. The hasty and clever escape from the Andrettis had only taken about an hour and a quarter in his fast plane. The journey would have been ten times longer by road. His group felt pleased with themselves, reckoning that their pursuers had been left fuming back in San Raphael wondering where the hell Santos had jetted off to. Little did they know.

On arrival the Almirante Marcos A. Zar Aeropuerto was almost deserted apart from a skeleton staff of workers on the night shift. Outside the terminal building Santos was met by Ernesto and Ruben, the couple on his pay roll based in this part of northern Patagonia. They looked after his bolthole but their main day job was at a nearby *estancia* where large flocks of sheep roamed over thousands of acres of low-quality grassland. As requested, Ernesto had brought along Santos's tank on wheels: his specially adapted Land Rover Defender with its powerful engine, armour plating and bulletproof windows.

Santos said he'd do the driving. Before leaving the airport confines, Ángel inspected the armoury store in the boot compartment. There were three AK-47 automatic rifles, the deadliest handheld weapon ever made with its curved box magazine capable of holding thirty rounds, one of the guns had a larger magazine capable of holding up to a hundred bullets. Underneath the Kalashnikovs, he found a Remington semi-automatic assault rifle and a metal box full of Glock pistols together with ammunition. Nestled on top of everything else, was the *pièce de résistance*, Ángel's favourite weapon, a Barrett M82 sniper's rifle with its bi-pod stand and telescopic sight.

Leaving his assistants to return home in a farm pickup truck, Santos sped out of the airport complex with Ángel taking up his usual position in the front passenger seat, the others were crammed in the back. At the first roundabout Santos headed right along the RN25, Dai Davies's farm was only six miles from Trelew. Inside the Defender all was quiet, the hour was late, everyone was tired but at the next roundabout, Ángel broke the silence.

'Turn back into town, boss, I think someone's following us!'

'What's that?' shouted a suddenly wide-awake Tomás. He'd half heard what had been said.

'You sure?' asked Santos. His eyes were fixed firmly on the road ahead.

'Don't look back but there's a truck, looks like a Toyota, about fifty to a hundred metres behind, it followed us out of the airport along with two other cars. They've gone off in different directions but not the Toyota,' was Ángel's reply.

'We're not long out of the airport,' said John. 'They could be heading the same place we're going.'

'That's why we're about to do a U-turn, see if they follow,' replied Ángel.

Santos did as his bodyguard suggested. The original plan was to take Tomás, John and Lola straight to the farm and drop them off. He'd then make for the Peninsula Valdés. Now he needed to have a rethink. Santos headed back into town along a main street, Colombia, before turning right into another road entitled

Pelligrini. Eventually he stopped his vehicle in a Carrefour hypermarket car park. As feared, the Toyota followed them, it stopped well before the large parking area but its driver and front seat passenger had the perfect view from across the street.

'Who the hell are they?' questioned Santos. 'If it's Andretti's men how did they know we'd flown down here? Has someone back in San Raphael put a tracking device on the plane?'

'Perhaps they were tipped off at the airport. Do you trust your pilot?' asked Tomás.

'He gets paid too well to let me down and he'd know the consequences of betrayal, Ricky's not stupid,' answered Santos. 'Our plans have to change. It would be madness to lead these people, and maybe the Andrettis, to your farm, Tomás. The consequences could be really bad!'

'What the hell are we going to do then?' asked a worried Tomás. His customary good cheer and hearty laugh had long deserted him.

Santos went on to say that they'd stay parked up outside the hypermarket for a short while, five minutes at the most. He wanted to see if the suspect car with its occupants stayed put and, when his Land Rover did eventually move off, what would happen. Would they be followed? Ángel used his powerful night-time binoculars to look across at the Toyota, there were two shabby looking men, in their thirties or forties he reckoned, inside the vehicle.

'You can't go to your farm Tomás, and we certainly won't abandon you here. Someone could follow you, others would come after Ángel and me,' said Santos.

'Well we can't stay here all night either!' exclaimed Tomás.

The man in the front passenger seat of the Toyota was on his mobile speaking to Bruno Andretti, still directing the Argentinian operation until older brother arrived. Bruno was heading south to Trelew in the helicopter, along with Chico and three others, as quickly as possible. Another guy had been given the unenviable task of driving the Jeep Cherokee through the night and into the morning all the way from San Raphael along desolate and dark desert highways. Bruno's instruction to his men in Trelew was simple: keep watch and follow whenever and wherever necessary. Both he and Chico were on their way south to join them, along with the big daddy of the outfit, Luca Andretti.

Santos and Ángel had agreed it would be crazy to split up and leave their friends by themselves. They could get a taxi even though it was late on Sunday night, it was only a short trip to the Davies farm but, as sure as day followed night, they'd be pursued. That could bring them and others into a heap of danger.

'I've made my mind up, we're all going to my hide-out on the Peninsula Valdés,' said Santos decisively. It was an order, it wasn't up for discussion. It would spare the Davies family from becoming involved and Tomás, Lola and John would, hopefully, be well protected from Andretti's mob.

'How far is this Peninsula Valdés place?' asked Lola. She'd been looking forward to a hot shower at the farm followed by a good sleep and was feeling a little irritated, but she fully understood the wisdom of Santos's decision.

'Sorry, Lola, it's about three hours away, over a hundred miles on slow roads. Look, we'll be safe if we keep together,' answered Santos, keen to reassure everyone.

The tough as teak little man from Brazil seemed totally unfazed at the idea of driving that distance even though it would soon be midnight. He turned on the ignition, followed by the lights, and hurriedly sped out of the car park. They'd been the only vehicle parked up so their hasty and noisy exit was easily spotted. Sure enough, as Ángel had expected, the Toyota started moving.

'There's your answer, Ángel, we ARE being followed. *Mierda!*' shouted Santos.

'You concentrate on the driving, boss. I'll keep my eyes on them and look out for any others.'

'Anything we can do?' asked John, trying to be helpful.

'Look over your left shoulder, John. You'll see a gap between you and the boot. Pass me one of the rifles and, if you can, take out a couple of pistols from the metal box, give me those as well,' replied Ángel.

'My God!' gasped John as he peered into the boot space. 'You've enough weapons here to equip a small army!'

'That might be the general idea,' was Tomás's rather despondent response.

Lola looked worried at the sight of all the weaponry and John felt astounded by their predicament but kept schtum about it. Tomás also kept quiet but wished he was somewhere else, preferably safely back home in Mendoza with Lucia watching a late-night TV show and sipping wine, even better would be tucked up in bed catching up with some much-needed rest. An equally taciturn but highly focused Santos drove out of Trelew following road signs that pointed towards a place called Puerto Madryn. The unflappable Ángel made sure that the guns in the front footwell were all fully loaded. He also kept a close eye on the vehicle following them while constantly glancing at the road sides for any would-be ambushers.

The men in the Toyota stuck doggedly to their tail keeping a steady fifty to a hundred metres distance between themselves and the Land Rover. It was one vehicle pursuing the other on a twisting Patagonian road. They ploughed on through the blackness of the night into the small hours.

30

The Peninsula Valdés is a World Heritage Site because its coastal waters are a haven for an abundance of marine life: mainly whales, orcas, elephant seals, sea lions and penguins. For those with a bit of imagination the peninsula's outline, if viewed on a map, looks like an Australian kookaburra or an English woodpecker, not that anyone would find either of those creatures living on this particular peninsula.

Inland, away from the cold waters of the South Atlantic, the area is a bleak, flat and semi-arid part of the world covered in scanty vegetation and pock-marked by deep hollows carved out over many millennia by the erosive power of the wind. Some have developed into impressively large dried-up lakes such as *El Gran Salitral*. The other massive salt-coated hole etched into the surface of the peninsula, *Salina Grande*, is a huge depression winnowed out to a depth of forty-two metres below sea level by the powerful and persistent Patagonian winds. Few people live on the peninsula and, as a result, it's an ideal place for any animal life that can survive the harsh conditions. Guanacos, rheas, grey foxes, dwarf picki armadillos and small rodents called maras, larger and uglier relatives of the guinea pig, live amongst the spindly grasses, short shrubs and sandy soils. Other than a few farmers living on isolated *haciendas,* and those connected to a growing tourist industry, the human population is noticeable only by its absence. When Santos was looking for an Argentinian hideaway that particular characteristic made the location ideal whenever he needed to escape from the dangers of his increasingly turbulent world. This intriguing lump of land that juts out into the ocean was a perfect haven for him.

Soon after by-passing Puerto Madryn, Santos turned onto a much narrower road off to the right, following the sign for the Reserva Provincial Peninsula Valdés. The Toyota wasn't far behind. The route was now much quieter, unlike the main highway where there'd been the usual overnight freight lorries and occasional police patrol car. A mile along the minor road Santos suddenly swung his Land Rover into a deserted lay-by. The car tailing them slowed down and came to a halt, the occupants were content to keep watch from afar. Santos had decided to lose their annoying stalkers. Time for confrontation.

'What guns have you got, Ángel?'

'An AK-47 and some Glocks.'

'Where's your favourite?'

Ángel turned around and asked John to hand him the rifle with the telescopic sight. Despite wondering what was about to happen, and fearing the worst, John did as he was told. The Barrett sniper's rifle was passed across into the front of the car.

'I hope you're not going to shoot them?' asked an incredulous John, fervently hoping to hear an answer that had the word 'no' in it.

'Don't worry Inglés, just watch!' Ángel climbed out of the vehicle, a powerful assault weapon cradled in his arms.

Tomás and Lola fidgeted about nervously in the back wondering what Ángel was about to do, both lost for words. They looked on apprehensively.

'Scare them first', ordered Santos.

Ángel duly obliged. With the AK-47 firmly in his grasp he sprayed a volley of automatic fire above the Toyota. Vivid yellow-orange flashes from the gun's muzzle lit up the night sky.

'*Mierda!*' screamed Tomás.

The men in the truck, terror written across their faces, ducked down below the level of the windscreen. The guys weren't used to gun battles, they lived a quiet life down in Patagonia. This wasn't the border country close to Bolivia or Paraguay, a favourite battleground for drug gangs. This was way out of their comfort zone, the Andrettis had somehow roped them into their criminal operations but these men were small fry, not hardened frontline fighting members of a drugs cartel. Whatever guns they might possess would be no match for the raging firepower of a Kalashnikov let loose on full throttle. Ángel passed the rifle back to his boss who was sat calmly in the driver's seat watching his main man at work. He was eager to use his sniper's rifle.

'Now shoot out the front tyres!' Santos shouted.

The Toyota was about a hundred metres away. Its scared driver was desperately trying to put the vehicle into reverse while keeping his head down at the same time but all he seemed capable of doing was crashing the gears. Both he and his companion were freaked out by the warning spray of fire that had thundered above their heads. Ángel now aligned his gun at the driver's side of the Toyota. A shot rang out and the front, nearside tyre immediately deflated, he repeated the process with the other front tyre. It was enough to cause the terrified men in the Toyota to spring out of the vehicle with their hands up.

'Please don't harm them!' shouted John. 'They've given up!'

'Leave them, Ángel,' ordered Santos. 'They won't be going anywhere soon. Come on, let's get out of here.'

Santos sped off and followed the solitary road that winds its way across the *Istmo Ameghino*, a narrow strip of land linking the Argentinian mainland with the Peninsula Valdés. People aren't supposed to visit the area after eight in the evening but Santos wasn't a tourist calling in to marvel at the sea life. He drove past the check point, it was late, no-one was on duty. The little village of Puerto Pirámides with its smattering of houses, hotels and restaurants soon appeared. All was quiet, it was the middle of the night. Another fifty miles on gravel roads, it was slow going as Santos headed for the most northerly place on the peninsula, the Punta Norte.

It was still dark when they arrived at their destination but dawn on Monday morning wasn't far away, the faint glimmer of light blue sky lining the eastern horizon out to sea signalled its approach. Near the head of the peninsula, nestled amongst rolling dunes, was an impressively concealed place of sanctuary. A handheld, remote-controlled device when pressed by Santos revealed an underground garage. The vehicle was driven down a ramp into a subterranean refuge, as the doors behind them automatically closed a light came on. Everyone disembarked, it was the end of the journey. They'd entered a hidden concrete bunker buried under the large expanse of sand dunes. From the garage a connecting door led into a living space with separate bedrooms and shower/toilet block at the far end. The only part of the bunker not buried under sand was a narrow window section with bullet-proofed glass that looked out towards the breaking waves of the Atlantic. Santos explained that when not in use his men, Ernesto and Ruben, piled up the plentiful supply of sand to cover the viewing area. A bulldozer parked nearby shifted the stuff. Once all were ensconced in the living area Santos got straight down to business.

'We stay here only for a short while. Andretti's men will be rescued. The guys in the helicopter will turn up, they'll search the peninsula knowing I've got to be here somewhere.'

'What's the plan then, Federico?' asked Tomás. 'You say we can't stay here for long.'

'The peninsula will be crawling with Andretti's men soon, on land, in the air, maybe even out at sea. We can hide for a while, this is a good place, we need to freshen up and get some sleep. I'll organise a helicopter to pick us up, we shall fly to an airport where my jet will be waiting.'

'The boss is right, it's important we rest up for a few hours,' said Ángel, 'we're all tired. Later today we'll get well away from here.'

'Where are you intending to take us?' asked Lola.

'Well, Lola, it's not been much of a holiday for you and John so far,' replied Santos with a broad smile.

'And I haven't visited my farm to meet up with Dai,' complained Tomás.

'The main thing is that we have given those guys following us the slip, at least for a while. We'll make a quick exit, probably early afternoon. When the time is right we leave this bunker and head along the coast, for a few kilometres, to meet up with my pilot. Andretti's men will be scouring the peninsula. Fortunately, it's seventy kilometres long and fifty in width,' said Santos.

'That's three thousand, five hundred square kilometres of territory, not an easy job, even with a helicopter!' Ángel looked impressed by his powers of mental arithmetic.

'But there's not a lot of cover to hide under. I've seen no trees anywhere, not many bushes either, only bits of grass dotted around the place. It'll be an easy place to search from the air,' commented John.

'You're right,' said Santos. 'That's why we plan our departure carefully. We'll travel along the beach, I've checked, the tide is out this afternoon. We can hide behind rocks or in the dunes if we see anything or hear a helicopter that isn't mine.'

'Federico, please tell me, where are you planning on taking us?' asked Tomás.

'To Bahia Blanca, two hundred miles north along the coast. The Andrettis have their helicopter so we need a good start over them. They'll follow us to Bahia if they see us leave, we must have enough time to transfer to the plane once we're there.

'Where are we then going to, Federico?' asked Lola.

'Brazil! But I intend getting you into America eventually. I have important business with one of my partners somewhere else, after that we'll go to California. You will have the best holiday of your life, Lola. Have you ever been on a boat ride through the jungle?'

'No, can't say I have. Sounds great, it's something I've missed out on. Only hope we can stay alive long enough to enjoy it though!' she added, somewhat sardonically.

Tomás returned from one of the bedrooms. He'd disappeared earlier to ring up his wife. He'd shamefacedly told Lucia that he'd changed his plans and decided to have a few days of sightseeing, holiday time, on the Peninsula Valdéz. Unbeknown to her, even though they'd been married for thirty years, he'd always had an interest in penguins apparently. After joining the others, he was rather taken aback to hear the news that they were heading to Brazil. It looked as if he'd be taking an unexpectedly even longer vacation and one fraught with all sorts of dangers he could do without. *Yet more explaining to do to Lucia.* He asked Ángel to pass him one of the Glock pistols, he'd take it to bed with him in case any uninvited guests turned up. After receiving instructions on how to use it he retired, a tired and worried man, to the bunker's bedroom area.

All of them followed except for Ángel, he would be on guard for a while before Santos took over. Soon they'd be leaving, it would be time to spring into action again.

31

Two scruffy looking men, dressed in dirty white vests and tatty blue jeans, stood forlornly by their pickup truck. Its front tyres had been destroyed. Unfortunately, the vehicle had only one spare wheel. They were marooned in the back of beyond along a lonely road, in the middle of the night, on the windswept Peninsula Valdés. There was nothing to do until help arrived so they sat down on a nearby rocky outcrop and gazed into the distance across the choppy waters of the *Golfo Nuevo,* both just thankful to be alive. They'd contacted Bruno Andretti to relay the news of what had happened. He told them to wait by the Toyota, he was on his way. The original plan, going to Trelew, was now unnecessary. Instead his helicopter was heading for the Peninsula Valdés, by his reckoning they should arrive early Monday morning around daybreak.

Luca Andretti had caught an American Airlines plane out of JFK at 22.30 hours on Sunday night. It was a fast, non-stop flight, scheduled to land in Buenos Aires by ten-thirty on Monday morning, Argentinian time. He'd catch the next departure to Trelew to meet up with his brothers and then search the Peninsula Valdés for Santos. He wanted his quarter of a million dollars' worth of cocaine back or that amount of money, together with $25,000 interest for his troubles. The lives of Santos and his pals would then be spared but they'd be left somewhere nasty, there were plenty of potential dumping grounds in the wastes of Patagonia. If he didn't achieve his goal, Santos and his pals, all tied up and gagged, would be dropped over the Atlantic, food for any passing sharks and other sea life that fancied a meal.

Dawn was indeed breaking when Bruno landed next to the stricken Toyota. He ordered the men to wait a little longer, a breakdown service, based in Puerto Madryn, were on their way to fix things with two new tyres. Bruno would fly on across the peninsula with Chico, three other gang members and the pilot. Their other guy was still busy driving the Jeep Cherokee down from San Raphael hoping to arrive about mid-day. In the meantime, they'd search the area and drop in on any settlement they could see from the air, not that there were many of them. Puerto Pirámedes, the only village on the peninsula, would be the starting point followed by isolated farms.

After snatching some rest and recuperation Santos and his companions were up and about having breakfast. Sipping a mug of coffee, the drugs lord was busy as usual on his mobile. Reception wasn't great but he'd managed to contact his pilot. Ricky was told to land the jet in Bahia Blanca and fill it up with fuel. He then had to hire a helicopter and fly it south to the Peninsula Valdés to pick them up. They'd be waiting a few kilometres to the west along the coast from Punta Norte. Ricky was to look for the wide and flat rock platform there, it would act as a suitable landing pad for the chopper. He was warned that Andretti's men would be scanning the peninsula in their helicopter and maybe a couple of vehicles, the Jeep and a Toyota. Ricky would have to keep an eye out for them too, if seen anywhere near the Punta Norte he must abort any landing plan unless told otherwise. Ricky was an intelligent man and quickly assimilated his instructions, for now he was at Puerto Madryn airport having made the short flight from Trelew after having dropped off his boss the previous evening. Not wanting to waste time, he jetted off to Bahia Blanca, a large city along the coast.

Bruno Andretti didn't have any luck in the peninsula's only village. Originally built over a hundred years ago as a small port for transporting salt from the inland brine lakes, its main *raison d'être* today is catering for the steady flow of visitors interested in the local marine life, especially whales. Six hotels, a bakery and coffee shop were visited but no-one reported seeing five strangers, four men and a woman, in a Land Rover Defender. Looking down from on high, Bruno decided to follow the gravel road to Punta Delgada, a hamlet at the southern tip of the peninsula. The place would be easily spotted from the air with its luxury *estancia*, Faro Punta Delgada, once the site of an old lighthouse perched on a clifftop. Perhaps Santos and his friends had booked in for the night and were enjoying some breakfast, he'd love to give them a nasty surprise. On their short, fifty miles journey they passed over the wind-scooped hollows of *Salina Grande* and *Salina Chica*, dried-up salt lakes, excavation sites for extensive deposits of sodium chloride in the past. He doubted that Santos would have chosen to spend the night in either of those God-forsaken places.

If unlucky at Punta Delgada they'd work their way northwards along the peninsula. Being a well organised man, Bruno Andretti had compiled a list of settlements to visit, not that there were many, much of the area was uninhabited. After the village of Puerto Pirámides and the *estancia* at Punta Delgada, a sheep ranch, Estancia La Postosa, would be the next stop, followed by the tiny hamlet of Valdés on the east coast situated close to a giant lagoon. Nearby was a restaurant, *La Ernestina*, frequented by tourists and day-trippers. Another couple of *estancias* existed further north around Punta Norte. Bruno reckoned there weren't many places where Santos could hide but maybe he was camping out somewhere, or perhaps he'd parked up his Land Rover Defender and was pretending to be an awestruck visitor. In the helicopter Bruno thought they'd easily cover the whole peninsula by nightfall. Santos only had a few places to hide and a handful of roads to travel along. The vegetation cover was minimal. Finding him should be a doddle, he was hoping he could present a captured Santos to Luca later in the day.

While Bruno was searching the southern tip of the peninsula Luca had arrived at a busy Ezeiza airport in the south-western outskirts of Argentina's sprawling capital. He rang his brother's mobile, reception was crackly.

'Hi, Bruno, is that you? Can you hear me?'

'Just about, what do you want?'

'I'm in BA, but I can't get a flight down to Trelew today or anywhere else close by for fuck's sake! The only goddam plane left earlier this morning, there isn't another till tomorrow. It leaves at six thirty, I'll be in Trelew two hours later, get someone to meet me. Find Santos today, capture him and the rest, but keep Chico away from all of them, that includes the lady!'

32

Everyone stayed cooped up in the bunker, safe under the coastal dunes until about one o'clock in the afternoon. They'd heard nothing outside other than the noise of Atlantic waves crashing down on the nearby shoreline, coupled with far less soporific snorting and wailing sounds emanating from the sea lions and seals piled up on the beach. John and Lola would have liked to walk along the coast to view its natural wonders but this was hardly the time. Punta Norte was bound to be visited by the Andretti mob, best to remain in their subterranean hideout.

But Santos had no intention of staying there much longer, moving on from the peninsula was vital. He told Ángel to have a look around, find out if it was safe to venture outside, so he went off on a recce and returned with good news, there was nothing to worry about, either on the ground, in the air or at sea. He'd seen only a small group of day-trippers accompanied by their tour guide.

Santos phoned Ricky who was now heading south in a hired helicopter with instructions to look out for them, he confirmed they'd be a short distance along the coast to the west of Punta Norte ready for picking up at 13.45 precisely. Any problems and Santos would warn his pilot.

Ángel emerged from the refuge first, he was dressed in fresh attire: XL size, desert army fatigues in various shades of yellow and brown to mould in with the surrounding arid landscape of rocks, stones and sand. The four others followed, similarly decked out, but in smaller sizes. The underground bunker carried a stock of such clothing, Santos was a man who thought of everything.

The powerfully built Ángel carried the sniper's rifle across his left shoulder, an AK-47 in his right hand and a Glock pistol in a holster under his left armpit. Tomás, John and Lola followed with either a rifle or pistol. Santos was the last to leave, all were well equipped for any trouble.

As Santos and the others left the bunker the Andretti brothers, plus accomplices, were about thirty miles away to the south down the coastline at Caleta Valdés. They'd visited the nearby restaurant and questioned both staff and guests. No-one had seen anyone resembling Santos and his party. Meanwhile, the driver of the Jeep Cherokee was approaching the peninsula with instructions to head for Punta Norte where he'd be met by the rest of them.

'Come on, Chico, let's get aboard the chopper, we'll move onto Punta Norte, Santos has got to be in that area, he don't seem to be anywhere else, there's a few *estancias* nearby,' said Bruno to his younger brother.

'If we find him in this shithole can't we just shoot the son of a bitch and get the hell out of here?' asked the hot-headed Chico.

Bruno looked disdainfully at his younger brother before replying.

'Hell, no! Luca's given explicit instructions. Harm no-one! He wants to mete out his own justice. He also wants his cocaine back, or its value in money! All we have to do is catch Santos, plus his friends, nothing else.'

All five climbed aboard the helicopter, Bruno ordered the pilot to fly north. They'd look in at more places and take a scout along the north coast. Punta Norte was only fifteen minutes away.

The party of would-be escapees scampered their way through the undulating dunes. The area was quiet, the only animal life were the resting seals lounging about on the beach enjoying the early afternoon sunshine, but tranquillity was about to end.

'Quiet everyone. What's that noise?' whispered John.

'It's our helicopter, I can see it, look up there!' exclaimed Santos gazing at the sky. 'It must be Ricky.'

'That's not Ricky, boss. He'd be coming in from the north across the sea, that chopper's approaching us from the south.' It lost altitude and became much clearer. 'Look at the colour, the Andrettis have a blue helicopter. It's them! Quick, get down behind these rocks and keep real still.'

They hid behind some ocean battered rocky outcrops that poked out of the sand like old and gnarled fingers. Ángel reckoned the incoming chopper was heading for Punta Norte but it didn't look as if it was planning on landing, maybe they were just snooping around along the coastline. With his keen eyesight he could see the Andretti gang clearly, they were staring down at the rocks where they were trying to hide. They'd been spotted, the helicopter was coming in their direction.

Santos decided drastic action was called for, he muttered something hurriedly in Spanish to his bodyguard. In response Ángel hoisted the rifle off his shoulder and slotted a few bullets into its magazine before focussing the powerful telescopic sight on the approaching menace in the sky.

'My God, what are you going to do?' asked a worried looking Tomás.

'Shoot it down, Ángel!' ordered Santos. The chopper was now less than a kilometre away and descending fast.

'Surely you'll never hit it at this range?' questioned John.

He was clueless when it came to the incredible power of certain rifles and especially the Barrett M82. In the right hands it could shoot the proverbial balls off a gnat from one to two kilometres away. Ángel watched intently as the helicopter continued towards them. When the chopper was about five hundred metres from where he was standing, sheltered from view behind a large, barnacle encrusted lump of rock, Ángel pulled the trigger and fired off three rounds in quick succession. Within less than a second the bullets had ripped into the fuel tank housed at the back of the cockpit compartment. It exploded immediately. A giant ball of orange flame lit up the sky, the helicopter fell like a stone and hit the beach with a sickening thud. Another smaller blast followed, thick black smoke started billowing out of the mangled, blazing wreck, the intense heat from the fireball had twisted metal and melted glass, plastic, leather and rubber components. Worst of all, blackened, wizened and charred beyond recognition bodies burnt slowly but surely amongst all the fiery flames and dense smoke. From where Ángel was standing it looked like there were four persons in the cockpit but he couldn't be sure.

'We need to get out of here, quickly,' shouted Santos. 'Where the hell's Ricky got to?'

Tomás, John and Lola were shocked and left speechless. They'd never seen anything like it except on television or at the cinema, but this was for real.

'It had to be done.' Santos sounded dismissive, as if it was all in a day's work in his business. 'It was either us or them, that's the way it is in these situations. If we'd been captured they'd have killed us. At least they had a quick death!'

Another noise was heard above them and attention was drawn away from the horrendous scene, it was Ricky's helicopter high above the ocean. Within a couple of minutes, he'd landed on the solid if rather wet and slippery rock platform that had been left uncovered by retreating ocean waters, the tide was well out. Santos and his companions clambered aboard, destination the port of Bahia Blanca before continuing their journey to Santos's isolated cattle ranch in the depths of Rondônia, on the southern edge of the Amazon Basin.

'Adiós Argentina, Olá Brazil,' commented John lamely. He was still stunned by what he'd just witnessed.

They climbed upwards and headed north, over the sea, leaving behind the smouldering wreck of the Andretti's helicopter to burn itself out on an isolated, wind-blasted stretch of Patagonian coastline. The seals resting along the shoreline seemed oblivious to what had happened and the rolling waves of the Atlantic, illuminated by the afternoon sunlight, crashed down onto the beach, as they'd done since time immemorial.

33

Bruno Andretti had heard the noise of a loud explosion coming from somewhere near Punta Norte. At the time he was standing outside an isolated *estancia*, a few miles to the south and slightly inland from the coast. Together with one of his men he'd been dropped off at the farm earlier. Bruno's plan had been for Chico, two other gang members and the pilot to search the northern shoreline of the peninsula before then coming back to pick him up. Hearing the sound of the blast coming from the coast worried Bruno. *What the hell had happened? Had Chico found Santos? Had he disobeyed orders?* He knew what an impetuous and reckless act-now-think-later fool his younger brother could be at times. *Had he discovered Santos and decided to lob a few grenades into his hideout? Maybe that was what all the noise was about. But had the helicopter crashed?* The last option didn't bear thinking about. An anxious Bruno contacted the driver of the Jeep Cherokee and told him to head for the *Estancia San Lorenzo*. He needed picking up, urgently, they'd then head off to Punta Norte to see what had kicked off up there.

By late afternoon a distraught Bruno was surveying the charred remains of his helicopter on the north coast of the Peninsula Valdés. An acrid smell filled the air, a mixture of burning paint, rubber and worst of all, human flesh and bones. Chico had died in the explosion along with two of the gang and the pilot. *Shit, what a godawful mess!* With a heavy heart he rang his older brother. When he answered the call, Luca was onto his fourth pint of lager in a downtown *boliche* (night club) in the centre of Buenos Aires, accompanied by a couple of men of dubious character, local drug pedlars and pimps. Three scantily dressed, middle-aged women propped up the bar alongside them.

'Bruno, is that you? What the fuck's happening? Have you got Santos yet? There was a momentary silence. 'Bruno, ... are you there, for Christ's sake?'

'God, I'm so sorry, Luca, something awful has happened. Our helicopter ... it's been shot down. Chico was on it ... with three others ... they're all dead, Luca!' He broke down and cried.

Luca, usually not a man to be short of words, was quiet for a few seconds while he took in the full implications of Bruno's news.

'Where the fuck's Santos? I presume he was responsible!' he bellowed.

'I've been told he got away. I was elsewhere. Some tourists, soon after the explosion, saw another helicopter arrive. When it left it headed off north, where to, we haven't got a clue!' bemoaned Bruno.

'Shit! Shit! Shit! If Santos thinks he can get away with this he's oh, ... oh, so fucking wrong!' replied a fuming but also distressed Luca. 'Get the mess cleared up, Bruno, no point me travelling down there now. Once you've sorted it head back to New York, that's where I'll be going tomorrow. Hell fire, I'm too upset and far too fuckin' pissed to do anything today,' he concluded before abruptly ending the call.

Luca hailed the barman and ordered a double whisky. He intended to get really hammered, sleep it off overnight and catch a plane to JFK on Tuesday. In the light of developments, he had plans to make with business contacts throughout the Americas, he needed to call in a few favours. Most of the Andretti's drug dealing involved the Eastern Seaboard states from Maine down to Florida but he had friends and accomplices in Mexico, parts of Central America, the Caribbean islands as well as both Argentina and Colombia.

As Luca swigged downed his drink, he swore he was going to track Santos down if it was the last thing he did on planet Earth, the Brazilian would pay dearly for killing Chico. He might have been one stupid dumbass but he was his kid brother. Luca was the head of an Italian-American family and that mattered more than anything to him. Chico's death had to be avenged, it would be expected, it was a question of honour.

34

After taking off from the Atlantic port city of Bahia Blanca, Argentina's answer to Liverpool, Santos's jet landed at the small and relatively quiet airport of Ji-Paraná in the centre of the Brazilian state of Rondônia. Not that long ago the area surrounding it would have been covered with pristine rain forest but nowadays things are very different due to fifty years of rampant deforestation. The western limits of the Serra dos Parecis uplands, on the southern edge of the vast Amazon region, has the dubious distinction of having one of the highest rates of forest clearance anywhere in Brazil.

From the sleepy provincial airfield Santos and friends were whisked off in a pickup truck to the remote cattle ranch that he owned close to the Rio Jiparaná. After turning right in the town of Jarú the Toyota followed a series of bumpy farm tracks for many miles before reaching his property. Their incredibly eventful day was nearly over but before its conclusion talking filled the still night air. Santos, together with his chief bodyguard, his long-standing friend and wine merchant, an ex-doctor on the run from the law and a lady sommelier were sitting outside on the veranda of a wooden farmhouse situated in the middle of nowhere. Surrounded by patches of forest and much larger areas of recently created pasture land they mulled over the dramatic events of Sunday and Monday. A lot had happened since they'd left Mendoza in Tomás's Range Rover. Plans for the coming days were discussed with Santos acting as chairman of the group.

'We'll spend a few days here, I've a lot of thinking to do before we move on.' Santos liked having to make decisions and when he'd made up his mind acting decisively.

'Federico, I could do with returning to Mendoza, back to my business, wife and family,' complained Tomás. 'I can't keep telling Lucia I'm on holiday when, unbeknownst to her, I'm flitting around South America trying to avoid gangsters. I was supposed to be visiting my farm in Chubut and then heading home but here I am, somewhere, God knows where, in remotest Brazil!'

'Such is life, Tomás. You worry far too much,' replied Santos.

'And Lola and I were planning on having a vacation in Patagonia, horse riding in the wilderness and eating Welsh cakes in little tea houses. Instead, well, it's been a holiday with a difference. Certainly not one advertised in the travel brochures,' added John with a laugh.

'I told my bosses I'd be away for maybe a fortnight,' said Lola, 'but I can ask for some more days off. I'm owed plenty of holiday.' Lola was quite an adventurous lady and secretly she'd quite enjoyed all the drama of the last week since John had come into her life but she'd hated witnessing the helicopter crash with its tragic consequences.

The night wore on, it was past midnight, but the drinks and conversation continued to flow.

'John, Lola, you should enjoy time in the Amazon, have a look at some of its wonders, I have a riverboat you can use. Tomás, you can stay here if you want, but I shall understand if you wish to return home. We'll only be here a short time, Ángel and I have important business to sort out in Central America, we shall be going there soon. I suggest John and Lola travel with us, extend their holiday, we'll get them safely to California before too long,' said Santos. He glanced across at John and Lola. A candle flickered and danced in the gentle breeze, its burning wick illuminating their faces as well as the pile of empty drink cans and glasses littering the table top.

'You reckon we're safe here do you, Federico?' asked John.

'As safe as you'll ever be when you're with a man like me. Together with my underground bunker in Patagonia, and my home in Rio, none of my enemies know about this place.'

The talking went on until after one o'clock. When they'd all retired for the night the heavens opened and torrential downpours cascaded down from an overcast sky full of clouds, warm raindrops hammered onto the corrugated iron roof of the farmstead. The dark Amazonian night was both hot and humid on the southern fringes of the Brazilian *selvas*, the world's largest rain forest, almost seven million square kilometres in area and twenty-eight times the size of the United Kingdom.

Santos, along with thousands of his fellow countrymen, some rich like him but most of them poor peasant farmers, had decimated the forests of Rondônia over the past half century. Much of the trees, indigenous tribespeople and animal life had long gone from this neck of the woods. All along the main highway a once beautiful landscape had been blitzed by destructive tides of humankind eager for land. Swathes of dense forest had been cleared and replaced by wide open vistas where herds of tough Zebu cattle, suited to the climate and resistant to tropical diseases, grazed poor quality grassland that had come to supersede the ecologically diverse forest. Etched into the man-made grasslands innumerable small tracks led to isolated *estancias* where their owners and *gaucho* workforce lived. Pioneer settlements had sprung up along the main highway in the seventies and grown rapidly. Today, fifty years on, they are post-pioneer towns with services such as schools and hospitals together with houses of different qualities and status. Ramshackle shanty settlements are commonplace along the fringes of these new towns. Hastily constructed saw mills, timber yards, transport depots, shops, seedy hotels and sweaty brothels have replaced the magnificent forest, the untrampled beauties of nature supplanted by the greed of humanity ever eager to make money in whatever way possible. Natural beauty, formed over millions of years, has been replaced by an ugliness that only the hand of man can inflict upon the land.

When the following morning dawned, it was pleasantly warm with the temperature in the mid-twenties. The heat and humidity levels would start rising as the day wore on. An uncharacteristically grumpy Tomás, who'd hardly slept due to the incessant drumming of the rain beating on the iron roof, as well as conditions made worse by a lack of air conditioning, had decided to leave for Argentina as soon as possible. He'd had enough and was busy figuring out the best way to return to Mendoza. It wasn't going to be easy. He'd be taken to Ji-Paraná to catch an internal flight to Cuiabá, capital of the neighbouring state of Mato Grosso and gateway to the wetlands of the Pantanal. From there he'd fly to Sao Paulo where another plane would take him to Mendoza. Santos said he could have use of his jet but Tomás politely declined. The Andretti gang would be on red alert looking for that particular plane. *Best he kept well away from it.* He discussed his plans with John and Lola.

'My son, Juan, will pick me up from the airport. It's a long and tedious journey but at least I'll be home in Vistalba. It's been, how shall I say this? ... an interesting last few days, but I've had more than enough of excitement and danger.' Tomás let out one of his customary hearty laughs followed by a sigh, he felt exhausted.

'Lola and I have decided to travel on with Federico and Ángel. They've promised us a trip to a tropical island paradise in the Caribbean,' enthused John.

'Eventually we shall spend some time at your Californian winery, Tomás, then it's back to work in Argentina for me,' added Lola.

'Yes, well, that all sounds great, but remember that wherever Señor Santos goes, danger follows! Are you really sure you want to stick with him when you could return safely to Mendoza with me,' pleaded Tomás.

He was right to be concerned for their future well-being. Many of Santos's acquaintances had a low life expectancy. Tomás tried hard to persuade Lola and John to travel back with him. It would be a much safer alternative but both his friends, despite the horror witnessed, had enjoyed the excitement of travelling around South America. They felt safe being looked after by the wily Santos and the bodyguard extraordinaire, Ángel. Tomás expressed his feelings to his gangster friend but he was dismissive.

'Once again, you worry far too much Tomás. We'll look after them. They've been promised an interesting time where we're going! Life is to be lived, and if you die along the way well that's too bad, we all end up dead one day anyway. Better to live forty exciting, fun-filled years than eighty boring ones!'

John and Lola would continue with their adventure. Soon it was time to bid their fond 'goodbyes' to Tomás, recent events had brought them all much closer together. One of Santos's ranch hands would drive Tomás the fifty miles distance to the airport. Before leaving he promised to meet up with John in the Napa Valley and see Lola at his favourite Mendoza restaurant. As for Santos and Ángel, it would be when next they were in Mendoza or maybe at a River Plate football match in Buenos Aires but, while lying awake in his hammock during the hot and sticky tropical night, Tomás had decided he'd have to start distancing himself from these two dangerous men for the sake of both his safety and sanity.

After the parting of ways, John and Lola spent a leisurely morning moping around the farm. Despite the searing heat, they decided to take a leisurely walk across what had been rain forest not long ago. Burnt tree stumps, the legacy of forest fires started by man, stuck out like unwanted warts on the surface of open pastures that stretched in every direction from Santos's farm. It was a sad and sobering experience. Where majestic trees had once stood and animals, birds, insects and indigenous tribes had lived in harmony with their environment modern 'civilised man' had, in a relatively short time, destroyed what the wonders of natural evolution had created over many millennia. John and Lola were determined to discuss such issues with Santos at an appropriate time. He might not like to hear their opinions but they agreed it was a situation that couldn't be ignored. It would be a suitable topic of conversation one evening over drinks and dinner.

After lunch John and Lola were taken down to where the Rio Jarú met the larger, wider and deeper Rio Jiparaná. A riverboat belonging to Santos was kept near the confluence. He'd promised John to take them out on the river but thought it better to leave the lovers to themselves.

'Do you know how to use one of these things, John?' asked Santos as he looked down at the boat moored next to the river bank.

'You don't need to worry, Federico, my father owned something like it, a smaller one maybe, but it ran on the same principles. He kept it on a lake in Wales, I learnt a lot from him.'

'Take it for a day, take Lola off on a trip into the jungle. You'll find food and drinks in the fridge in the cuddy cabin along with other things but I don't expect you'll need to use the guns!' joked Santos. After the laughs had died down John responded:

'Are you sure? The boat I mean, not the guns.'

'Go on, off you go, enjoy yourselves.'

'Wow, that's brilliant, Federico! Many thanks, we'll return it to you tomorrow.'

John started up the Yamaha outboard motor at the stern of the boat. Santos had assured him there was plenty of fuel stored in a couple of large metal containers kept below deck in the cuddy.

'Oh! One other thing,' added Santos. 'Best you stay on the boat, don't go ashore, too many snakes and other creatures. And keep out of the water, you'd possibly be safe but maybe not, look out for nasty things swimming about, especially the caimans. The black caiman is six metres long, a real mean son of a bitch he is, you can't miss him.'

'What about insects?' asked Lola.

'Yeah, they're another hazard. Keep away from any swampy areas and slow-moving waters. You'll find sprays below deck, sun cream also, plus a good medical kit. You're in safe hands, Lola, Señor John is a doctor remember.'

'Thanks, Federico, you can be such a nice man when you want to be!' she beamed.

'Take the boat down river, go as far as a place called Iracema, it's about thirty kilometres away. There's a large double meander there, you'll recognise it. Don't forget, when you come across islands in the river channel always take the route to the left, the water's deeper on that side but we are not in the dry season. I've been told it's rained heavily for weeks so you should be alright. From June things are different.'

After thanking Santos for his generosity John opened up the throttle of the outboard motor and headed off downstream while Lola sat on the top of the cuddy cabin intending to act as navigator. They'd spend the night moored somewhere in the middle of the river with the undisturbed rain forest that was the Reserva Biológica do Jarú to the starboard flank of the boat. On the port side things would look very different: damaged and desecrated tracts of rain forest had been cut into and exploited by loggers and farmers over the last five decades. Much of the forest had gone, only a few narrow strands lined the river bank between wide open areas where cattle roamed and the River Jiparaná. The thin strip of trees was a dividing line and poignant reminder of a lost world. It was a case of clearance and exploitation on one side of the river with rain forest on the other bank.

John and Lola had the rest of the day and the forthcoming tropical night to spend together. It promised to be a magical time, the two of them all alone surrounded by the incredible wonders of the equatorial rain forest.

35

The remaining Andretti brothers looked out over central Manhattan from their top floor apartment on West 72nd Street. It had been a bad time for the family and the business. Their younger brother's body, or what was left of it, had been brought back from Argentina and a funeral service had been organised. Luca Andretti was in a sullen but grimly determined mood. Revenge consumed his mind, it had been ever since Bruno had imparted the dreadful news about what had happened to the helicopter, Chico and other gang members on the coast of the Valdés peninsula.

'We get this fucking funeral out of the way, Bruno, show some respect for Chico, put on a show for the family, all that kind of shit, then we go looking for Santos again!' He spat the last few words out angrily.

'Do you really want to continue this vendetta?' asked Bruno.

'Are you serious? Our brother's death has to be avenged.'

'OK, OK, fair enough, message understood, Luca. We still go after Santos. Look, I've been checking with our guys in Mendoza, there's been no sign of him around his home or offices.'

'Where's that son of a bitch got to? We need to find him, quicker the better,' snapped Luca.

'I've got men looking for him everywhere. No-one's seen him in Buenos Aires or Rio. We've our Argentinian boys out searching. Pozzo is organising things.'

'What about Mexico City where Santos has accomplices? He owns some place in the hills nearby for Christ's sake.'

'Nothing doing in Mexico either,' responded Bruno forlornly.

'What about those fucking banana republics in Central America then? I believe he knows some dude called El Bigote who hangs out in Guatemala, El Salvador, Nicaragua also. Some kind of intermediary for Santos between South and North American markets is what I've heard.'

'I've got our man there, Randy Lister, looking into things. He knows all about this El Bigote, real name is Jorge Hernandez. He's some Mexican who plays ball with some of the big players from Colombia and is very matey with Santos.'

'Our boys can cover New York down to Miami. I've got them looking for him all over town, also in Washington and Atlantic City,' added Luca.

'Looks like we've got most bases covered,' said Bruno, trying hard to sound upbeat.

'The bastard's got to crawl out from under his stone before long and when he does we'll catch him, and then kill the little fucker!' screamed Luca.

Bruno Andretti had been back less than a day in the 'Big Apple'. His older brother, after recovering from a giant hangover courtesy of the downtown Buenos Aires bar he'd recently frequented, had beaten him to it and had been in contact with business associates all over the Americas. He'd been spreading the dirt on Santos: how he'd stolen $250,000 worth of cocaine from him in Argentina and how his bodyguard had shot down their helicopter with kid brother Chico on it. He was offering $50,000 for information that led to Santos's current whereabouts and subsequent capture. He must not be harmed or killed by anyone. That particular pleasure was to be reserved for Luca. Bruno had reluctantly agreed to be present if and when that happened. He was not an evil man, unlike Luca whose mind had been twisted and contorted by a lifetime of violence. He just happened to live in a family that for several generations had been firmly embedded in a world full of criminality and the resultant ongoing savagery and bloodshed that accompanies those who deal in illegal narcotics, people trafficking, protection rackets, prostitution and the black market. The Andrettis had become wealthy on the back of their nefarious activities but at a cost to all concerned. Bruno was essentially a decent human being but one trapped by family circumstances. He did many things only to please his older brother and keep in with other gang members.

Secretly, he hoped that he wouldn't have to witness the last few hours of Santos's life. His brother, Luca, although a clever and powerful leader, was a deranged psychopath capable of all sorts of unspeakable, wicked deeds. His deceased younger brother, Chico, was more of a violent thug. Any man who followed his way of life stood every chance of an unpleasant death and being turned to toast in a shot down, burnt-out helicopter was always on the cards. If it hadn't been a helicopter it could have been a plane, a car, or even while asleep in bed in some house discovered by an enemy to be subsequently attacked and torched.

In order to exact a suitable and compensatory revenge Luca was capable of horrendous actions. Bruno, from past experience, was well aware that Luca enjoyed slicing off bits of his still alive victims and roasting them over an open fire before pretending to eat the cooked flesh. It was a barbaric custom that some of the indigenous Native American tribes had reserved for captured enemies in previous centuries. Luca normally used a secluded forest in the Adirondack Mountains, up in New York state, it was ideal for such a cruel and brutish activity. Psycho that he was, he'd talked about putting Santos's body through electric shock treatment or maybe finger nail extraction but a favourite torture method was to push a victim's head into a barrel full of effluent until they choked to death on it. During Luca's latest demonic rant Bruno had been told exactly what his evil brother planned to do once Santos was caught. His last moments on planet Earth would be spent tied up in a trough full of excrement. From Luca's point of view, he saw it as a fitting end. He'd laughed like a maniac at the thought of Santos being force-fed a whole pile of the stuff.

36

Watling had been promising to take Jill on a break to their favourite hotel in the Lake District but that would have to wait a little while longer. He'd decided to take a week off but he wanted to devote time to something else before any trip to their favourite English holiday destination. After his visit to Argentina he'd arrived home in Cambridgeshire tired and frustrated. Yes, he'd met up with John Ripley, and Watling genuinely believed the ex-doctor's account of what had happened at Fen View Cottage back in 1991. Ideally, Ripley would have been brought home for further questioning and a possible court case, but the big guy with the pistol had put a stop to that. Ripley had been let off the hook. However, on reflection, it was perhaps better that the ex-doctor kept well away from his homeland given the circumstances of what he'd done in suddenly deserting, without any explanation, both his wife and job. Watling realised that Ripley wouldn't be returning to England any time soon, if at all.

Another important matter was on the horizon: the forthcoming trial of Benny Hayes. Watling would be needed in court. He was looking forward to it, he'd been liaising with the Met in London for several weeks, a very good case against Hayes was being prepared by the CPS, especially since new key witnesses had been found down in the capital.

One of Watling's first tasks, on his return to England, was to meet his colleagues: DI Rigsby, DS Collins and DCs Cooley and Carmichael, the detectives who'd worked on the Fen View case with both him and Lester. He briefed them about the trip to Argentina as well as making it clear that Hoskins had insisted the investigative aspects of the case were now closed. Other incidents needed looking into but, secretly, Watling didn't want to let things drop. On the long flight home, he'd discussed his plans with Penny. He intended to visit Bob Hemingway, the farmer who once owned the land where Fen View Cottage had stood, that would be his first port of call. Watling, during the investigations, had become fascinated by the possible supernatural happenings associated with the cottage and, as a result, he also wanted to meet up with an old friend, Professor Michael Dunlop from Christ's College. Watling's long-standing friendship with Mike went back twenty plus years. They'd meet for a game of tennis whenever free from their busy, responsible occupations, it would usually involve three sets followed by a couple of pints at a favourite pub. Given Watling's intentions, Mike Dunlop might be an extremely useful man to know as he was a leading member of the famous Ghost Club.

Dunlop had told Watling that the venerable club was established in 1862 by fellows of Trinity College, Cambridge in order to discuss paranormal phenomena. The Victorians were fascinated by the afterlife and anything to do with the supernatural. Seances and fortune telling became fashionable in many social circles from the 1860s, the mid-Victorian era, onwards. Past members of the Ghost Club included famous Victorian writers such as Charles Dickens and Sir Arthur Conan Doyle. The Irish poet, W.B. Yeats, joined the Ghost Club in 1913 to be soon followed by the war poet, Siegfried Sassoon. Other more recent members have been the leading writer of Black Magic thrillers, Dennis Wheatley, as well as Peter Cushing, lead actor in many of the wonderful, if now somewhat dated, 1960s Hammer horror movies.

Watling was relaxing by himself after dinner at home. His wife had nipped to a neighbour's house to comfort a friend who'd recently lost her husband after a long illness. His mind was made up, he'd begin his own private investigation, it would be nothing to do with official work, he'd devote some of his spare time to it. As usual he had his mobile close at hand on the lounge window sill next to his favourite armchair. Time to phone Bob, he tapped in his number. It was the farmer's wife, Janet, who answered the call.

'Hello, Mrs Hemingway, DCI Watling here, I was hoping to have a word with your husband, if he's free.'

'Oh, righto, I'll go and fetch him, please hang on a minute.'

He was soon on the other end of the line.

'George, what can I do for you? I thought the Fen View Cottage case was over and done with.'

'It is, Bob, but there's a few loose ends I wanted to tie up. Any chance of me popping over tomorrow for a chat? I was also wondering if you have any details on the history of the place, if so I'd be pleased if you could share them with me.'

'I'll be here at the farmhouse after lunch. Come and drop by then if you like, how about two o'clock?'

'Sounds great, Bob, see you then, look forward to meeting again. Bye for now.'

Watling turned his attention to Professor Dunlop. He lived with his wife in a terraced Georgian property not far from college, he too was at home.

'Hi, Mike, George here, I was hoping we could meet for a beer and a catch-up one evening.'

'Good to hear from you, old boy! It's ages since we met up, bit early in the year for tennis though, too bloody cold for me,' was Dunlop's jaunty reply.

Mike Dunlop had been to an expensive public school in his youth and was very much a product of the upper middle classes in the way that he spoke with a clipped, rather posh accent and the somewhat archaic expressions he frequently used such as referring to a male friend as an 'old boy'. He often went shooting, fishing and horse riding at weekends and was a regular attender of up-market sporting events and venues such as the Henley Regatta, the Burghley Horse Trials and the Bisley Shooting Ground in Surrey. Watling's family background was far less grandiose, but the men got on like a house on fire through their shared interests of tennis, fine French red wines, real ales and vintage cars. Watling sometimes drove an old Jaguar Mark 1, inherited from his maternal grandfather, Dunlop had a 1968 Aston Martin DB6, both desirable in their own ways, but the latter model more valuable than the former.

'Mike, how are you fixed this week?' asked Watling. 'I'm taking Jill away on holiday before long so I was hoping we could meet up as soon as possible.'

'I can do tomorrow night if you like,' replied Dunlop helpfully.

'Great, let's meet at the Maypole.'

'Sounds good, George, see you 6.30, toodle pip, old boy.'

Watling had his next day sorted: shopping with Jill in the morning followed by a visit to Bob's farm in the afternoon and drinks with Mike in the evening. He was keen to hear what both had to say, one about the old cottage and the other about the paranormal. He wanted to know as much as possible about the history of Fen View including any ghostly and other supernatural happenings, not only in the late sixties when Benny Hayes and his hippy gang hung out at the place, but also through the years ever since its construction. As for the Prof, well he was a mine of information on things that most sane and sensible people are wise enough to leave well alone ... the supernatural.

37

John and Lola spent the rest of the daylight hours heading steadily downstream, John confidently controlling the boat and Lola, perched on top of the cabin roof, proving to be an excellent navigator. They avoided the occasional sandbanks and the hull of the vessel was kept well away from any shallow water where rocky outcrops might damage the craft. After travelling for about an hour they decided it was time to survey the awe-inspiring scenery that surrounded them. Lola lowered an anchor, attached by a cleat to the bow, into the muddy waters. Time to soak up the wonders of the jungle and to drink some water, it would be easy to become dehydrated in the oppressive heat.

They sat together at the back of the boat and listened to all the different bird noises that were punctuated at regular intervals by the racket of screeching howler monkeys high up in the trees. Lola pointed out a scary-looking caiman lounging on a sandy beach near the river bank to their right, John noticed a couple of toucans, with their massive, multi-coloured bills, perched high on one of the emergent trees sticking out above the canopy but his gaze was averted elsewhere when a large and noisy flock of green parakeets flew across the river past the front of the boat to eventually disappear amongst the foliage. Another group of exotic birds, with glistening blue plumage, settled on various shrubs that lined the river banks, Lola thought they were curassows, there must have been well over a hundred of them.

The lovers just watched and listened, keeping quiet and motionless for ten minutes or more, both astounded by the wonder of it all. They'd never experienced anything quite like the tropical rain forest, they were all alone in a magical, primeval wilderness. No traffic noise, or sirens going off, or people rushing about along crowded city streets plagued by air pollution. They were surrounded by the mind-blowing vastness of the Amazon in all its glory. Dense woodlands, in various shades of green, enveloped them, individuals totally enchanted by the immense power of mother nature. The hypnotic sounds of birds and monkeys echoed and reverberated throughout the lush forest. It felt as if they'd been transported back hundreds of thousands of years to a time long before man ever set foot on planet Earth. They were touched greatly by it all. Both felt overwhelmed and deeply affected by the sheer atmospheric and visual beauty of a world, unique and ancient, they'd been privileged to enter into.

'This is one incredible place,' said John. 'I can't believe that so many Brazilians want to destroy all this in the name of progress, economic development I think it's called.'

'I shall speak to Federico,' responded Lola. 'With all his power, he needs to do something useful, something to look after this amazing forest and other parts of South America like it. He could do some good with all his money.'

'We'll both have a word with him, perhaps he can be persuaded, all of this needs protection for now and the future. What a fantastic planet we live on!'

'Are you going to risk a swim?' asked a smiling Lola. She wasn't serious as she had no intention whatsoever of jumping into the water. The boat represented safety, the river was the complete opposite.

'Are you joking? Didn't you listen to Santos? Caimans lurk on the banks and in the shallows. Something called black pacu live in these waters, the buggers are over a metre long as are the vampire fish with their razor-sharp teeth. And what about piranhas? Look, if you want to cool down, Lola, take your clothes off, I'll be happy to rub in some sun tan lotion, all over you if you want.'

Lola gave a seductive smile and started to peel off her T-shirt and shorts. In the stifling afternoon heat she stripped off completely apart from a skimpy black g-string. In response John decided to throw off his white polo shirt and khaki shorts. It wasn't long before they decided to retire to the privacy of the cubby cabin and that's where they spent quite some time. It was turning dark when they later appeared back outside.

John decided he needed a drink, he opened the small fridge and took out two bottles of ice-cold *Brahma* beer. He jokingly put one of them on Lola's bare back and the sudden shock of it made her scream. John said she sounded like one of the howler monkeys and suggested she'd better join them in the trees. Lola laughed and pretended she was going to knee him where it hurts. Eventually, after fooling around, they sat closely curled up together, both in the nude, sipping cool beer and listening once more to the cacophony of sounds around them while also watching the magnificent sights of the rain forest, a tropical wonderland that has been around for millions of years. Sitting at the back of the boat they felt a great empathy with their natural surroundings. Mankind, despite its billions of people, was only a very small, if hugely influential, part of a huge biological cycle of creation, life, death and decay. Humans were responsible for protecting this complex, inter-connected web and they neglected to do so at their peril. Being alone together in the vastness of the Amazon had been a spiritual and life-changing experience for both John and Lola. They'd made up their minds, whichever future path they took in life they were determined to do all they could, however small that might be, to protect this precious ecosystem and others around the world like it. Losing the rain forests, sometime soon in the future, didn't bear thinking about.

After finishing their drinks, the lovers returned to the snug cuddy cabin and made sure their sleeping area was covered by a mosquito net, they didn't fancy being bitten, malaria was a hazard best avoided. Both John and Lola had taken anti-malaria tablets since their arrival in the Amazon but the netting was a sensible, extra precaution. The ensuing tropical night, roughly equal in time to the daylight hours, was punctuated at first with heavy showers but, entwined together under a thin sheet, they were soon fast asleep. The ensuing heavy rain, streaks of forked lightning that lit up the sky, followed by loud thunder claps didn't disturb them.

When they awoke dawn was breaking and a wispy layer of early morning mist hung over the river and parts of the surrounding forest canopy. It would soon be time to head back to where Santos had arranged to meet them at the confluence of the Rios Jiparana and Jarú. Twelve noon had been mentioned.

The ride south back upriver was just as breathtaking as the previous day's journey north downstream. The ubiquitous howler monkeys screamed in the tree tops, tamarins bounced and leapt along the sturdy branches of tall trees, a giant ant eater was spotted next to the river bank and a scarlet macaw with its bright plumage flashed across the river channel. John hoped he'd see the elusive big cat, the jaguar, but it wasn't to be. Although surrounded by animals, birds and insects the human race wasn't seen at all, it was only John and Lola returning up-river. John wondered whether they might see some indigenous tribespeople. Santos had advised against instigating any social interaction, best keep themselves to themselves. Most of the natives were friendly but some weren't and they might not differentiate between eco-tourists and belligerent land grabbers and loggers keen to divest the tribes of their ancient rights to territory that they and their ancestors had roamed across for many centuries.

By eleven o'clock, on a hot and humid morning, they were approaching journey's end. Once there, John tied the boat to an old wooden stake that jutted upwards from the end of the short pier that cut across the silty river channel. Santos was waiting for them. After thanking him for the loan of his boat and saying what a wonderful experience they'd had it wasn't long before both John and Lola started discussing their concerns for the future of the forest. On the ride back to the farmstead Santos listened attentively but was unapologetic for the attitudes of so many of his fellow countrymen and leading politicians.

'Bolsanaro is an ex-military man with strong opinions on many things, he is supportive of forest clearance and the need for economic development but other politicians like Lula da Silva are the exact opposite. It is difficult to know who is right but only one option makes money.'

'But you can't just let this wonderful forest shrink and disappear!' appealed Lola.

'It would not only be bad for Brazil, think of the whole world!' added John demonstratively.

'My ranch covers thousands of acres. We've been clearing land for many years but I tell you what I'll do. I won't expand it anymore, at least for now, and I'll fund some extra protection for the conservation of the Nature Reserve you saw. I'll employ rangers to guard it, the government provide some but they're not enough.' Santos had been impressed by their persuasive arguments against economic exploitation and, during their time together, had grown to like both his guests.

'How much of Rondônia is protected?' asked Lola. The short trip into the rain forest had convinced her to become an environmentalist.

'Quite a bit, more than you think,' replied Santos. 'Nature reserves are all over the place and in the centre there's a huge area that's protected, the lands of the Uru-Eu-Wau-Wau people.'

'But from what you've told us I expect the government and local officials turn a blind eye to many of the infringements into these lands?' asked John.

'Too right, there are cassiterite mines outside the capital, Puerto Velho, and gold mines too. Tin is big business. Thousands of poor peasant farmers are looking for land in order to make a living, illegal logging operations are going on all the time.'

After discussing the need for conservation, Santos began to discuss his own plans. Ricky, his faithful pilot, would be meeting them at Ji-Paraná airport, they'd be whisked off thousands of miles north, destination Central America to Nicaragua, in order to meet an associate of Santos in Bluefields, a sleepy Caribbean coastal town. He had important business to discuss, John and Lola could continue their holiday in the colourful fishing port. Centuries ago it had been a den of iniquity for motley teams of Dutch, French and British pirates who plundered ships heading back from the Spanish Main laden with gold and other treasures. Today there are none of the pirates of old but Bluefields is still a town full of interesting characters as both John and Lola were soon to find out.

38

Luca and Bruno Andretti had been busy. Chico's funeral, held at the family cemetery on Long Island, was a solemn and respectful occasion played out in a chilly sea fret sweeping in off the cold waters of the Atlantic. Fortunately, their young brother had no wife or kids, but the guy was only in his thirties and his untimely death was mourned deeply by ageing parents and an elderly grandmother. The event was attended by the wider Andretti family, as well as associates from a criminal community that stretched all the way down the east coast into other parts of the Americas. Some big shots from Miami, relatives of the brothers, had flown in that morning. Met by some heavies in a black limo, they were driven to the church service in the Hamptons at the far end of the island.

Another member of the circle, Randy Lister, controller of operations in Central America, thought it prudent to show up, best to keep his boss happy he reasoned. Carlo Pozzo, head man in South America, made the long trip from Argentina.

Once the memorial service was out of the way Luca held a meeting at the family's statement property that backed onto the ocean, the main topic of conversation was Federico Santos.

'Any of you guys have an idea of where Santos is?' enquired Luca menacingly as he looked around the table at the assembled throng of family and gang members.

There was an anxious hush, nobody wanted to set the ball rolling on this particularly sensitive topic. From brief, informal chats at the funeral wake they all knew that Luca was seething about the matter. He could be touchy at the best of times and no-one wanted to upset him any more on what was a sad day for him and his immediate family. It was Pozzo who broke the awkward silence in the room.

'He don't seem to be anywhere in Argentina, boss. We've had all bases covered and his known whereabouts checked out. There's no sign of him in Mendoza, his house is under surveillance 24-7, business offices are closed, builder's yard also. No sign of the big Brazilian bodyguard either. Wherever Santos goes, he travels with him.'

A tall, broad-shouldered man, part of the Miami brigade, was the next to speak.

'He's nowhere in Florida, boss. We know the guys he deals with, some of our boys paid 'em a visit, broke a few things to show we're seriously pissed off, roughed up one or two. They swore he'd not been around for months.'

'He has places in Buenos Aires and Rio,' said Bruno, 'We've a watch on his apartment in BA, unfortunately we don't know where he lives in Rio. Rumour is his wife and kid are stashed away somewhere in the Copacabana district, we don't know where, but we're working on it. If we find them we sure as hell find Santos.'

'I have men in Rio,' added Pozzo. 'They're on the case right now.'

'How about you, Randy?' asked an increasingly disgruntled Luca.

'We know he shifts most of his drugs through Nicaragua. He has some hideaway outside Mexico City, up in the hills, we're trying to check it out but no news as yet.' replied Randy.

'How's he get stuff into Nicaragua?' asked Luca.

'The same as we all do I suppose, along the Caribbean coast. It's quiet with hardly no fuzz about,' answered Randy.

'I heard he has an associate who works there, some guy called El Bigote,' said Luca.

'That's right. Real name, Jorge Hernandez. He has an amazing moustache, that's how he got the name El Bigote. Fucker looks like a modern-day version of Zapata, the revolution guy from way back, but this dude has a beard too.' Randy had an ugly grin smeared across his face, amused at comparing El Bigote to Emiliano Zapata.

The room laughed with him sharing Lister's joke. The thought of a Zapata look-alike shifting narcotics in Nicaragua entertained them all. Perhaps the revolutionary, assassinated at the end of the Mexican Civil War in 1919, had been reincarnated as a drugs dealer.

'Keep tabs on this character. Where's he hang out, Randy?' asked Luca.

'The guy don't seem to have no fixed abode but he spends a lot of time on the Caribbean coast in a town called Bluefields,' replied Randy.

'That's a place we need to concentrate on then. Make sure it's done,' concluded Luca.

After drinking their way through over a hundred bottles of Corona beer and finishing off another three bottles of Van Brunt bourbon Luca brought the meeting to a close. Chico was dead, they'd paid their respects. His death was Santos's fault, the top priority for everyone now was to find the little Brazilian, capture and keep guard over him, and inform the boss. He would then swing into action. Luca Andretti would supply the *coup de grâce*.

39

It was a typical March day in England. The weather veered from bright blue skies and pleasant sunshine to dark clouds accompanied by heavy showers. A strong but mild wind, a south-westerly, blew across the open fenland as Watling, wearing a rain coat over his casual clothes, knocked on the door of Bob Hemingway's farm house.

'Well, hello, DCI Watling, come on in, before it throws it down with rain again.' Bob was his customary affable self.

'Please call me George,' replied Watling as he walked through the open doorway.

'What can I do for you this time, George?'

Watling went on to let Bob in on some of the events of recent weeks, but there was no mention of meeting up with John Ripley in Mendoza. He didn't want that out in the public domain, it was private information that had to remain inside the walls of police headquarters, at least for now until he'd visited Lucy Ripley and Addenbrooke's Hospital. Ripley's wife should be the first to know about his trip to Argentina and the meeting with her errant husband.

'I'd like to learn as much as possible about the old cottage please, Bob. Anything you've got, or that you can remember. You've already given us some useful information but I was hoping you could go further back than the 1950s.'

'Well, as you know, I was born soon after the war and my earliest recollections of people living in the place are of Norman Field, his wife and their two lads. Back in the fifties, I used to play with the sons all around the farm, happy days they were. Time moves on, *tempus fugit* and all that, when the boys grew up they moved away. The parents are long dead,' he mused.

'What about before the war or even during it? Can you remember anything your parents or grandparents told you about the house and the folk who lived there?'

Bob went on to say that he'd recently been searching through some old farm records that his father and grandfather had kept, they dated back to before the Great War. He lifted himself out of his chair and walked across the room to pick up a pile of battered ledgers and diaries. He opened them, he'd already selected certain pages by inserting bookmarks in the appropriate places.

'Here's some stuff you might find interesting. Everything's hand written, no computers or even typewriters it seems in them far-off days.'

Bob handed the old records of life on the farm across to Watling. The ledgers mainly contained information about the costs of various purchases for the farm, in old-fashioned pounds, shillings and pence, as well as the prices received for goods, mostly arable crops, fruit and vegetables. One of them listed details of some roofing work done on the cottage back in 1934, costing only £5 for the materials and £10 for the labour. However, one particular page, highlighted in yellow marker pen by Bob, really caught Watling's eye and his initially lukewarm interest in the old manuals suddenly became ignited. There were details recording the names of the cottage's residents ever since its construction in 1882. Watling already knew that the Fields had lived in the place during the 1950s but he could see that their tenure went back to 1946, the year after World War Two had ended. During the war years a small group of Land Girls were living in the cottage, four female names were listed. They'd all been evacuated from London and had worked on the farm. Watling turned over the page to discover more interesting facts.

Before the war a family of five, the parents and three children, had been in the cottage. They'd moved in during 1928 and left ten years later. Bob mentioned that his now deceased father was born in 1921. Both his dad and granddad would have known the Watkins family. He added that his long dead grandfather had been born in 1895. Before the Watkins, the Hudson family were the tenants for the twenty years from 1907 to 1927. A note in the book mentioned the sad loss of their eldest son, Ernest, killed on the Somme in July, 1916. According to the notes the young lad used to help on the farm before enlisting in the army during

1915. The records went right back to the 1880s: lists of names and, fascinatingly, a record of births, marriages and deaths. Bob had worked out that there'd been 15 births in the house, a total of 10 marriages of farmworkers' children had been recorded plus 16 deaths, some young babies and children from killer infant diseases such as diphtheria and scarlet fever in the days before vaccinations. A few adult deaths were the result of consumption or tuberculosis.

'This is a fascinating piece of history, Bob. Do you mind if I take a photograph of it all?'

'Be my guest,' answered Bob, helpful as ever.

Watling wanted to move on to the topic of the supernatural.

'During our investigations people spoke of strange happenings in and around the cottage. You haven't any records of that sort of thing, have you? An old lady, dressed in black, carrying a candle was mentioned by more than one person. Bit of a ghost cliché that is, I know, but I was wondering if you'd maybe heard or read anything?'

'Well, George, I've never seen or experienced such things myself either at this farmhouse or at any of the cottages that were once part of the farm. I also don't remember my parents saying anything. But come and have a look at this, it's something I came across last night, while going through the old diaries.'

Bob opened up the farm diary for 1930 and pointed out an entry for Tuesday, November 18th. In faded black ink it read:

Strange happening last night. Pete Watkins he reported his wife Emily she gone up stairs of Fen View Cottage after nightfall to check on children. She seen some sort of ghost at top of stairs female figure dressed in black rags she said. Awful appearance no eyes scratched bloodied face but present for only few seconds, Emily she distressed, fortunately her screaming it don't disturb the kids. Never heard of a ghost before in the cottage very strange!

The scribbled insert had been signed by Ted Hemingway, Bob's late grandfather.

'That's interesting! Maybe there is something in all this stuff I've heard about. Do you believe in ghosts, Bob?'

'Not really, I reckon it's a load of old baloney, nonsense people dream up to scare others, it always makes for a good story though,' he replied with a chuckle.

'I didn't believe in ghosts either, until I heard one.'

Watling went on to recite his own supernatural experience. Bob smiled politely at the story but didn't seem convinced. After a second cup of tea Watling thanked him for his time and warm welcome. He left the farm and hurried home to see his wife before meeting up with Mike Dunlop.

At six-thirty that evening Watling greeted his friend in the Maypole. After ordering a couple of pints of *Sparta*, a real ale produced locally at the Milton brewery, they found a quiet corner. Following opening pleasantries about the forthcoming tennis season, the latest football results and the dire state of British politics the old mates got down to the main reason for their get-together.

'Mike, you know why I want to see you, I need to pick your brains on the subject where you're an authority, apart from botany that is!'

'My knowledge of things that go bump in the night I believe, George,' replied Dunlop with a smile.

'One of my latest inquiries has supernatural happenings associated with it and I'd like to seek your advice, your expert opinion.'

'Fire away, old boy!' enthused Dunlop. 'I'm always interested in any matters that science hasn't an answer to.'

Watling went on to describe the Fen View case. The academic listened attentively while sipping his beer. After Watling had finished his intriguing story Dunlop was keen to get involved.

'A fascinating tale, George. You and I must go out to the Fens, have a bit of a scouting mission, get a feel for the place. Pity the cottage has been knocked down, we could have spent a night in it, what!'

Dunlop laughed so loud that some of the other customers turned around to look in their direction, wondering what was so funny. Without saying so, Watling wouldn't have fancied spending the dark hours in a dingy and derelict Victorian farm cottage that might be haunted out in the middle of nowhere. He suddenly felt grateful that it had been knocked down.

'Are you free either tomorrow or the day after?' asked Watling. 'Preferably during the day.'

'Night would be best, old bean. You get a much better feel for the spiritual world when it's dark, it's the right time of the month, there'll soon be a full moon, we'll be able to see more. I'll try to bring along one of my friends, he's a spirit medium. He's no phoney operator. Quite a few of my fellow Ghost Club members have used him to great effect. The clergy are always contacting him to exorcise poltergeists and malignant presences in houses throughout the country.'

'Right, OK, night time eh! If needs must I suppose, Jill's going to love this, good job I've promised her a holiday soon.'

'How about tomorrow then, George, along with an old chum of mine? My Parisian friend, Michel, he now works and lives in Cambridge. He's a Modern Languages lecturer, but a medium also, one of the best, old boy. We could spend a night together at where this Fen View Cottage used to be. You say a new place is going up but no-one's moved in yet so it shouldn't be a problem.'

'My detective sergeant, Penny Lester, is interested as well. She's on a rest day so maybe she can join us?'

'OK, George, let's all meet here again tomorrow at seven o'clock, that's if Michel can accompany us, I'll give him a ring.'

Michel responded immediately to the call, he was indeed free the following night and was happy to join them. Watling then rang Penny, she was delighted to be asked and agreed to meet up. A team of four would convene for dinner at the Maypole before heading out to the Fens. An investigation with a difference was about to begin. Watling felt excited but his anticipation was tinged with a good deal of apprehension. He'd been advised in the past that the paranormal was best left untouched. Delving into matters supernatural was an extremely dangerous road to travel down.

40

Federico Santos's private jet touched down in Bluefields late on Saturday morning. Ángel was the first to descend off the plane after being asked, as usual, to survey the scene. Everything looked OK, he gave a nod and a thumbs up to Santos sitting in the front of the cockpit. The others could follow him into the sunshine. John walked down the steps onto *terra firma*, followed by Lola. Last person out was Santos, dressed in his customary attire of black shirt, slacks, shoes and sunglasses. It was late March, the dry season, the best time of the year to visit this part of the world. Although hot the humidity levels were thankfully low.

Ángel collected a hire car but Santos did the driving. He'd visited Bluefields on many occasions and knew the place like the back of his hand judging by how he sped out of the airport and along the surrounding roads. They headed for the centre of town, destination the top hotel, *Casa Royale*, positioned near the water front. Their journey took them past a motley mixture of houses, many were no more than shacks. The better constructed buildings had a colonial look about them, a residue of overseas influences from times past in the area once known as the Mosquito Coast. Attractive palm trees of varying sizes and shades of green, planted between adjacent properties, swayed to-and-fro in the strong onshore breeze.

Bluefields is an archetypal Caribbean coastal settlement. Like much of the West Indies, the east coast of Nicaragua is a cultural melting pot, a polyglot of people with varied skin colours speaking in different languages and dialects. Most are either Creoles, people of mixed Negro and European stock, or Mestizos, an ethnic blend of European with indigenous groups. Some are plainly Negro and others native such as members of the local Miskito tribe. A few are of Chinese origin or at least mixed Chinese. Over the centuries, ever since slaves were brought into the region from the sixteenth century onwards, indigenous tribes have mixed with the Spanish, British and Dutch as well as descendants of the original negro slaves imported from West Africa.

The immediate impression of Bluefields, often conveyed to first-time visitors, is one of poverty. Santos, always a fountain of knowledge, told his companions that the port dated back to the 1630s. A Dutch pirate, Abraham Blauvelt, established a tiny settlement on a sheltered inlet at the time. That's how the place got its name, Blauvelt eventually morphed into Bluefields. The location became an ideal base for raids by buccaneers on Spanish shipping, laden with riches, heading home from the New World to the Old.

Lola, to her dismay, remarked that children weren't wearing shoes and John commented on the numbers of young men lounging around menacingly on street corners. Many of the buildings they passed, painted in vivid and garish shades of pink, blue and purple, had been bleached and blistered over the years by the powerful tropical sun. They journeyed on into the town centre. A busy scene greeted them with old fashioned cars slowly winding their way along concrete topped streets and people, of all ages and colours, going about their business, most of them shopping for everyday items like fruit and vegetables, or perusing the latest catches displayed on fishmongers' slabs. Others waited patiently to be served at roadside cafes and eateries. A colourful array of shops and outdoor stalls lined the broad pavements, it was typical Bluefields on a Saturday morning.

The comforts of the *Casa Royale* made it the go-to place for Santos whenever work brought him to the east coast of Nicaragua. The staff there viewed him as a successful businessman. Whether they were aware he was a major drugs lord was doubtful but, if they did, they'd probably be happy to ignore the fact. Drugs money had brought welcome cash to Bluefields in recent decades, either through the hurriedly discarded bales of cocaine that periodically washed up on the beaches or from those drug dealer benefactors in the local community who pumped much needed funds into the town's economy. It's not uncommon for drug runners in boats, operating along the Caribbean coastline, to throw plastic parcels of cocaine overboard if they feared being intercepted by the drug control enforcement agencies patrolling offshore waters. The so-called 'white lobster' is sometimes washed ashore, deposited by breaking waves along the coastline. Locals search for this welcome gift from the sea and the dealers buy it off them for a good price, but one well below its market value in cities like Miami or New York. The Nicaraguan government take a fairly liberal attitude to drug smuggling activities, especially in backwaters like the Caribbean coastal region. Their *laissez-faire* policy avoids the conflicts and killings that can happen when police and armed forces decide to take on the cartels.

Santos, as usual, was hungry and decided it was time for lunch and so, after checking in, they headed straight for the hotel's restaurant. Apart from easing his hunger pangs Santos, forever thinking ahead, wanted to run through his latest plans.

'I'm meeting Jorge this afternoon but Ángel is free to show you two around. Take a *panga*, it's a small motorboat, travel up the coast. Show them the mangrove swamps, Ángel, go up the Rio Escondido into the jungle, it's navigable for many kilometres inland.'

'Federico, there's one thing I've always been meaning to ask you. How come you speak such good English?' questioned John.

Santos smiled, pleased to be complimented for his ability to speak it so well.

'When I could afford it I went to night school in Rio. My teacher was brilliant and I practised hard. I also paid for extra one-to-one lessons. I knew I'd have to master the language to be successful in America. I was a young man with enthusiasm, commitment and a burning desire to succeed. After seeing all the poverty that surrounded me I always wanted one day to be rich and powerful. It took me several years of hard work to speak really good English.'

'Well you're pretty damn good at it now,' said John. 'Better than many English and American people.'

'You too, Ángel, you also speak it perfectly. How is that?' asked the always curious Lola.

Ángel smiled and was happy to answer the question:

'I've an American mother, she was born in Florida, it's where I spent my youth. My father is Brazilian, he was an officer in the army and often away from home. We had an apartment in Rio as well as a house in Miami. I followed in my father's footsteps and joined the Brazilian army but I travelled to England and spent a year at the Sandhurst Royal Military Academy where I learnt many skills with the British army before returning to Rio. That's where I met Federico and he pays me ten times more than what I could earn as an honest member of the public serving my country.'

'OK, so now we know. Lola and I would be delighted to be shown around by Ángel. We'd be in safe hands.'

'Most of the people here speak English,' said Santos. 'Bluefields is more Jamaica than Nicaragua. The Spanish live in the west of the country and up in the hills, here along the Caribbean coast people use English, pigeon English maybe, or various native languages.'

'You sure you're OK by yourself for the afternoon, boss?' asked Ángel.

'No problem, I'll be fine, I'm staying in the hotel, I'm not wandering off anywhere, Jorge is coming to meet me later, we have lots to discuss. I'm not expecting trouble. The Andrettis haven't a clue where we are and the different gangs try hard to get along with each other. It's not in anyone's interest to start shooting people. This town has an edge to it but it's a lot friendlier than many other parts of the world,' was Santos's dismissive reply.

After lunch in the hotel's Bay View Bar and Restaurant Santos was left all by himself in his room with plenty to keep him occupied. He'd plans to construct as well as calls to make. Later he'd be expecting a visit from Jorge Hernandez, his main partner in crime in the Caribbean region.

The others left the hotel and headed down to the seafront where rows of *pangas* lined the shoreline. Ángel spoke to a young man of mixed race, a mestizo. Cash was exchanged, John and Lola were told the boat had been hired for four hours. They'd travel north across the bay towards the mouth of the Rio Escondido and head inland. As the *panga* cut through the placid waters of the lagoon they glided their way past broad sweeps of mangrove forest growing out of the brackish sea water along the coastline. Inland of the swamps, coconut palms swayed in the breeze. John spotted banana trees with bunches of unripe green fruit and a sugar cane plantation appeared further along the shore. At the mouth of the Escondido they headed upstream into the steamy heat of the jungle. It was a very different world compared to the residential sprawl of the coastal area where a rash of urban development, both planned and unofficial, extended into the surrounding hills and along the seafront.

While his travelling companions played at being tourists, Santos was awaiting a visit from Jorge Hernandez, a tall, swarthy Mexican, better known to friends and enemies alike, as El Bigote, the moustachioed one. He was a popular man in these parts because he donated money to local charities, he supported the carnival in May and provided drugs industry jobs in a town where the unemployment rate was usually well over fifty per cent. Most of the honest men with no connections to the trade in narcotics were either relatively poor fishermen, farmers or storekeepers. When in Bluefields, Hernandez stayed with friends he could trust and certain hotels, but he owned two properties in different parts of Nicaragua. Like Santos he was a man always on the move. El Bigote had been married twice but soon ended up divorcing both women. He eventually decided that he didn't want to add his name to the long list of middle-aged men with a wife, kids, dog and a mortgage to worry about. Ever since his mid-thirties he'd remained single, he now preferred the casual company of different women, reckoning that sex without commitment or any strings attached was more exciting. He never took his mistresses to the secret abodes, he couldn't have relied on any of them to keep quiet. Jorge Hernandez trusted very few people but his old friend and business partner, Santos, was an exception to the rule.

The wall clock in Santos's room indicated a few minutes after three o'clock. A sudden, hard knock startled him, he wasn't expecting a visitor just yet. Always a cautious man, Santos took a loaded gun out of its holster and slowly headed towards the door but never at any time was he in line with it. Forever cool and calculating in the face of potential danger, he was in self-preservation mode, it was second nature to him. Walking straight up to a door when you didn't know who was on the other side of it would be a dumb move. He also never sat by a window in full view to the outside world as he quite rightly reasoned that he'd be a sitting duck target for a would-be assassin. In a restaurant, or any room for that matter, he always sat with his back to a wall, preferably a thick one made of bricks, so that he could observe all that went on and more importantly who was coming in and going out.

'Who is it?' he asked guardedly.

No answer so he repeated the question, a little louder.

'WHO IS IT?'

Santos stood behind the solid wall to the left of the door, pistol in his right hand.

'Room service.'

'I haven't asked for room service.'

'I have message, from Señor Hernandez,' was the response from whoever was outside the door.

'I'm busy, go away!' Santos sounded annoyed.

He'd been expecting a visit from Jorge but not for a while, he certainly wasn't anticipating some messenger turning up and acting on his behalf. If there was a problem Jorge himself would have contacted him. Also, if Hernandez had been at reception a message conveying that information would have been sent via his room telephone. The mystery guy outside the door was a dubious intrusion, Santos was suspicious. No way was he going to open the door. He retired back into his suite and sat down in an armchair before ringing his friend. There were no more knocks, his unexpected visitor had presumably given up and walked away.

'Hi, Jorge, Federico here.'

'*Hola! Señor Federico, mi amigo,* what is it?'

'Did you just send someone to my hotel with a message for me?'

'No way! I'm expecting to see you in about an hour. Hotel reception, as usual, will let you know when I arrive.'

'I thought so, thanks Jorge, see you soon.' Santos ended the brief conversation.

It confirmed what he'd suspected and feared. Someone, an enemy no doubt, must know he was in town, it was bad news. He tapped Ángel's number. The call wasn't answered, it was highly unusual for his bodyguard not to respond immediately to his boss. There must be no reception along the Escondido. Santos started to wish they'd all stayed together, that policy had served them well since leaving Mendoza. Normally he didn't have any hassle in Bluefields, it was a sleepy corner of the Caribbean. Drug dealing was part of the local economy, even if nobody liked to admit it. In recent times the small port had become a pit stop for the flow of narcotics out of Latin America on its journey northwards.

Santos reasoned that an enemy must know of his whereabouts, the uninvited guest was proof of that. He wondered if the Andretti mob were on to him. He wanted Ángel, John and Lola back in the hotel urgently, for their safety as much as his, but if they were still in the middle of the jungle they'd be uncontactable. It looked as if Santos would be requiring El Bigote's assistance, he possessed plenty of muscle in this part of the world. The unexpected intrusion had been a warning. He felt convinced that Andretti, or one of his Nicaraguan associates, was onto him and when Santos had a hunch about something he wasn't usually wrong.

41

After dinner at the Maypole the would-be ghost hunters climbed into Watling's car and headed out of Cambridge, destination the fenlands to the north of the city. It was the end of March, the clocks had just gone forward, the light of the day had not yet dimmed but, half an hour later, it was almost dark when they arrived at the isolated site where Fen View Cottage had once stood. In the twilight they could see the shell of a new property taking shape, parts of its exterior that were metallic glinted in the moonlight but the build was a long way from being completed.

Investigators of the paranormal, a couple of seasoned veterans and two rookie newcomers, made their way across the empty and rather eerie building site.

'We'll have a jolly good walk around, George, old boy, get a feel for the place,' said Dunlop jauntily.

'That's fine, Penny and I will follow, you're the experts.'

'OK, but first you must show us where the bodies were found. If I remember rightly you said the area was a patch of wasteland, not part of the garden or any field,' Dunlop remarked.

They trooped towards where the swimming pool was going to be. Watling headed for the deep end to show Dunlop and Thibault where Sara Barrington-Webb's body had been discovered the previous October. He then moved a few metres to the side of the excavated hollow and indicated where Suzy Wong's remains had been dug up more recently. The distance between the two locations was less than ten metres.

'What do you think Michel? Are you feeling anything, any presence in this area?' asked Dunlop.

His French friend, Dr Michel Thibault, stood still and silent for about half a minute deep in thought after having first climbed into the intended pool area at the exact spot where the first body was found back in the autumn. After clambering out with help from the others he did exactly the same thing where the second body had been discovered by the cadaver dog team. He looked at his companions.

'*Non, rien ici*, nothing here, *mes amies*, but we could try something, ... later perhaps.'

For quarter of an hour they toured the site in the gloom. There was not much to see other than the shell of a new house together with a few silted-up waterways lined by reeds and bulrushes. In the distance, poking out above the flat farmland, were occasional trees and the odd hedgerow. However, certain features of the landscape were starting to fascinate Thibault. He showed great interest in the decaying wreck of an ancient wind pump as well as a copse positioned on top of a hummocky, undulating patch of land. Any hill, however small, was an unusual feature for this part of England.

'We need to look at the old windmill,' said Thibault. 'I have a strange feeling about it.'

They made their way across to the ageing wreck of what was in fact a late eighteenth century wind pump that had long ceased to function as such. They walked around the monument of a by-gone age searching for an entrance, all they found was a narrow doorway that was half open. What was left of the sails had collapsed and were propped up along one side of the building. Thibault carefully surveyed both the outer and inner walls. He then turned to his companions.

'I'm convinced that evil has taken place here!' he exclaimed. 'Have you noticed what I've seen?'

Watling and Lester remained silent, all they saw was a derelict and decaying wind pump but Mike Dunlop had spotted faded markings scrawled on the outside wall of the building, about six feet above ground level.

'I've seen something, it's rather disturbing I think.' He pointed to an area on the wall. 'Look, there's the vague outline of a shape, it's now weathered with age but if you look carefully you can see its form. It's one that has been used by devil worshippers, in many countries, over the centuries.'

'You're right, Mike, ... the shape of the pentacle!' Thibault replied excitedly. He went on to explain the meaning of the symbol. 'The pentacle is a five-pointed star contained within a circle. It's supposed to have magical powers, the points represent wood, fire, earth, metal and water. An indication that sometime in the past this building was used by people into the dark arts, or black magic as it is often called.'

Thibault wondered if the wind pump had at one time been a meeting place for devil worshippers. Black masses had occurred throughout the ages, there are many historical accounts of such events. He laughed and joked about the French having been particularly fond of such gatherings. His attention then moved on to the large copse. The intrepid foursome trooped towards the silhouetted shapes of dormant, leafless trees. As if wanting to add to the feeling of unease nocturnal creatures were on the move. An owl flew out from a large oak tree and a swarm of bats could be seen circling above the slumbering plant life. The odd rustling sound from the undergrowth and occasional, sudden gust of wind only added to the spookiness of the surroundings.

'I'm wondering why's there such a large patch of woodland out here on the Fens?' asked Dunlop. 'This area is supposed to be covered by fertile soil, ground ideal for farming.'

'Maybe it was planted as a windbreak,' ventured Watling.

'Or as an area for foxes to build their dens,' added Lester. 'Woodland was planted as cover to attract foxes, back in the days when hunting was popular and legal.'

'Both good points,' said Dunlop, 'another possibility is that the area is a patch of stony ground, dumped thousands of years ago by a decaying ice sheet, a legacy of the Ice Age perhaps?'

Thibault listened attentively to the different theories put forward but then came up with another, far more chilling explanation.

'What you all say is possible of course but I feel uneasy in this space. I feel the spirit world strongly. Have you ever heard of plague pits?' he asked somewhat dramatically.

'You're not suggesting that this was once the site of a mass burial, are you?' asked Watling.

'It's possible, I think this patch of woodland might have been here for centuries. Knowledge of its history will have been lost with the passing of the years and generations. The area might have been a burial site, maybe at the time of the Black Death in the middle of the fourteenth century, trees were then planted over it, much later, for the reasons you've already mentioned,' replied Thibault.

'Bob Hemingway, the farmer who owns most of the land around here, he showed me some old maps of the area. They went back to before the cottage was built in 1882. I can definitely remember seeing this patch of woodland on an 1870s map. It was the only area of trees, it stuck out like a sore thumb,' said Watling.

'There are restless spirits in this area, I can't see them but I feel their presence. I'm confident that, long ago, this will have been a burial place,' insisted Thibault. 'We need to have a séance, we must do it tonight, by this wood,' he added rather abruptly.

Penny looked shocked at the idea. Mike too seemed taken aback and apprehensive at the thought of trying to contact the spirit world on a cold night out on the Fens beside a patch of woodland. Watling was the first to reply:

'Right, let's do it!'

42

Ángel returned the *panga* to its owner and led the way from the waterfront back to the hotel but on approaching the Avenida de 19 Julio he slowed down to allow his companions to catch up. Without turning around, he then whispered quietly:

'Don't look now but we're being followed.'

Although alarmed by Ángel's words, John and Lola kept on walking, ignoring an understandable urge to turn their heads. Without stopping they strolled back towards the hotel as if nothing untoward was happening. Eventually Ángel ushered them through its entrance before he glanced back at their pursuers. A couple of men, first spotted after returning the motorboat, were still trailing them. They were roughly fifty metres away with their eyes fixed on Ángel. Both looked like Creole locals, early twenties, maybe younger, no more than kids from a gang tied up with the drugs trade. One of them was on his phone, maybe to a more senior guy higher up the food chain, probably asking what to do next.

Once inside the hotel's lobby Ángel followed John and Lola up a few flights of stairs to Santos's room. He'd been expecting them, Ángel had phoned ahead to let his boss know they were back in town and would be with him soon. John knocked on the door.

'Hi, Federico, it's John.'

Always ultra-careful Santos asked for the pre-agreed security code.

'656 ... Caiman,' replied John.

Santos let them in. Ángel told his boss they'd been followed by suspicious-looking youths, he thought trouble was brewing. Santos confirmed his fears. He was convinced that someone, possibly connected to the Andrettis, had been keeping tabs on them. He mentioned the mystery caller earlier that afternoon.

It was not unreasonable to assume the Andrettis had used contacts in the Caribbean to track them down.

Earlier, as planned, Santos had met with Jorge Hernandez. The major topic was the latest shipments of cocaine being moved in motorboats from various Nicaraguan coastal hideouts up to Miami but the ongoing threat posed by the Andrettis was also discussed. Hernandez assured Santos that he'd a team of twenty-four men working for him in and around Bluefields, everyone a tried and trusted gang member, they knew the consequences of any disloyalty, all were now at Santos's disposal. Hernandez had recently seen unfamiliar faces in the town, including a white guy, an American called Randy Lister. Jorge said he'd travelled from León, Nicaragua's second largest city, a place from where the Andrettis controlled the clandestine movement of narcotics northwards through Central America into southern American states such as New Mexico, Texas and Florida. After asking around he'd been informed that Lister worked for an American drugs gang with its headquarters in New York. To Santos it was all the confirmation he needed, the Andrettis were onto him yet again. They'd infiltrated his territory on the Caribbean coast, he was in a tricky situation once more, but El Bigote and Santos had hatched a plan for the evening.

'Jorge and I, we've put something together for later tonight,' said Santos. 'We've arranged to meet at a night club. We'll all go there, we need to stick together, at all times from now on, I reckon we'll have to make a rapid exit from Bluefields. We're being watched so we'll be followed wherever we go. My friend, Jorge, will have his men stationed both inside and outside the joint. Also, some of his guys will be down at the waterfront with a *panga*. Another group will be on the coast with a fast motorboat.' He looked at the others before adding: 'Because my friends, tonight, I think we'll need to get the hell out of here pretty damn quick.'

'So, what do we do for now?' asked John, concern written all over his face.

'We stay here, but only for a short time. I've asked reception to ring immediately if someone asks for me. It looks as if they already know I'm here so we'll be moving to another room right now. Someone's on to us, that's for sure, we've got to keep one step ahead of them.'

At half past nine precisely Ángel led the way to the *Cima Club*, it was a short walk of less than half a mile from the hotel. The night club has two distinctive, contrasting parts to it. Downstairs is an open terrace bar frequented by the locals, often hard-drinking fishermen and several ladies of the night looking for opportunities to make some money. Upstairs is the more respectable area where a varied mixture of Latin pop, rock and reggae are played.

Santos headed up the stairs. The moustachioed El Bigote was sat near the bar talking to a very large man, propped up on a stool, who looked like a cross between a boxer, with his broad, flat nose, and a body builder who spent half his life lifting weights. Huge, tattooed biceps bulged out from below the sleeves of a grey T-shirt. The big guy was introduced as Xavier, it turned out he was Jorge's deputy. After introductions, they all congregated around a couple of tables, cocktails were ordered, piña colada for Lola and gin martinis for the men except for Ángel, the committed teetotaller, who preferred lime and soda laced with plenty of ice and lemon. El Bigote reassured everyone that his men had the place surrounded, all entrances and exits were covered. They'd bide their time, enjoy the drinks and wait for the enemy to make its move.

It didn't take them long. Xavier received a message to say that rival gang members were downstairs but some were moving upstairs. All seemed more interested in observing the goings-on than buying any drinks, joining in the dancing or trying to pick up women. El Bigote's attention was drawn towards a white man dressed in a pale blue cotton shirt and beige chinos sitting at a table on the other side of the room. He looked like an average sort of guy, medium build and height, but what made him stand out was his piercing blue eyes and swept back, gelled, blonde hair. Both his arms were heavily tattooed and another piece of body art extended its way from his neck down to his chest. From a distance it looked like it could be a bald eagle, maybe he was proud to be American. Perhaps he'd another tattoo, one of 'Uncle Sam' etched onto his back.

'That guy over there with all the body art, the one that looks like a gringo, he keeps looking at us,' said El Bigote.

'You want me go over and engage him in conversation?' asked his deputy, 'find out what he's staring at.'

'Hell, no!' interjected Santos. 'Let's not go looking for trouble.'

'Not until we've at least enjoyed our drinks,' added El Bigote with a laugh.

'What's the plan if trouble starts?' asked John. It seemed like a sensible question. He was worried not so much for himself but for Lola.

'When things kick off, which they will, Jorge and his men will tackle the problem,' replied Santos. 'We four, meanwhile, head for the fire exit to our left, one of Jorge's men will meet us there, once outside we hurry down to the waterfront, a *panga* is on standby, ready and waiting to take us out of Bluefields.'

Apart from the loud reggae music and noise of conversation things remained quiet for half an hour, a second round of drinks was bought, no-one as yet had made any move but things were about to change. A large, black guy wandered over and said that his boss would like a word with someone called Santos. He turned and pointed to his superior, it was the blonde American festooned in tattoos.

'You go tell your boss that I'm busy with my friends,' was Santos's dismissive reply.

'He want speak with you mister, like now! He say it important,' added the large negro aggressively.

'Well that's just too bad, clear off and leave us alone,' replied Santos menacingly.

Santos looked annoyed, he didn't appreciate strangers coming up to him giving out orders. The rebuffed messenger wandered back over the busy room to his boss and whispered in his ear. Lister stood up and walked downstairs, the big guy followed him.

'What the hell do we do now?' asked a concerned John. He was becoming more worried. He'd appreciated all the help from Santos and Ángel but he was starting to realise that both he and his girlfriend were being increasingly dragged into the highly dangerous world of drug smugglers. Rather naively perhaps he'd been hoping that they would be taken to California with as little hassle as possible while having a great holiday together along the way. John had planned on renewing his duties at Tomás's Napa Valley winery during the coming week, Lola would spend a few days with him before returning, even if temporarily, to her sommelier work in Mendoza. The prospect of all that happening was not looking so good. John started to wish he'd taken the safer option, both he and Lola should have returned with Tomás to Argentina when they had the chance a few days before.

'Look, someone is out to get us but it's mainly me they're after,' said Santos, 'but we all need to stick together. I don't want trouble, no shooting or aggro of any kind.'

'Don't worry Federico, I have enough men here if it came to that, we can take care of the American and the big guy, anyone else for that matter,' Jorge said reassuringly.

'We can't stay here too much longer, boss, they could be waiting for the Andrettis to show up,' said Ángel. 'Then there will be a scene. We need to clear out, sooner the better I reckon.'

Randy Lister had moved outside flanked by his bodyguard. Leaning against a palm tree he was on his mobile, Luca Andretti was on the other end of the line.

'So, you've found the little fucker, he's in a Bluefields night club you say! You keep a good eye on him, Randy, track him for now. Don't lose him! Bruno and I will get over to you as soon as we can. We're on our way.'

Luca and his brother were in Miami. The Andretti brothers, on hearing that Santos was in Bluefields, hired a private jet. They'd be heading straight to Nicaragua, it was only a short trip across the Gulf of Mexico in a fast plane.

43

It was approaching eleven o'clock and Watling was wishing he'd worn a chunky jumper under his winter coat, not just a long-sleeved rugby shirt. The night was becoming increasingly colder. Darkness had fallen a few hours ago but the light from the moon meant that the flat fields of the fenlands were visible well into the distance. Watling started to think that he'd been mad to agree to this nocturnal adventure into the unknown but, nevertheless, he was determined to persevere. Together with the others he continued to tramp around the bleak landscape, enveloped as it was by a chilly blanket of Arctic air.

Michel Thibault, expert medium, one of the best in the field, led the way. His reputation had been built up over three decades of psychic investigations. The French academic was part of that rare group of people seemingly able to communicate with the spirit world. He'd already confessed to feeling the presence of 'evil' in the area by the wind pump and was convinced that there'd been a mass burial at some time underneath a patch of ancient woodland. If this had been official police business Watling would have called the cadaver dog team in by now.

'God, it's cold,' complained a shivering Penny Lester. 'How long do you think this is going to take?' Her enthusiasm, initially high earlier in the evening, was starting to wane rapidly with every passing minute.

'As long as it takes I'm afraid,' was Thibault's blunt and somewhat dismissive reply. It did nothing to lift Lester's sagging morale. Brought up in suburban Manchester, she was someone who had no affiliation to the countryside, especially on a night with the temperature only a degree or two above zero.

Thibault, in charge of operations, decided it was time to open up four small fold-away chairs and position them next to the copse of trees. They were strategically placed so that each one was in line with the cardinal directions on the compass he was carrying in his right hand. Time for a séance he said. After arranging them accordingly, Thibault sat in the seat that faced from east to west, Dunlop was instructed to sit opposite him, looking to the east, Watling was politely asked to sit down in the north seat that looked south and Lester occupied the south seat. Thibault then asked everyone to hold hands and insisted there must be no talking or moving about, they also needed to keep their eyes closed. Only he would speak from now on. He wanted to try to contact the spirit world, energy from the dead, people who hadn't fully passed on to the other side was how he put it. Nothing happened for more than ten minutes. Only the sounds of the countryside and the occasional gust of wind punctuated the scary silence, but Thibault eventually stirred. He grew restless and started to speak in a laboured, guttural sort of way. It unnerved both Watling and Lester but they followed his instructions: no speaking, no moving about, keep your eyelids shut and hold hands with those to the left and right. Thibault was now mumbling to himself in a slow and deliberate manner. It went on for several minutes. Eventually his mutterings became louder and clearer:

'You, ... want, ... to, ... tell, ... me, ... what?' The bizarre episode was become increasingly more frightening. 'Something, ... terrible! Tell, ... me, ... about, ... it.' After a pause Thibault's tone of voice changed, his words became less audible, he started to whisper, but all of a sudden something that had been conveyed between him and whoever he was in contact with made him speak more loudly. 'YOU WANT TO CONTACT ONE OF US!' He sounded surprised.

The conversation between Thibault and the dead went on for another couple of minutes. Eventually it was all a bit too much for Watling, he opened his eyes. He looked towards Thibault who seemed half-asleep, but the link between the medium and whoever he was talking to had been broken. Lester had heard more than enough, she was starting to shiver uncontrollably, the result of both the cold and the creepiness of the situation. She also opened up her eyes. To her right Thibault had come out of his trancelike state and told everyone to relax and disjoin hands.

He seemed exhausted by conversing with a spirit, or maybe it was spirits, plural.

'That was incredible! A woman, her name was Elsie, spoke to me. She lived in these parts, she was murdered here.' They stared in disbelief at Thibault. 'By the way, do any of you come from Manchester?' The stunned silence was broken by Penny Lester:

'Yes, I do, but so what?'

'This woman, the spirit, she once lived there. She wanted to contact one of us, to ask about the place, she worked in a cotton mill but moved to this area, somehow she knew that one of us had connections with the city!'

'Bloody hell! How did she know that?' Penny felt herself shivering even more uncontrollably.

'This woman, she told me she was murdered by her husband. She had a lover, the husband killed him and then her.'

'And when was all this supposed to have taken place?' asked an intrigued but somewhat sceptical Watling.

'Long ago, the 1860s she said, on land where the cottage was until a few months ago.'

'Perhaps it happened in a house that has long since disappeared, maybe it was knocked down to make way for the last Fen View,' said Dunlop.

'Possible I suppose,' added Watling. 'This is amazing stuff. It could explain the occasional ghostly sightings.'

The cold and shocked ghost hunters returned to Watling's car and headed back to Cambridge. They'd discuss things again tomorrow, it was after midnight, they were all tired and mentally drained. It had been a strange evening to say the least, certainly one to remember. Watling told everyone he'd be doing some research on murders in the area during the 1860s, he'd take a look at police archives. He also wanted to find out if there had been a cottage that preceded Fen View, the recently demolished property had been built in the early 1880s, a few decades after Elsie's supposed murder by her husband.

For one of the ghost hunters, the evening's drama was not yet over. The men all lived in Cambridge but Penny didn't. Together with Dunlop and Thibault she was dropped off in the city centre by Watling before he drove home. As it was late the men gallantly accompanied their female companion to her car parked opposite the closed for the night *Maypole* pub.

Penny Lester, shattered after a day at work followed by all the evening's antics out on the fenlands, climbed into her new Ford Puma. She only had a short drive, half an hour at most, back to Huntingdon but it would turn out to be a journey like no other she'd ever taken before. On her way home, she suddenly felt a presence in the car, it was as if someone was sitting beside her on the front passenger seat. She glanced over to her left. Nothing there. *What the hell's happening?* Penny, normally confident, felt uneasy but put it down to lack of rest and what she'd witnessed a few hours before. She checked in the rear-view mirror to see if any vehicles were following her … nothing, there were no headlights, it was early morning, the carriageway was quiet. A wispy mist had formed across the surrounding fields, it was starting to waft about, the air disturbed no doubt by the gentlest of breezes. Soon the mist might turn into a much thicker fog. It made Penny keen to return home as quickly as possible and retire to the safety of her bed. She put her foot down on the accelerator despite the worsening visibility. After travelling along a straight section of road Penny braked hard and turned her steering wheel to the right in order to navigate a sharp bend.

A sixth sense forced her to check the rear-view mirror again, she was convinced something was behind her and following her, she felt sure of it. What she saw this time completely freaked her out and sent a sharp shiver down her spine and her mind into a spin. To her horror she saw a female face staring back at her, its pale complexion smeared in congealed streaks of blackened blood. The lady looked like someone from a by-gone age. Piercing, penetrating light blue eyes glared out at her. The apparition broke into a sickly smile and its sallow, facial skin began to crack apart, the woman then faded and disappeared. Penny was stunned. Normally fearless in the face of danger, she was now terrified.

'What the ffff…!' she screamed.

Penny turned her head around for a second time, only momentarily, to take another look, nothing there, but with her mind not focused on her driving she lost control of the car. The nearside front wheel crashed against the kerb, the raised edge of the highway caused her vehicle to career off the tarmac and tumble down a steep embankment. After several noisy somersaults down the grassy slope and over a narrow drainage ditch it came to rest on its side in an arable field. All went quiet.

44

Santos decided it was time to leave the packed-out interior of the *Cima Club*. They'd been there long enough to check out the opposition, but no sign of the Andrettis. They might already be in town. He reckoned that Randy Lister and his gang, a motley mixture of local youths desperate to earn a few dollars together with more seasoned drug smugglers, were waiting for their bosses to turn up before the real action started. For his part, Santos didn't want any trouble in the centre of a place he often visited or at a busy night club full of innocent people. He'd discussed his escape route with Jorge Hernandez earlier in the afternoon, he was now waiting for the right moment to start things moving. Over recent drinks together he'd gone through the plan once more with Jorge and his right-hand man, Xavier, he wanted things to run smoothly, no hitches, no cock ups. John and Lola were also fully aware of what was about to happen, all were primed and ready to spring into action when given the nod by Santos. That moment had arrived.

A disturbance, a diversion, was about to start. Suddenly a couple of El Bigote's men ran into the crowded bar area screaming and bawling, there was a fire in the toilets they shouted, and it was spreading fast. One of them had set off the alarm in the corridor outside the men's room in order to convince customers it was genuine and not a stupid prank staged by drunken idiots. Xavier yelled over to the bar staff for someone to ring the fire service before bellowing at everyone to get the hell out of the place. In the general panic and stampede for the emergency exits Santos made his move.

'Time to go, follow me!' he ordered.

Santos sprang up off his seat and headed for one of the less conspicuous ways out of the club, it was a small door that opened onto a metal staircase fire escape attached to the outside of the building. It had been closely guarded by one of El Bigote's heavies who'd told customers it was unsafe and out of action, go use another exit was the message, but Santos and his companions left this way. Once outside at ground level their lightning fast getaway was obscured by throngs of frightened night clubbers who'd burst into the street expecting the building to go up in flames at any minute. In the confusion Santos and the others hurried away from the scene. Down the street they ran, passing the *Blue Star* casino on the way where a crowd of gawping onlookers had gathered wondering what all the commotion was about. They dashed past the Moravian church before continuing downhill to the harbour. No-one seemed to be in pursuit. At the waterside, as planned, a *panga* was waiting for them, ready to make a swift getaway. As they all clambered in, Ángel took over the controls from a young man who seemed more than happy to disappear into the night well away from any trouble.

'Where we off to?' asked John.

'Safety!' replied Santos emphatically.

'What are all the guns and knives for?' asked Lola fearing the worst. She'd noticed a couple of rifles and four large knives resting on the boat's hull.

'Hopefully we won't have to use the guns but we'll need the machetes,' was Ángel's reply.

The hullaballoo back at the club was beginning to die down. The place had been emptied, everyone evacuated into the street. No fire had been discovered and a modicum of calm had returned. Jorge and Xavier had watched the drama unfold with broad smiles of satisfaction over their faces. Santos had left the area during the fifteen minutes of chaos as panicked customers piled out of the club. Some had been knocked over and injured in the general rush to the doors, an ambulance was on its way. Quarter of an hour had been enough time for Santos's group to make their escape.

As the fuss abated a desperate Randy Lister knew Santos had done a disappearing act. He realised that the supposed fire in the toilets had been a diversion to facilitate the escape. He was a worried man, the Andrettis were on their way and landing at the airport soon. Luca would not be pleased to hear that Santos had escaped his clutches yet again. Panicking about the possible consequences of his incompetence, Lister urgently ordered his men to search the town and check if Santos had returned to his hotel.

Santos was far too cute to outstay his welcome in Bluefields, he was busy controlling his hurried departure in the harbour.

'Ángel, head north towards the mouth of the Escondido.'

'OK, boss, will do.'

'What's the plan when we've left Bluefields?' asked John.

'We're heading for a small lagoon, we ditch the *panga* there, and make our way across land to the coast. I've arranged for a speedboat to meet us close to the beach, then we get well away from here,' answered Santos.

The *panga* proceeded to plough a furrow through the calm waters of the bay as it headed out of the port area, the small light on the boat's prow helping Ángel to navigate his way in the dark. While John and Lola sat huddled together in the stern of the boat the small figure of Santos stood next to them, Glock pistol handy in case he needed to use it in a hurry but no-one was following. They'd made another perfect escape courtesy of meticulous planning.

'Ángel, we're coming close to the river mouth, take the channel over to the right, it leads into Smokey Lane lagoon. Once inside, just keep going straight on,' he ordered.

The *panga* passed through a narrow entrance into the brackish waters of the lake. Santos barked out more instructions. Ángel was to head for the dim outline of a peninsula in the distance called Punta Bay Point, it stuck out like a long and very bony finger. He was told to steer the vessel into a wide inlet and look for a suitable spot to park up. It would be about a mile on foot to the Caribbean coastline. They'd have to find a way through a densely vegetated bar of land that separated the lagoon from the sea. That's where the machetes would come in handy, they'd need to hack a path through a mixture of mangrove and scrub.

When the Andretti brothers arrived at the airport Luca was told the bad news. He was spitting feathers. The unenviable task of informing him had fallen to Lister. He told his boss that Santos wasn't anywhere to be seen, at his hotel, or in any of the pubs and clubs around town. However, some of Lister's men had been questioning owners of *pangas* in the harbour, one man said he'd seen three men and a woman hurry off out across the bay not long ago. Hoping to appease his irate boss, Lister quickly arranged for a posse of speedboats to sweep the area, two to the north and another couple to the south, all with armed men on board. Lister himself was in the lead boat urgently heading towards the mouth of the Rio Escondido.

Not too far away Ángel switched off the *panga's* engine and let the vessel quietly drift into the waters on the side of the Smokey Lane lagoon. He turned off the small light on the prow and, when they reached the shallows, Santos and John jumped out of the boat to drag it towards the shore before hauling the vessel onto a shingle covered beach.

As they did so, in the distance on the other side of the lagoon, less than half a mile away, the noise of a powerful outboard engine penetrated the warm night air. Looking out across the water they saw the dark outline of a speedboat. A bright searchlight, positioned on top of its cabin, was sweeping across the bay before becoming fixed in their direction. The craft was heading straight for them, at a worryingly fast rate. John was convinced they'd been seen, Ángel said there was no doubt about it. They were trapped between the fast approaching speedboat and thick mangrove.

'Quick, get the machetes and the rifles out of the boat,' ordered Santos.

As they grabbed them from the hull a gunshot rang out from the pursuing boat. No harm done, it was only a warning shot that thudded into a nearby tree trunk and ricocheted away to safety. Loud words crackled from a handheld megaphone:

'Santos, you're cornered. Stop or we shoot to kill, the lady gets it first!'

It was the American guy, Randy Lister, in an accent that was pure Texan drawl. Standing alongside him was his large negro friend, the one who'd irritated Santos in the night club. To make matters even worse there were another two gang members on board, both armed with high velocity rifles.

45

It was an early morning dog walker who first noticed Penny Lester's car flipped over on its side in the field adjacent to the main road. The young man with his golden retriever was soon followed at the scene by a long-distance lorry driver who'd scampered down the grassy embankment to help out. Penny was lying motionless but alive, the combination of seat belt, front and side airbags, had saved her.

The men had opened the driver's door but sensibly refrained from dragging Penny, unconscious, from out of her seat. Instead the dog walker dialled 999, within ten minutes paramedics, together with a police patrol car officer, had arrived. Penny was rushed to hospital, blue lights flashing and siren sounding on the speeding ambulance. After first being admitted to Accident and Emergency, Penny underwent tests to determine the extent of her injuries. By two o'clock the doctors had discovered three broken or cracked ribs and a dislocated right ankle but, thankfully, there didn't seem to be any brain damage or spinal injuries and come the middle of the afternoon Penny was sitting up in bed, on pain killers. Her worried parents had rushed down to Cambridge from Altrincham. Later, a group of friends from the local hockey club arrived. Her next visitor was a concerned looking Watling. Sitting next to her bedside he was full of apologies.

'I'm so, so sorry about all this, Pen. It was me who dragged you out on such a cold night and the evening ends up with you being freaked out by some awful apparition, I feel really guilty about getting you involved. I'm just so relieved that you're going to be OK, things could have been so much worse.'

'Don't worry, boss, I can handle it,' Penny attempted to smile but it was more of a grimace. Despite all the pain killers, damaged ribs and a dislocated ankle were a major discomfort.

'Look, Pen, I've decided to let all this paranormal stuff drop for now. I might look into things again when I'm back from the Lake District. There's Benny Hayes's trial coming up soon, I have to concentrate on that. Pen, you'll need time off, take things easy for a while, don't rush back to work.'

After a bit of banter about their visit to the site of the old cottage, and some details of a new murder case involving yet more drug dealers operating throughout the county, Watling wished Penny well. He'd call on her again as soon as he returned from holiday, in the meantime he'd keep in touch by phone. He didn't want to tell her but Watling had decided to follow up the leads from the previous evening. Thibault's revelations were both remarkable and worrying in equal measure. Watling would be checking out the nineteenth century murder case records from police archives as well as other things. *Was there a woman called Elsie who lived in the Fen View Cottage area back in the 1860s? Did she originate from Manchester? Was she murdered by a jealous husband?* He also wanted to consult Professor Dunlop and Monsieur Thibault about the unbelievable happenings in Penny's car.

He wished her goodbye intending to head for the exit but as he was about to leave the ward a large guy, dressed in a fireman's outfit, burst through the doors with a huge bouquet of flowers and rushed over to Penny's bed. She introduced him to Watling. His name was Danny, he'd been seeing Penny on and off for about three to four months since their initial meeting up at the local hockey club's Christmas party. Watling, despite a close working relationship with his colleague, knew nothing about him. It looked as if Penny had a boyfriend, it was something she'd kept quiet about which was fine in Watling's book. He was old-fashioned and believed that someone's private life was meant to be just that and not something to be broadcast.

Watling drove home to discuss holiday plans. Although looking forward to a long overdue break from his police duties, with all its stresses and anti-social hours, he was infatuated by the Fen View Cottage case and was keen to delve further into its mysteries. He'd love to pay Benny Hayes a visit to ask him more questions but with his trial soon to take place that was out of the question. Hayes had disclosed as little as possible to the police during his interviews last autumn. He'd only told them a few snippets of information about his time at the old cottage. It had helped clear his ex-girlfriend, Janey Harrison, of any involvement and to fix the blame for the death of Sara Barrington-Webb firmly on someone else who was long deceased, while also keeping himself out of jail, ... but Benny Hayes knew a whole lot more about Fen View Cottage than what he'd divulged so far.

46

Santos used his machete's sharp-edged blade to slice open a passage into the dense vegetation alongside the beach on the side of the lagoon. As he hacked an escape route through the mangrove both John and Lola followed him. Ángel, meanwhile, sent a couple of rifle shots into the air above Lister's speedboat to let the enemy know they were armed and dangerous. His next shot shattered the craft's powerful searchlight. It had the desired effect, the boat slowed down and turned off course to the right rather than heading in a straight line directly for them. Ángel took the opportunity to hurry after his companions.

Perspiring heavily due to the heat and humidity as well as physical exertion, Santos frantically cut a path through the tangled plant life and much to his relief a relatively clear patch of open land soon appeared in front of him. He started to run and the others did the same. They were about a hundred metres along their escape route when Randy Lister's boat came to a halt on the shoreline of the Smokey Lane lagoon, not far away from the abandoned *panga*.

Lister and his men leapt out and ran along the shingle beach intending to follow the pathway obligingly cleared for them by Santos. They were four men in a hurry, but that was a bad mistake to make given it was dark and they were in unfamiliar and potentially dangerous territory. Suddenly, a loud scream pierced the still night air. They all froze and looked down in horror. The right leg of one individual had been clamped tight by a solitary caiman, a hazard at all times, but especially so at night in the shallow waters and on the beaches of the lagoon. The victim let out another agonised cry. Reacting quickly to the situation, Lister fired a couple of bullets into the caiman's head, between its eyes, and the big negro released the poor guy's leg from the jaws of the dead reptile. His lower limb looked a mess and was bleeding badly. Lister ordered his pal to drag him back to the speed boat where the medical kit could be used to bandage up his ankle. Lister and his henchman would press on.

Ángel had now taken over from Santos, his machete scything a routeway through bushes and saplings. It was tough physical work and John volunteered to assist. Santos, in the rear, fired a few shots into the sky above the heads of their pursuers.

'You keep clearing the jungle. I'll wait here and hold them back. Get going, I'll join up soon. Ángel, make sure you look after Lola and John!'

The men took turns to hack down the plant life that hindered their escape to the coast, Lola looked after Ángel's weapons. Not far behind them Randy Lister could see Santos in the distance but he hadn't a clue where the others were, he guessed they must have gone on and left Santos by himself. He knew he was armed but had no idea what guns and how much ammunition his adversary possessed. Lister decided to shout an instruction across the open patch of ground:

'Give yourself up, Santos!' he bawled out. 'You can't escape. The Andrettis are here, they want to speak with you. Think about the lady and her man friend. You don't want to see them harmed, do you?'

Despite the warning Santos had no intention of surrendering:

'If you're a sensible guy you'll turn around, head back to Bluefields, don't bother getting yourself killed,' he shouted defiantly.

For Lister it was an impasse situation. Santos had a gun, maybe more than one. *Was it safe to rush him?* The Texan was well aware that Luca Andretti desperately wanted Santos captured alive. If he could bring him in he'd be flavour of the month, but if he failed once more the consequences would be unpredictable. *Hero or villain, which was it to be?* Lister ordered his companion to move off to the left. They'd split up and crawl their way through the undergrowth towards Santos, Lister with a front on approach engaging him in conversation while his mate, unseen and hopefully unheard, would circle around and corner Santos from the rear. The man dressed in black, still perspiring profusely due to both the high humidity and fear factor, watched their progress intently but he soon lost sight of the negro, he'd disappeared out of view somewhere to his right. *Where the hell was he?* He could see Lister crawling his way slowly towards him. When he was only about thirty metres away Santos shouted out:

'That's far enough, buddy!'

Lister stopped moving and started talking, shouting more like, at Santos. It was threat after threat. Santos listened patiently, his eyes were fixed on where Lister was huddled behind some dense bushes, but his thoughts were elsewhere. He was becoming increasingly anxious about where the big black guy had vanished to. It all went quiet for a while, a strained situation became tenser as the seconds ticked by, the only sound was the steady hum of insects somewhere in the distance. Then, unexpectantly, the nervous silence was shattered. Screams of agony filled the night air again, they emanated from a dense thicket off to Santos's right. It must be the big negro, it sounded as if he was in major trouble. *Had he stumbled and injured himself? A broken leg maybe? Perhaps a wild animal had surprised him? Had he been attacked by pesky mosquitoes, there might be plenty of them about in this watery area?* Various thoughts flashed through Santos's brain.

He'd been bitten alright but not by a vicious, four-legged animal or by any insect. Lister's companion had been unlucky enough to stumble and fall over. He'd tumbled, head first, into a hidden depression covered by leaf litter, twigs and other debris on the pitted woodland and scrub infested ground. As he fell, his terrified, bulging eyes had observed, only for a brief moment, the head of a snake and its menacing forked tongue. But this wasn't any old snake, it was the most feared and most venomous species in the whole of Central America: the poor man had the misfortune to disturb the *bothrops asper*, or pit viper, better known as the fer-de-lance. The creature showed no mercy, its fangs lanced into his facial area. His outstretched arms, neck and chest soon followed. The pitiful cries continued, but it wouldn't be for long. The powerful venom works quickly, the big negro was dying and would be dead within five minutes. Anti-venom is available but not out in the wilds, somewhere between the Smokey Lane lagoon and the Caribbean coastline. Santos's voice broke the silence:

'Looks like your mate might have got unlucky,' he said coldly. 'That leaves only you and me.'

'Where the fuck's Ángel? Where's the other guy? And the girl?' shrieked a panicked Randy Lister. He guessed what might well have happened to his companion although he hadn't a clue that he'd come face to face with the most dangerous snake in Nicaragua.

'They're sorting out my boat, I'll be joining them soon enough. You need to get smart, turn around, go home, Mr Lister, ... clear off, ... while you still can,' advised Santos in a calm and assured voice.

It was a choice that a wise man might have taken but any retreat from the current situation would be regarded as cowardice by Luca, worse still, betrayal. Lister had to somehow capture Santos all by himself and then deliver him to his boss. Retreating back to his speedboat to join the others, one of them badly wounded, was not an option. Lister sprang up from off the ground and dived to his right. He rolled over several times before taking refuge behind some dense shrubs and tall grasses. The adversaries were now no more than twenty metres apart. Santos glared to his left trying hard to peer through the dark, his eyesight wasn't as sharp as it had once been. *Where was he? Lister was far too close for comfort, he knew that much. Damn, he couldn't see him.* All of a sudden Lister appeared in Santos's eye-line, only ten metres away, and fired off a round from his pistol. The shot hit Santos, he fell backwards, it was his turn to scream out in pain. A triumphant Randy Lister stood up and walked across towards his victim. Santos was holding his shoulder, it was bleeding badly, he'd dropped his Glock. He was at Lister's mercy. Things looked bad.

'Get the fuck up, you son of a bitch!'

Santos stood up slowly clutching his left shoulder with his right hand. He looked in a bad way but the bullet wound was superficial. It was nowhere near as nasty as he was trying to make out. It was only a flesh wound, the bullet had nicked the point where shoulder meets arm, it had ripped away skin and made a mess. The damaged area was bleeding badly but no bullet was embedded in Santos's left shoulder and no major blood vessel had been punctured. Another sound filled the night air:

'Hold it right there, don't move, drop the gun, asshole!'

Surprised and alarmed, Randy Lister looked around. He caught a momentary glimpse of a man with a rifle, it was pointed straight at him. Lister panicked and pushed his luck too far, he decided to take a shot but was too late. The top half of his head was blown away, the rest of his body crashed down onto the forest floor. Santos stared up at the smiling figure standing behind him. It was his bodyguard, the self-anointed *Ángel de la Muerte* had chalked up another victim.

'I was beginning to wonder where the hell you'd got to?' shouted Santos still clutching his shoulder.

'You're not badly hit. Come on, follow me, boss. Let's get out of here.'

Santos picked up his pistol and followed the path that had been cut all the way to the coast. John and Lola were standing by the shore, concern written across their faces. Waiting in the shallows were two speedboats. On board the larger vessel was El Bigote in his own personal boat, he'd left all the confusion back in Bluefields.

'Let's get you aboard, Federico,' said John. 'I'll patch up your wound, payback time for the holiday!'

The injured Santos was helped onto the boat. Lola hurried below deck and returned with an impressively equipped medical kit. She passed bandages across to John together with some sterile padding and antiseptic wipes. After donning disposable rubber gloves, he cleaned up the wound before stemming the bleeding with the padding.

'Look what I've found,' said El Bigote.

It was a box full of surgical hooks and needles together with threads. Within half an hour Santos was all patched up, the wound had been stitched together or sutured as John preferred to call his skilled handiwork.

The speed boat was now well out to sea far from the Nicaraguan coastline.

'Where we off to?' asked John.

'A place called *Las Islas del Maíz*. That's what the Spanish speaking government calls them, but around these parts they are known as the Corn Islands,' answered El Bigote.

'Why there?' asked Lola.

'One of Jorge's homes is on Big Corn, but I shouldn't be telling you that,' replied Santos.

'Hell, this is supposed to be a holiday,' said John laughing.

'Well apart from veering from one danger to another it's been fantastic,' added Lola.

'How far away is this Corn Island place?' asked John.

'About another forty kilometres,' replied El Bigote.

'What if the Andrettis guess where we're going and follow us?' asked John.

'They may do, it's the obvious place but we'll arrive before them and my house is hidden well away from the busier areas, it's not easy to find,' said El Bigote reassuringly.

'The Corn Islands, eh, sounds interesting,' said John.

'You'll have a great time, you and Lola,' said Ángel.

'They're the best places belonging to Nicaragua, Great and Little Corn are tropical paradises, I've holidayed on both with my wife and son and I've always felt safe,' added Santos.

El Bigote retreated downstairs and brought drinks from the fridge.

'Here's to the Corn Islands!' Santos exclaimed.

'The Corn Islands!' they all shouted in unison.

Luca Andretti surveyed the scene of havoc on the patch of land between the Smokey Lane lagoon and the Caribbean coast. More men had been killed in his dogged pursuit of arch-enemy, Federico Santos. One had been bitten to death by a venomous snake, the other man's head had been shattered by a bullet from a high-velocity rifle. His main man in Central America and his deputy had been killed. Luca was far from happy. His brother, the more placid Bruno, stood beside him.

'Isn't it about time to forget this vendetta, Luca, at least for now?' asked Bruno, more in hope than expectation. 'We're bound to come across Santos in the future, we can surprise him and sort him out then.'

Red with rage at the thought of letting Santos get away with all he'd done, Luca was apoplectic in his response:

'We don't fucking drop it until Santos is dead!' he screamed in anger. 'I reckon he's headed out to the Corn Islands. I've suspected for a while that Jorge Hernandez, that Mexican bastard, lives there. That's where we're heading next.'

47

APRIL

It was time for a holiday. George and Jill Watling spent four nights at their favourite hotel in the Lake District. They enjoyed walks on the fells as well as leisurely lakeside rambles. The trip concluded with a stroll along the wonderful solitude of the River Eden valley before the long journey home.

Watling returned to Cambridge a man refreshed, keen and eager to prepare for the fast approaching trial of Benny Hayes. The Met had come up with plenty of new information gathered from the many witnesses discovered and interviewed down in London. All were people who remembered life with Hayes's commune in the late sixties. They'd volunteered details to the police after all the media coverage back in the autumn. Adding considerable weight to the prosecution case would be all the forensics evidence prepared by the Cambridgeshire team, it was both extensive and damning. Hayes would have a lot of explaining to do in court. Although looking forward to the trial Watling was still fascinated by the site of Fen View Cottage.

He had a few more days off before returning to work so decided to devote some time to researching the Cambridgeshire and Huntingdonshire police records. However, his first task was to discover any old maps of the area. He rang both the Cambridge University Library and County Council and was in luck. The council had one that went back to the 1860s, drawn up not by the Ordnance Survey but by a local land surveyor. Watling booked an appointment at the Archives Department for that afternoon. When he viewed the map, the Hemingway's farm was clearly marked and various small cottages were shown dotted about on the land close to it. Some had names, some didn't, Fen View Cottage was in the same location as the most recent incarnation had been until last autumn's demolition job. *So, there was a previous Fen View Cottage, it preceded the 1882 version only recently knocked down.*

His next task was to find information about who'd lived in the cottage in the middle decades of the nineteenth century. Watling had a useful contact, a retired colleague who regularly used online family history websites. After a chat on the phone, ex-Detective Inspector Ken Palmer said he'd look into things and returned the call later that evening. He'd managed to find several families who'd lived in the various farm worker's cottages tied to Fen View Farm according to the 1851, 1861 and 1871 censuses. He'd been asked by Watling to look out for a lady, probably in her twenties or thirties, with the name of Elsie. Ken Palmer had come across two females with that name. One was elderly, aged sixty-four in 1871, married to an Albert Tate. She was mentioned on all three dates but she was too old. The other possibility sounded far more promising, the second Elsie was aged twenty-two in 1861, her full name was Elsie Summers, married to a Henry Summers. They had no children, maybe they'd only been married a short time. This Elsie had been listed on the 1861 census, her birthplace, in 1839, was Ancoats, a district in Manchester full of cotton mills by the 1850s and 1860s. Interestingly, on the 1871 census for the Fen View farm estate there was no mention of an Elsie Summers or indeed her husband, Henry. Ken Palmer had carefully checked their names on the 1871 census and there was no record of them living anywhere else in England or Wales. *Maybe they'd both died?* … but there wasn't any Death Certificate evidence. *Perhaps it was something more intriguing?*

Watling had warmed to his task and marvelled at Monsieur Thibault's incredible ability to contact the dead. According to the old map a Fen View Cottage did exist back in the 1860s, a precursor to the last one, and with the help of his ex-colleague it had been found that a young lady called Elsie Summers had lived at the farm, in Fen View Cottage itself, during 1861. Her husband, Henry, was listed as a farm worker on that year's census. *Time to delve into the local police archives.*

On the following day Watling was back in his study soon after breakfast with several numbers to ring, all different archivists connected to the police. His discussions eventually centred on three publications: an article in a copy of the Police Gazette of 1867, the County Assizes Records for Cambridgeshire and lists of prisoners in Huntingdon County Gaol. The Gazette had a report on the murder of a young lady by a jealous husband who'd accused her of having an affair with a man from a nearby village, the woman's name was Elsie Summers! The County Assizes for 1868 recorded the trial of a Henry Summers and his resulting conviction. The lists of prisoners in Huntingdon Gaol included the same man, aged forty, incarcerated there and awaiting transportation to Birmingham's Winson Green prison to be hanged for murder. Watling had all the evidence he needed. He eagerly rang up his tennis and drinking buddy, Professor Dunlop.

'Hi, Mike, have I some interesting news for you!' he enthused.

'Bet it's about Fen View, old boy.'

'Your medium, remember he got in touch with someone called Elsie from Manchester.'

'How could I forget! It was quite a night, how's your young colleague by the way? Is she making good progress? Damn lucky not to have been killed, poor girl.'

'She's fine, but still uncomfortable nursing bruises and broken bones. She's back at home taking it easy. Fortunately, Pen will be alright, she's a tough cookie. Anyway, this Elsie woman that Michel managed to contact, I've been doing some digging, and bloody hell, Mike, it looks like she really did exist back in the 1860s and lived at Fen View. I've used maps, old censuses, police archives, records of trials, that sort of thing and it appears that an Elsie Summers was murdered by her jealous husband in 1867! He was later found guilty and hanged in 1868.'

After a brief pause to take it all in Dunlop replied:

'Well, I did tell you, George, old boy, that my man, Thibault, was pretty damn good! He's no fraud, no con artist is Michel. One of the best in the business. God knows how he does it but the chap has a reputation for being able to communicate with the dead. So, this poor woman's spirit still stalks the site of her murder. It's beyond belief! This is why I'm interested in such matters, George. I'm a man of science, a Professor of Botany, but there are some things that science just can't explain.'

'It's unbelievable, Mike.'

'Best keep all this to ourselves, George, dear boy. If the bloody press gets hold of it they'll have a field day and the farm site will be plagued by them and hundreds of sad buggers who haven't anything better to do with their lives, some people just love poking their noses into other people's business. Your farmer friend will have the world and his wife trapesing all over his land, the new owner of the site will be well miffed.'

The thought of the smarmy property developer, Charles Black, being inundated with unwanted sight-seers momentarily pleased Watling. He'd disliked the man from their first meeting last autumn but, being the responsible and sensible citizen that he undoubtedly was, Watling was in full agreement with his academic friend's sentiments.

'This will go no further than between you and me. You'd better congratulate Thibault though, another one chalked up to his amazing powers.'

'OK, George, let's keep it between us and Michel, that sounds pretty damn sensible. We must meet up soon for a three-setter and a few beers now that the weather's improving at long last.'

'Will do, Mike, but I'm back at work tomorrow and I've the Benny Hayes case coming up next week. Thanks for all your help, I'll be in touch, see you soon.'

Since his return from Argentina, Watling had been busy, both at work and on holiday, but he hadn't neglected to perform two important tasks. He'd visited Addenbrooke's Hospital in Cambridge to put Dr Ripley's employer in the picture about why their well-respected consultant had left in such a hurry. In particular, he wanted to see the senior nurse, Mary Waring. Her invaluable assistance had helped track down Tomás Rodriguez and John Ripley, she deserved to know what had happened in Mendoza, even if he did give her a watered-down account of events in the Parque San Martin. Before all that though, his most important duty was to visit Ripley's deserted wife, Lucy. He explained everything to her in as delicate a way as possible and in a fashion that painted her husband in as good a light as was feasible. She was naturally shocked and very disappointed with John. He should have confided in her, it was an awful secret to have kept to himself but, after much reflection, she had come to terms with John's reasoning, even if she didn't agree with it. Lucy Ripley was a tough woman, she'd endured an unhappy first marriage, then she'd met John. She believed he was essentially a good man despite his past misdemeanours. Up until last autumn he'd been a faithful and kind husband as well as a good step-father to her children but Lucy had reconciled herself to the fact that John wasn't ever coming back to England, she had to move on with her life, she'd returned to work as a primary school headmistress, a job she loved, and was busy with local community business as a parish councillor.

For the next few weeks, Watling's priority would be the forthcoming court case. He'd have liked to interview Benny Hayes again with regards to his time at Fen View Cottage, especially on anything that could be considered paranormal, but Hayes's interest and involvement in such matters might have to remain a thing of mystery for ever.

48

Benny Hayes was seated in the plush lounge of his expensively decked out Stoke Newington apartment along a gentrified street in North London. Unable to keep still, he nervously tapped an antique mahogany coffee table and kept on anxiously glancing down at his wrist watch. Hayes, now into his seventies, was a man in trouble. He was due to appear at Cambridge Crown Court later in the morning after being charged with some very serious offences relating to events that had occurred over fifty years ago during his wild and disreputable youth. Feeling increasingly on edge Hayes shot out of his chair and started marching up and down his lounge. He was waiting, restlessly, for his lawyer to arrive. His partner, Judy, told him to calm himself and sit down, he'd wear a furrow in the carpet.

Hayes was a wealthy man, not that he'd had much to do with earning his rich status. His financial clout had been inherited rather than earnt by any hard work or great enterprise on his part. Both his late parents had enjoyed high powered, well paid employment and his father had come from a seriously moneyed background with properties in England, Ireland and Monaco. Despite a life of privilege that had involved education at an expensive private school and a place at Cambridge University, Hayes had lived a feckless existence ever since he decided to drop out of mainstream society and become a hippy back in the 1960s. His life had spiralled out of control from then onwards as he followed a hedonistic but ultimately self-destructive path of excessive alcohol consumption and Class A drugs abuse associated mostly with cocaine and LSD. A promiscuous sex life had only served to compound his problems. His existence on planet Earth had been dominated by complications of his own making punctuated only occasionally by fleeting, short-lived periods of contentment.

Wealth had not brought Hayes much happiness. Since the mid-sixties, after dropping out of university, he hadn't been employed in any meaningful and useful way. He'd drifted aimlessly through the decades since his younger days as a long-haired hippy and 'wannabe' rock star. Over the years a depressingly extensive list of criminal charges from both possessing and selling illegal drugs to being under their influence while driving a motor vehicle had come his way. Hayes had also assaulted two ex-girlfriends and beaten up a man in a Hackney bar room, in North-east London. An unfortunate tendency towards violent outbursts had led to him being found guilty of ABH (Actual Bodily Harm) on several occasions. Periodic bouts of rage had even resulted in him assaulting the woman he'd loved most during his lifetime, the fellow Cambridge drop-out named Janey Harrison. This particularly unsavoury incident, in 1975, had led to the ending of their eight years of being together as a couple.

Hayes was due to appear on trial for an offence which, according to the CPS, amounted at least to manslaughter, maybe even murder. He had also been charged with perverting the course of justice by his involvement in the unlawful burial of a young woman's body. Hayes had violated the Burial Act of 1857 in disposing of the corpse. The litany of crimes committed by Hayes over the years painted a dismal and damning picture of the man's character. Remarkably, given his many minor misdemeanours and several far more serious felonies, Hayes had spent very little of his life behind bars other than a couple of short custodial sentences for drug and alcohol offences in the 1980s and another prison stretch of six months in Strangeways, Manchester following the Hackney bar room brawl in 1998. Fortunately, he was able to afford the best defence attorneys that the legal world had to offer, otherwise the number of his incarcerations in prison would have been much greater.

Benny's latest lawyer was a swaggering barrister with the name of Peter Quentin Hindmarsh, a man well-known amongst the rich and powerful criminal community in London and surrounding Home Counties. Such people knew that if you were ever in need of escaping charges and a possible long-term prison sentence then Hindmarsh was the person to call. He didn't come cheap but that was the least of Hayes's worries. If found guilty of manslaughter, or heaven forbid murder, he'd be going down for a long stretch, there'd be no wriggling free from the power of the law, he'd probably spend the rest of his life locked up in some God-awful prison surrounded by habitual, hardened criminals. His life would be hell on Earth. The prospect of a long custodial sentence made him feel ill, it had even caused Hayes to think seriously of ending it all, a combination of vodka, whisky and barbiturates, topped off by snorting plenty of cocaine, should do the trick.

At the end of last year Hayes's sordid past had caught up with him. The badly decomposed body of a young woman had been unearthed close to Fen View Cottage, north of Cambridge. After demolition of the rundown property it had been discovered by builders in the surrounding grounds. The ensuing police investigation, together with all the forensics evidence, proved that the human remains had been lying in its unofficial grave since the late sixties, a time when Hayes and his motley entourage of assorted hangers-on had lived in the cottage. After interviewing him, initially at his London home, the Cambridgeshire Police's homicide team quickly decided to pull Hayes in for further questioning at their Huntingdon headquarters.

After early denials of any involvement in the case, Hayes eventually broke down and told the experienced detective team of DCI Watling and DI Rigsby what had happened on one fateful day in the spring of 1969. In the weeks and months since the autumn Hayes's life had been on hold. He was released on bail and forced to report every week into his local police station. His passport and driving licence had been confiscated. He was effectively restricted to his London home and its immediate surroundings. During this time of confinement, the Cambridgeshire police, together with crucial assistance from the Met in London, had built up a formidable case. The CPS were now swinging into action, the day of reckoning had arrived for Hayes. At his hearing he'd pleaded 'not guilty' to charges of murder and manslaughter but he'd owned up to helping someone bury a dead body.

Just before eight o'clock, Peter Hindmarsh arrived at Hayes's address close to Clissold Park. A chauffeur driven, gleaming black Range Rover SV petrol hybrid parked up outside the apartment, it was the sort of car favoured by government ministers. The flash, flamboyant and foppish Hindmarsh believed that if it was good enough for the Prime Minister and his Cabinet then it was suitable for him also. Anyhow, he wouldn't be paying the rental for it, Hayes would pick up the bill, money was no object when you had the stash of cash that he possessed.

After entering Hayes's first floor apartment and seeing his client's shambolic appearance, Hindmarsh advised him, given the circumstances, to change his attire before leaving for court. A scruffy orange T-shirt and faded blue jeans wouldn't look great, a smart suit, shirt and tie would be far more appropriate. He was also advised to shave off his grey stubble and put a comb through his unruly, thinning hair. After a wardrobe change and a facial tidy-up, Hayes, sitting next to Hindmarsh on the back seat of the hire car, with Judy looking glum in the front next to the driver, made his way out of London's suburbs to head north along the M11 to Cambridge.

'For God's sake, Benny, stop worrying! I've got people off far worse charges than what you're facing,' said the super-confident Hindmarsh. 'You need to look smart, smile nicely at the judge and jury, act remorseful and apologetic. Also keep cool, calm and collected. Leave the rest to me and my team. The police think they've a good case against you but, believe me, they've not enough hard evidence and certainly no eye-witnesses to say that you were actually involved in the death of this unfortunate young woman.'

'Yeah, right, Peter, but those bastards have got it in for me, they always have!' replied Benny dejectedly. An air of desperation was all too apparent in his voice, he knew that he was in big, big trouble. The police file on him was a long one and it didn't make for good reading.

'Just because you've smoked a few illegal drugs and drunk too many alcoholic drinks in your time, that does not make you a murderer, Benny,' declared Hindmarsh firmly but reassuringly. 'You're being tried on possible, I emphasise possible, manslaughter and murder charges plus the illegal disposal of a body, not all your previous offences. The jury will not be informed of your past record, they are judging you solely on what the CPS can come up with on this one particular case, and what I have to say in your defence, which I can assure you will be plenty.'

Hindmarsh was a classic narcissist who always believed that he was in the right, the type of man who thought he had the answer to everything and, in fairness to him, his record of defending the seemingly indefensible was indeed highly impressive. It was why he earnt the big bucks from his somewhat unsavoury clientele. By nine-thirty they were approaching the university city of Cambridge and soon they were parked up in East Street outside the Crown Court building. The area was busy with the media brigade: journalists and photographers. Proceedings were due to start at ten-thirty, after forcing their way through the scrum they'd grab a coffee before the trial began and have a final briefing with Hindmarsh's support team of three young lawyers, all of them eager to impress their revered leader.

An hour later, with the trial about to commence, an even larger congregation had gathered. A sea of bobbing faces stared down from the courtroom gallery as the tall, thin figure of Benny Hayes was led by the Custody Officer to stand in the dock. The opposing legal teams were sat patiently at the front: Mr Andrew Bannister KC led the Prosecution, Mr Peter Hindmarsh KC sat proud as a peacock at the front of the Defence attorneys.

The media gallery was packed, public interest in the case was high. The local television station, *BBC Look East,* and radio station, *Cambridge 105* were in attendance. The number of hacks from the written press was impressively large. Journalists included representatives from the *Cambridge News* and *Fenland Citizen* but there were also several from the British popular press publications: *The Sun, Daily Mail, Daily Mirror, Daily Express* and *Daily* Star, all no doubt hungry for a story to thrill their readers with. The free London dailies, *Metro* and *Evening*

Standard, were present too. The reporters had been accompanied by a posse of pushy photographers, waiting outside the court building's entrance doors, all eager to capture pictures of Hayes. Older members of the local community who remembered the hippies had turned up, but some in the public gallery were there out of sheer curiosity. The story of the discovery of a dead girl's body on the Fens had been reported in the media since before Christmas and the goings-on at Fen View Cottage in the late sixties had been well publicised. The wider public, not only those in Cambridgeshire, were eagerly awaiting more sordid details and general tittle-tattle about the disreputable behaviour of Hayes and his gang of dropouts. The more tales of 'sex, drugs and rock-n-roll' the greater the newspaper sales. The media vultures always chased a good story, the more salacious the subject matter the better. Until something else turned up they'd hover around Cambridge.

After having been asked to rise the assembled throng waited almost thirty seconds before the judge, Mr Justice David Pugh, made his entry. A deferential hush descended as he sat down. Those present then took their far less opulent seats and, after some initial murmurings, the room settled. After the judge's introductory rulings, the prosecution gave details to the twelve members of the jury regarding the allegations made against the defendant. The CPS set out the charges and the basic facts of the case.

It was clear that the police prosecution team had to prove, beyond all reasonable doubt, that Benny Hayes had been an accomplice to, or possibly even the person responsible for the death of the unfortunate Miss Barrington-Webb and whether it had been a tragic accident, and thus manslaughter, or a premeditated murder. A few months earlier, during his interviews with the Cambridgeshire police, Hayes had been vehement in his protestations that he hadn't been guilty of any of the offences he'd now been charged with, but he did eventually and reluctantly own up to being culpable of helping someone bury a dead person. After steadily building up a case against Hayes the police team, led by Watling, had become increasingly convinced that he hadn't told them the whole truth. What they'd gleaned, with the help of forensic experts, pointed to either murder or manslaughter having been committed. Watling's homicide team reckoned that such a terrible offence was not beyond the bounds of possibility given Hayes's depressingly long criminal record. However, that couldn't be brought up in court against him, he wasn't being tried on past crimes but his unpredictable, volatile character would be a point of discussion.

For the first few days a long list of police witnesses gave evidence. Andrew Bannister built up a strong case for the prosecution and Peter Hindmarsh, in his cross-examination, did his best to knock it down. Watling was the first person into the witness box, followed by Helen Sharp, the leading forensics officer of Cambridgeshire Police. Whereas Watling went through the factual details and history of the case, Sharp concentrated on the extent of the injuries suffered by Miss Barrington-Webb and doubted that they could all be explained away by a solitary fall down some stairs in the old farm cottage. Unfortunately, the place had been demolished prior to the corpse's discovery and no photographic evidence existed. The nature of the staircase and its inherent dangers were all down to hearsay. Helen Sharp discussed the cranial injuries, some of which looked like they could well have been caused by the hard impact of a blunt instrument such as a hammer. Both Watling and Sharp were convinced that Miss Barrington-Webb had been killed before her dead body had been thrown down the stairs to make it look like she'd died in a nasty fall. They painted a fairly damning picture and the odds of a conviction on the charges were steadily being stacked up against Benny Hayes.

Local builder, Frank Watson, the man who'd first dialled 999 to inform the police of the grim revelation of the buried body, gave evidence as did Bob Hemingway, the local farmer. He recollected many of the seedy shenanigans back in the sixties and was more than happy to tell all sorts of lurid stories about what had gone on there. Anecdotes about life at the cottage in the late sixties both amused and shocked the court in equal measure. His memories were avidly devoured by the media brigade as, no doubt, it would be by their listeners and readers.

Also present giving evidence was a man called Gerald 'Gerry' Yates. He'd contacted the Met after reading stories in the press, he now lived in the Croydon area of South London. Back in the sixties he'd been a good friend of Benny Hayes, they'd played in the same band but had fallen out due to musical differences over their group's direction. Yates, who grew to hate his one-time friend and wasn't into drugs, knew that Hayes had an explosive personality and was given to uncontrolled rages especially after a cocktail of drugs and drink. He gave evidence in court to this effect, it was something that the prosecuting team were very much hoping would count against Hayes and help greatly in his eventual conviction.

A key witness for the prosecution was local motor mechanic and occasional farm worker, Stephen Tyson. His family had lived in Fen View Cottage for over ten years after Hayes had moved out. Andrew Bannister bombarded him with questions. The main part of his interrogation came when he asked Tyson to relay to the court an incident dating from the late sixties.

'Tell us, Mr Tyson, in detail please, what you heard your late father say to your mother when you were hiding from them in the pantry of your home in Cottenham, a short time before your family eventually moved into Fen View Cottage, after Mr Hayes had been kicked out by the owner.'

The painfully shy Tyson mumbled his way through an answer and was asked on several occasions to speak up by the judge. He told the courtroom that his late father had watched Hayes assist Tyson's long dead older brother, Roger, bury a body under a patch of waste ground next to the back garden of Fen View Cottage. He said his sibling had confessed to their parents that he'd accidentally pushed a girl down the stairs, Roger was drunk at the time and his mind had been badly affected by taking the drug LSD. The girl was tragically killed by the fall, it had been a spur of the moment event, it hadn't been planned, it wasn't a premeditated, cold-blooded murder. Unfortunately, Tyson's father was long deceased and his frail mother was in a Wisbech nursing home suffering from Alzheimer's, they couldn't confirm his story.

A month or so before the trial began Stephen Tyson had agreed to give the police a DNA sample. Watling wanted some information as to whose DNA was on the blanket that had been used to wrap up Sara Barrington-Webb's body before its burial. Two sets had been found on the remains of the blanket used to cover the body, one belonged to Hayes's ex-girlfriend, Janey Harrison. It was, after all, a blanket that had been taken off her bed in the cottage without her knowledge as she was absent visiting her parents at the time. Watling reckoned the second DNA sample could possibly belong to Roger Tyson but he was long dead, killed when his car careered off the road into a watery drainage channel one foggy night on the Fens. The DNA of his brother, Stephen, if it showed a good match, would corroborate Hayes's story about Roger Tyson wrapping up the body and carrying it to its grave. When the test results came back they confirmed that there was a strikingly good match between the second sample from the blanket and Stephen's DNA. A 49% match was apparent in inherited gene variants between the DNA of Roger on the blanket and the actual DNA of Stephen. In the eyes of the CPS this was the evidence that Roger Tyson was indeed involved in the burial of Miss Barrington-Webb.

The trial continued into a second week during which the judge decided to ban all media reporting. They would have to wait until after the verdict had been delivered. It looked as if Hayes would be found guilty of manslaughter at the very least but his defence team, skilfully and methodically, built up a solid argument in his favour based partly on what they referred to as 'insufficient forensic evidence', but mainly upon the fact that there were no longer any totally reliable and impartial living eye-witnesses to the events of fifty plus years ago other than the openly hostile Gerry Yates, who obviously hated Hayes with a vengeance, and ex-girlfriend, Janey Harrison. She was called upon to give evidence of what life was like at Fen View and was questioned about her relationship with Hayes. Harrison confirmed that she was away visiting her parents in Warwickshire when Sara Barrington-Webb met her all too soon and grisly death. The account of her time with Hayes was particularly damning but Mr Hindmarsh drew attention to this when questioning her and addressing the courtroom. According to him, here was a bitter woman with a particularly large axe to grind and Miss Harrison had been more than happy to bury the hatchet, metaphorically speaking, deep into Hayes's head. Hindmarsh insisted that her blatantly biased and over emotional ramblings could not be believed as true and impartial facts. Could the jury really trust all that she'd said about her former lover? Hindmarsh had a very persuasive manner about him. His oratory was impressive, it sounded convincing. He dismissed Yates's evidence as inconclusive and anecdotal. Here was a "Hayes hater", how could he be believed to impart the real and unbiased truth of life at the cottage?

Witnesses for the defence were few and far between. Judy Carston, Hayes's partner spoke of how he was a changed character, a man who'd jettisoned his past and Vanessa Eustace, the lady who lived in the apartment below Benny and Judy, commented on what a kind and good neighbour Benny had been in the six years that she'd known him. As the legal proceedings wore on it looked as if the lengthy time lapse between the alleged offences and the trial was going to act in Hayes's favour as did the fact that there had been no impartial eye-witness accounts of what actually did happen on that fateful night in May, 1969.

But things were about to change. The CPS said they had another witness to the events at the cottage, a certain lady who'd been unavailable for the last month, she was away on holiday in Australia, but she'd be ready and willing to testify the following week after returning to her home in London. Judge David Pugh announced that the trial would reconvene in a week's time, a new witness for the prosecution would be entering the courtroom.

49

The *Islas del Maiz,* or Corn Islands, named after the first commercial crop introduced in 1778, are probably the best part of Nicaragua. The islands are two small lumps of rock perched high enough on a triangularly shaped submarine platform, the Nicaraguan Rise, so that their heads lie above sea level. Surrounded by clear, turquoise, shallow seas, bordered by pristine white sands, fringed by palm trees and topped by bright blue skies for much of the year it's no wonder that tourism, although small scale, is beginning to rival fishing in the local economy.

Jorge Hernandez's main home was in Managua, the capital, far away to the west in the Spanish-speaking part of the country, but his second secret abode was on the north coast of Great Corn hidden amongst an exotically named group of houses known as Sally Peachie. After successfully rescuing Santos and his party from the dangers on the mainland all were in ebullient mood as the boat carrying them sped through the waters along the quiet east coast of Great Corn. By daybreak, Sunday morning, they were safely on dry land.

Santos had never been to El Bigote's Great Corn hideaway in all the time he'd known him and was looking forward to it. John and Lola were keener to explore the island's sandy coves and offshore coral reefs teeming with shoals of exotic fish. It would be yet another adventure, courtesy of a drugs lord who'd become their good friend.

If the newcomers to Great Corn were expecting to visit some grandiose palace in the sun they were soon disappointed. After leaving the boat moored alongside a jetty they headed the short distance inland to El Bigote's residence. It was one small house and a couple of rather shabby-looking shacks along a narrow lane shaded by palm trees and dense tropical vegetation, a modest home for a man who could easily afford much better. Next to one of the huts a rusted, dirt and dust smeared Ford saloon, at least twenty years old and parked in a weed infested driveway, completed the impression that El Bigote wanted to convey to both the locals and any outsiders that might come snooping. As far as Hernandez was concerned his place blended in with its surroundings and didn't scream out to all and sundry: this is a rich man's house, maybe even the home of a drugs smuggler. There were plenty of smart detached properties nearby. If the Andrettis, or other enemies, came looking they wouldn't think El Bigote lived in such a humble abode. Surely, no-one would suspect that a leading player in the drugs trade had chosen to live in such a dilapidated group of buildings and that was exactly how Jorge wanted it. This was definitely downmarket, but just the sort of refuge that a man in his industry needed at times.

'Welcome to my little house on Paradise Island!' joked El Bigote.

'I like it, Jorge,' replied Santos. 'It's ideal, a poor man's home, it reminds me of my youth, my days in the favelas of Rio. I once lived in tin shacks.'

'Ah, but hold on a minute, wait until you see inside,' retorted El Bigote.

He opened the front door and walked in, the others followed. As alluded to it was far more lavish indoors. Comfortable furniture on well-polished parquet flooring adorned the lounge and various expensive white goods filled the kitchen. A modern, large screen television dominated the living room. Other than that, it was a fairly spartan, single man's house, without any feminine touches, but it was clean and tidy. Up the stairs were three bedrooms and a basic bathroom at the end of the landing. They'd have to share the facilities. It wasn't anything near even three-star hotel standard but it would suffice for a few days.

'I think this place is great, Jorge,' said John trying to be polite. 'I'm looking forward to our stay.'

For the next couple of days Santos and El Bigote kept a low profile, they took shelter and made business plans in the little house tucked away along the lane close to the island's north coast. John and Lola, on the other hand, were keen to explore and make the most of their short stay. Before going off gallivanting Santos told them to wear sunglasses and hats, apart from the necessary sun protection they best disguise themselves as much as possible. El Bigote gave directions to a nearby diving store, *Dos Tiburones*, where they could hire snorkelling equipment. He told them about the remains of an old steamship in the shallow waters not too far from the local beach and an even older Spanish galleon off Waula Point just along the coast. John and Lola were looking forward to swimming in the invitingly warm waters as well as exploring the reefs that ringed the island. After a light breakfast they walked to the dive shop, paid an assistant for snorkelling gear and continued their stroll down to the sea.

'Come on, John, let's swim out to the old wreck, it's supposed to be full of fish, we can have a look at the coral reef as well,' enthused Lola.

The couple spent a magical morning observing shoals of exquisitely coloured sea creatures: blue and yellow angelfish, parrot fish, doctor fish and the wonderfully named French Grunt with its characteristic yellow and white stripes, but the highlight was a couple of inquisitive leatherback turtles that swam close by them. Lola had been worried about having a brush with a black-tipped reef shark but this fairly docile and harmless species was noticeable only by its absence. The dive shop staff had mentioned to look out for barracuda, a thin, long and ugly-looking fish with sharp teeth but none were noticed. They too are usually relatively harmless but their aggressive appearance suggests that might not necessarily be the case. After swimming and diving all morning in the offshore shallows, it was time for some lunch. El Bigote had recommended a place called *Comedor Maris*. They took his advice and both enjoyed shrimps sautéed in garlic before sharing a lobster al gusto washed down by delicious passion fruit mocktails, they felt as if they were on holiday at long last.

A short bus ride around the island followed during the hot afternoon. The leisurely journey took them to Brig Bay, the main settlement where an old-fashioned pedalo was hired for an hour. Later on, it was off down to Quinn Hill and Bluff Point in the south. They walked to the top of the hill and were rewarded by fantastic views looking out across the whole island onto to the blue waters of the Caribbean.

'We must come again sometime, Lola, by ourselves next time.'

'I love it here, we could hire a cottage, learn to use diving equipment and explore some of the offshore cave systems. For now, John, let's get to California, I can manage a short stay with you, but I must then return to Argentina. I can't have any more time off work, people will be wondering where I've got to.'

'The sooner we return to normality and safety the better. It's been one hell of a trip but we need to get away from the dangerous world of drug dealers.'

'It's been quite an adventure but you're right, we must find a safer existence but, strange as it seems, I've always felt OK having Federico and Ángel with us. I can't believe they're criminals, but we both know that's what they really are.'

'We must keep pressing Santos on his area of the Amazon. He should look after the place, not just exploit and wreck it.'

'We'll try and get him to concentrate on his legal businesses,' implored Lola.

'Best of luck with that!' was John's rather cynical response.

They spent the rest of the day strolling along the coastline occasionally stopping to sunbathe or swim in the crystal-clear waters. It was nearly six o'clock when they returned to El Bigote's little home tucked up the shady lane. A sunny day turned into a dark sultry night and everyone retired to the back garden where Jorge presided over the spicy jerk chicken, Jamaican style, accompanied by lime rice and garlic potato salad together with plenty of Red Stripe lager.

It was a convivial evening but, as usual, things were about to change. After a leisurely day under the Caribbean sun, Monday would be very different. A small plane from Bluefields had touched down at Corn Island Airport with a group of angry men hell bent on revenge. Paradise was about to be disturbed.

50

The time had arrived. The CPS were about to reveal what they hoped would be their trump card. A lady now in her seventies, Mrs Emily Jenkins, was to become the key player in the trial of Benny Hayes. During the late sixties, Miss Emily Alcott, as she had been back then, was part of the commune of drop-outs that flitted between three different locations: a rundown terraced squat along a backstreet in Cambridge, another similarly grubby place in Hackney, London and a remote farm house on the Fens. Mrs Jenkins now lived in a far more up-market property in Richmond-on-Thames, overlooking the river, with her ex-stockbroker husband and a dog. Emily was a retired social worker but half a century ago she'd lived a very different life as a swinging hippy, an integral part of Benny Hayes's warped idea of utopia.

Earlier in the year, Emily had been sitting quietly in the living room reading a newspaper. To her astonishment the centre pages had a story about life in the sixties at a place she remembered only too well: Fen View Cottage. News about the tragic death and illegal burial of Sara Barrington-Webb featured heavily in the coverage but the main focus of the article was the debauched setup at the cottage. Elderly locals in that part of Cambridgeshire had been happy to regale visiting reporters with all sorts of sensational stories, embellished and exaggerated by the passage of time. After reading the two-page spread in *The Mail on Sunday*, Emily decided it was time to do something she should have done years ago. On Monday morning, the day after reading the newspaper article, she walked to her nearest police station. At last she was to disclose information about what she'd witnessed on the evening of the fourteenth of May, 1969.

At reception a nervous but determined Emily asked to see a senior detective, privately, she wanted to make a confession.

Her astonishing story would later be used in court. Following her visit, the Met contacted Watling to impart some stunning information. Both police forces felt confident that Mrs Jenkins's evidence would help convict Benny Hayes of a major crime, but at the start of the trial Emily had been away on a long-haul holiday. However, once back in England, she was to be wheeled out as the prosecution team's star witness after the short break in proceedings.

Andrew Bannister KC was ecstatic when he first heard the details from the Met. Here was someone who was there when Sara Barrington-Webb died, she was inside the cottage and would be able to deliver a bombshell that would stun the courtroom and swing the case firmly in their favour. Emily was to be the last person questioned before the summing up by the judge.

On the day of the trial's resumption the courtroom was packed, there wasn't a spare seat in the house. An understandably anxious Emily walked into the witness box. She gripped its sides tightly before nervously looking at the jury, judge, lawyers, press, public and, most frighteningly of all, the man in the dock, Benny Hayes. She hadn't seen him for over half a century. Unsurprisingly, he looked older and frailer, but it was definitely him, he still had the arrogant swagger that she remembered so well. After being sworn in her ordeal began in earnest.

'Mrs Jenkins, please tell the court all that you saw and heard on the evening of Wednesday, May fourteenth, 1969, the night that the unfortunate Miss Sara Barrington-Webb died in Fen View Cottage,' said Andrew Bannister in a grave and serious voice. Emily took time to compose herself before recounting the story she'd told the Met:

'On that evening I was in the kitchen (she paused and took a sip of water from the glass in front of her), … I heard an almighty row, an argument going on upstairs. I knew that both Roger Tyson and Sara were in a bedroom smoking dope and drinking vodka.' She paused and looked across the courtroom at the sea of inquisitive faces before eventually fixing her stare upon Hayes. Emily had difficulty controlling her emotions, … 'Benny, he was up there too.' She paused yet again, best forgotten memories of the past churned up inside her and flooded through her brain. As Emily hesitated, muffled voices could be heard around the court. *That's interesting! Hayes had always maintained he was out in the garden.* Whispered murmurs filled the room. Emily's grip on the witness box tightened.

'Please take your time, Mrs Jenkins, there's no rush,' said Bannister sympathetically. 'When you're ready, do tell us, what happened next?'

After composing herself she continued:

'I rushed out of the kitchen … Sara, she was standing on the top of the stairs being hit by a bat, she came crashing down and landed in an awful heap. She was unconscious, … her hair, it was covered, … plastered in blood (Emily sobbed and produced a tissue from her handbag), … I called out to her but there was no response. I went into shock, … I'd realised she was dead!' Again, she had difficulty containing her emotions.

'I know this is very upsetting, but when you're ready, do please continue, Mrs Jenkins, then what happened?' asked Bannister.

'Roger was standing at the top of the stairs … he looked mad with rage, he was carrying a wooden bat, we used to play rounders in the garden with it, it was smeared in blood. I saw Roger hit Sara with the bat before she fell. Roger started shouting at me. Sara was dead next to my feet. By this time Benny had appeared, standing close to Roger. He too was going berserk, he was high on drugs and drink, he started threatening to kill Roger for what he'd done.'

The courtroom had been sitting in stunned silence but mention of Hayes by name caused more murmurs, the whispers became louder and were followed by a very audible outrage from the watching gallery. The Judge intervened:

'Quiet! Quiet in court! … please continue, Mrs Jenkins.'

The hullabaloo subsided.

'Eventually, … after screaming threats at each other, … both Benny and Roger calmed themselves. They realised that Sara was dead, there was no bringing her back. Roger had clubbed her over the head with the bat and she'd fallen down the stairs.'

'So, Mrs Jenkins, let's make this quite clear. You're saying that only Roger Tyson was responsible for killing Miss Barrington-Webb, by hitting her, on the head, with a rounders bat?' asked Andrew Bannister.

'Yes, that's what I saw, both Sara and Roger were upstairs as I've said, they'd argued about something, Sara fell down the stairs after Roger Tyson attacked her with the bat.'

'From what you witnessed, and have just told this court, I think we can safely assume that Roger Tyson was guilty of either murder or manslaughter while under the influence of drink and drugs. What I'm going to ask you next is most important, Mrs Jenkins: Do you believe that Benny Hayes had anything to do with the violence against Miss Barrington-Webb?'

'No, it was all Roger's fault, but Benny was with them. He must have seen what happened. Whether he and Roger planned the attack I just don't know.'

'Please continue, what happened then, after Mr Tyson and Mr Hayes realised that Miss Barrington-Webb was dead, Mrs Jenkins?'

'Benny and Roger, they argued about what to do, ... they had a body on their hands. They decided to make it look like Sara had fallen on the stairs so they hauled her back up to the top, and they (she sobbed), ... they threw her dead body back down the stairs (more sobbing), ... they wanted it to look like she'd died from a really bad fall.'

More noises emanated from around the room.

'And did this only happen once, Mrs Jenkins? How many times did it occur?'

'At least three, maybe four or five times, ... it was awful, ... it might have been more, they took turns.'

The judge had to call for order after which Andrew Bannister pressed on with his questioning:

'And what were you doing? What part did you play in the unfolding drama?'

'I did nothing, what could I do? I was totally shocked and told to shut up and threatened that if I said anything to anyone they'd both come looking for me, ... wherever I was, ... and I'd get the same treatment, … I too would be killed.' Emily Jenkins broke down in tears.

Gasps of horror filled the courtroom. A man in the upper part of the public gallery stood up and shouted: 'You bastard, Hayes!' An elderly lady followed suit and screamed: 'May you rot in hell for this, Hayes!'

Judge Pugh had to call for order yet again. Once all the shouting had stopped, Andrew Bannister stood up and resumed his questioning.

'Please continue, Mrs Jenkins, I know it's very difficult for you, but do go on. After this threat to your life, this awful, terrible threat to murder you, please tell the court, what happened next?'

Emily, determined to finish her story, continued:

'Benny and Roger, they decided they weren't going to call the police. There were illegal drugs around the place, they reckoned they'd be charged with possession as well as murder. Benny threatened me again, I mustn't tell anyone, if I did one of them would find and kill me as punishment. They agreed to bury Sara under a patch of land at the back of the garden, Benny said he knew an ideal place. Roger wrapped Sara in a blanket from off Janey's bed, and then they buried her.'

'I'll save the defence having to ask you this question, Mrs Jenkins, but why didn't you come forward sooner? I can understand why all the threats at the time made you wary but this was over fifty years ago. It took a Sunday newspaper article to make you come forward with this vital information.'

'I read, … in the paper, … that Roger Tyson was dead. I didn't know that until then, he was an unpleasant character, a real nasty piece of work. I thought he'd search for me if I said anything, he'd definitely have killed me, I had no doubt about that. He was a dangerous man. I found out that Benny Hayes was standing trial and on bail, I didn't know that until I'd read about it.'

'Thank you, Mrs Jenkins, I very much appreciate that you've lived in fear for all these years, it must have been a dreadful ordeal for you, I realise it took a lot of courage to walk into your local police station and confess to what you witnessed. What you've told this court lends considerable weight to all the extensive forensic evidence supplied by the Cambridgeshire police. I want to thank you again, Emily, you've been most helpful.'

Andrew Bannister sat down. Judge Pugh asked the defence counsel if he had any questions. A stunned Peter Hindmarsh stumbled out of his seat and stood up. He cross-examined Emily but, underneath his bluster and feigned confidence, he realised that all his questioning and rather excruciating and distasteful attempts to put a different spin on her awful story were futile. He knew that what Mrs Jenkins had said in court was damning evidence against his client. She was a reliable eyewitness to what had really happened, he could accuse Emily of lying but why should she want to do that? She was a reliable witness, she didn't have any personal grudge against the man on trial, she was just fearful of him, and the deceased Roger Tyson, and had lived with that dread for more than fifty years. Neither Hindmarsh or Hayes could talk their way out of this mess. Hayes was as guilty as hell. He'd assisted Tyson to illegally dispose of a human corpse, he'd mistreated that body beforehand, he'd threatened the unfortunate Miss Alcott, as she was then, with being murdered. Hayes didn't try to deny what she'd said, he couldn't say that she'd made it all up or that she was never at Fen View Cottage. Both Janey Harrison and Gerry Yates could testify to her regular presence at the commune. Hayes was up the proverbial creek without a paddle. Even Peter Hindmarsh KC, with all his skills as a barrister, couldn't come up with something plausible to drag his client out of the mire.

After the judge's summing up it didn't take the jury long to come up with a verdict. Benny Hayes was found not guilty of either murder or manslaughter but he was guilty of perverting the course of justice by illegally burying a deceased person. His leading role in the whole sorry affair, especially the mistreatment of the corpse and his reprehensible threats to Emily didn't help his cause. The Crown Court judge, Mr Justice Pugh, sent him to prison for five years. Peter Hindmarsh returned to London with his tail between his legs and his reputation tarnished, while Hayes was driven in an unmarked police van to Winson Green prison, in Birmingham, to serve out his sentence. History was repeating itself. It was an ironic twist, Hayes would be going to the same prison that Elsie Summer's husband, Henry, had been to over one hundred and fifty years before. The difference was that Summers ended up dangling from a rope in the days long before hanging was abolished. But Hayes was not a murderer, he'd be spending time in a prison cell instead. Roger Tyson was the one guilty of either murder or manslaughter, justice had been served on him many years ago when he met his end in a water-filled ditch one night on the Fens.

Watling headed back to Huntingdon a happy man, Hayes had eventually ended up where he belonged, his incarceration for a life of crime was long overdue. It was time to move on and focus on other matters. Watling had received an e-mail from Police Scotland, soon he'd be travelling to consult with officers in the Highlands. An academic from Cambridgeshire had been found dead up there. The victim had been dumped in a loch, a diving team had made the grim discovery. Watling wanted to examine the scene. A trip to the beauty of the Scottish Highlands would make a pleasant change from having a gun stuck in his back.

51

A WARM, SULTRY NIGHT FOLLOWED BY
A SUNNY DAY IN THE CARIBBEAN

Luca Andretti was convinced that Santos had escaped to the Corn Islands. The recently deceased Randy Lister had previously passed on details to his boss relating to several sightings of El Bigote on Great Corn. On the strength of that information, Luca reckoned that both Santos and his entourage had fled from Bluefields to one of the two offshore islands. He'd cover the larger one first. Neither were big places and Luca reasoned it wouldn't take long to search both if necessary. Bruno would accompany him, together with an unsavoury bunch of criminals all connected to his drugs gang.

Once off the plane they headed straight for *Darrien's*, one of the island's liveliest night spots, located just outside Brig Bay. Apart from observing all the comings and goings they were eager to question locals and staff there. Bruno approached the barman to ask if he knew of anyone called El Bigote, real name Jorge Hernandez. The circumspect barman had heard of him but wasn't going to admit that to a bunch of guys who, going by their looks, might as well have had the words "drug dealer" stamped on their foreheads. He lied and said he'd never come across either title but Bruno was pointed in the direction of an elderly looking customer who was sat reading a newspaper in the corner of the room. According to the bartender, Joseph was the fountain of all knowledge about the island, including many of its inhabitants. If you wanted to know anything about Great Corn he was the go-to man.

Now the Caribbean is one of the world's great cultural and ethnic melting pots, the legacy of centuries of immigration, some voluntary from Europe, but a good deal of it forced from West

Africa. Joseph was the living embodiment of its history. He was powerfully built and of mixed racial ancestry: over six feet tall with chocolate brown skin, greying beard and short Afro-style hair. He made a living from catching lobsters. Bruno ambled up to him and said that he and his friends would like to ask a few questions. He offered to buy him a beer. Joseph accepted the kind gesture, he was friendly, outgoing and happy to talk to anyone, especially when a free drink was involved. After passing a cold bottle of lager across the bar Bruno ushered the elderly islander towards a table where a brooding, overweight and bald-headed man was sat surrounded by four mean-looking heavies.

'Say hello to my brother, his name's Luca, Luca Andretti,' said Bruno cheerfully to Joseph.

'*Wah gwaan mon!* (What's up man?), said Joseph in Jamaican patois. Although now living on Great Corn his origins lay elsewhere.

'Just sit the fuck down, old man, and cut the Jamaican slang crap, I've some questions for you,' piped up Luca before Joseph had a chance to introduce himself properly.

Joseph didn't look too pleased to be addressed in such a rude manner but after glancing around the table he realised it would be a pretty dumb move to get into any argument over it. Luca continued:

'We're looking for a dude goes by the name of El Bigote, that's cos the fucker's got some over-sized moustache.' He laughed, his entourage followed suit. 'You know him?'

'Yeah, I heard of him, Mexican guy, he visits dee island from time to time. Big player in dee drugs trade, so I've been told.'

Luca leaned across the table and stuck his face about a foot in front of Joseph's.

'You know where he lives?' asked Luca menacingly.

Joseph hesitated and looked warily at the band of criminals in his midst. *No doubt about it, this lot were drug dealers, he'd seen these types on the island many times before.* Narcotics were always being moved along the coastline of Nicaragua. He thought he'd better give Luca a snippet of information, something to keep him sweet.

'People talk, gossip, you knows what I mean, mon. I never seen dee guy you talk about but you hear stories. I hear he live somewhere on dee south of dee island, Quinn Hill area. Ask when you get there. Best of luck with your search,' said Joseph. He quickly swilled back his beer and put the empty bottle down on the table in front of Luca. 'You can find me here most days of dee week, if you ever need me again dat is. Thanks for dee drink, mon.'

Joseph was eager to leave the hostile atmosphere that emanated from off this gang of hardened thugs. He stood up and walked purposefully to the exit without looking back. When outside he checked that he wasn't being followed and hurried off home to his colourfully painted fisherman's cabin by the bay, a place where he'd lived by himself for the past four years ever since his wife died, but he didn't stay for long. He rushed into his bedroom and took a fully loaded pistol and some spare bullets out of a cupboard. Joseph then dashed out of the house and disappeared amongst the surrounding houses and shacks.

* * * *

It was late, after midnight, but Jorge Hernandez and his guests were still sitting out in the back garden talking quietly and sipping ice-cold lagers straight from the bottle, but the evening's conviviality was about to be disturbed. Someone was approaching the narrow, unlit side street in Sally Peachie, their mission to visit Jorge's modest home. The uninvited visitor looked around to see if anyone was about, not a soul in sight, that was good. A gun was removed from its holster and checked, it was loaded. Time to walk along the dark lane and knock on a front door. Two hard knocks, no answer. Despite the blackness of the surroundings an old and rusted button bell was located, it was pressed twice, surprisingly it still worked. The mystery caller stepped well back from the door and waited patiently.

Alert as ever, Ángel was the only one to hear the chimes from the doorbell. He'd been drinking fruit juices, mango mostly with iced water all evening, the rest of them had consumed several bottles of some of the Caribbean's favourite lager.

'Quiet,' he whispered, 'someone's at the front door!' Ángel instinctively reached for the Glock pistol lying close at hand. Santos gave a concerned look towards El Bigote:

'You expecting visitors?'

'At this time of night, no way!'

'John, you and Lola, go and hide in that shed at the bottom of the garden. Here, take this, just in case you need it,' said Santos. He handed John one of his pistols. 'Ángel, go check out who the unexpected caller is.'

All did as they were told. After directions from El Bigote on how to navigate his way along a narrow alleyway that led to the front of the house, Ángel moved off stealthily to creep up on whoever was at the door. For the highly-trained ex-Special Forces man it was all in a day's work, a minute later he was at the front of the building, his Glock pistol with its silencer fitted and pointed at the silhouetted figure.

'Put your hands up mister, nice and slow, stay exactly where you are and don't turn around. Try anything and you'll have a back full of holes,' said Ángel coldly. 'What's your name? Why you here?'

The person followed the instructions before speaking.

'My name, it Joseph. I need see Jorge, Jorge Hernandez, he known as El Bigote, it urgent, mon! He know me. I'm friend of dee man.'

After being disarmed, and with the gun pointed at his lower back, Joseph was shown along the passageway to where El Bigote and Santos were waiting at the rear of the house. John and Lola had returned from the confines of the old shed at the bottom of the garden after Santos told them it was safe to come out of hiding, things were under control. When Jorge saw who was walking along the alley he told Ángel to put his gun away, it was someone he knew and trusted implicitly.

'Joseph, my friend, what the hell you doing here? Thought I'd told you never to come to this place.'

'I know, I know, I real sorry for dat, Jorge, but day is men on dee island, they looks for you, mon. I had let you know, soon as I could.'

Jorge went on to explain to the others how he and Joseph had met. Joseph fished the local waters but as well as catching real lobsters he sometimes found 'white lobster' floating out at sea or washed up onshore. He had an arrangement with Joseph to give him any discarded packs of cocaine that he came across, an act for which he was amply rewarded. Joseph made money and El Bigote made even more money, it was a mutually beneficial arrangement, a symbiotic relationship, everyone a winner. The fisherman had a lot of respect for El Bigote, the drugs dealer treated him well and paid him handsomely. In some months Joseph earned more from discarded packs of cocaine than he did from catching lobster. He thought it a wise move to warn his friend, if someone had come looking for him, well Jorge needed to know. Earlier he'd been more than happy to point the rude American to the wrong end of the island.

'I had to see you, Jorge. It urgent mon. Some men, day turn up at Darrien's like day own dee goddam place, day makin' quiries (enquiries) dee boss man said, day ask where day find man call El Bigote. Dee bartender, he tell 'em to ask me. You know, I sociable guy who spend most nights out drinking after long days at sea fishing my ass off.'

'Any idea who these men are?' asked a worried Santos.

'Day six mean sons of bitches. Two Yanks in charge. New York accents I reckons, other four look American too, or maybe *yardies* (gangsters), day over here from Jamaica, plenty of 'em in Kingston.'

'What did you tell them, Joseph?' questioned El Bigote.

'Little as possible. Don't worry, I point 'em in dee wrong direction, mon. I say I hear someone called El Bigote, he live at Quinn Hill, on dee other side of island. I'm scared, mon. They real mean dudes, not friendly like you, Señor Jorge.'

Joseph had been spooked by these people, he was worried for his safety and wanted help and guidance as to what he should do. Santos was the next to speak:

'It sounds like the Andrettis have turned up. I've been expecting them. Joseph, you say you told these men to head for a place called Quinn Hill.' He turned and looked straight at El Bigote. 'You know what, Jorge, I'm fed up with running, I'm done with it. I was hoping the Andrettis might back off and stop trying to find me. No such luck, so, things have to change, we need to find the Andrettis, sooner the better. Get things sorted out, once and for all, get them off our backs.'

Santos had made up his mind, in the morning they'd make the short journey onto the other side of Great Corn. Joseph was advised not to go back to his home. El Bigote told him to lie low for a while, he could use one of his friend's places that was empty, it was not far down the coast road, only about a hundred metres away, he pointed him in the right direction after giving him the key to the property.

'Disappear for a while, Joseph, stay out of trouble. I'll find you when we've sorted this shit out.'

* * * *

After a short sleep a gloriously sunny Monday morning dawned. As agreed the night before, John and Lola wouldn't be joining the search for the Andretti mob. Instead, they were to be dropped off by the side of Arenas beach, the longest stretch of sand on the island, with instructions to enjoy the day. They'd swim, snorkel and sunbathe along the beautiful shoreline. Several bars and restaurants were nearby. Jorge said they'd be picked up later, at six o'clock, outside the *Picnic Center*, a café he frequented from time to time. It had a well-stocked bar, he recommended lobster and shrimps in coconut sauce for lunch, a dish on the menu that went under the inauspicious name of *Rundown*, he joked that it tasted a damn sight better than it sounded. A feature of the café was its thatched pergolas and the place throbbed to the sound of reggae music. Santos said if they weren't picked up at six as promised, presume there'd been a hitch, they must then head back to the secluded house at Sally Peachie, taking great care not to be followed. He added that he'd arranged for Ricky to be at the airport for eleven o'clock. John and Lola must leave with him, by themselves if necessary, he would fly overnight to the lonely landing strip in the hills of northern California, not far from Sacramento, Ramon Fernandes would meet them. Hopefully, both Santos and Ángel could be on the flight but Ricky had been primed to travel without his boss and bodyguard if necessary.

John and Lola were dropped off on the kerbside alongside the impressive Arenas beach, the others then went off in search of the Andrettis. After travelling the short distance inland to the Quinn Hill area, El Bigote parked his battered old Ford in a quiet cul-de-sac. Today, Santos would be the hunter rather than the hunted. He reckoned he couldn't keep on running, it was time to be proactive instead of reactive. The Andrettis refused to go away. Usually, when it came to doing a deal or handling a tricky situation, Santos preferred working at night, especially when confrontation was likely but he yearned to see his wife and son in Rio, he wanted to return to Mendoza and wished he could meet with Tomás at a football stadium somewhere. He'd done enough running, it was time to be the aggressor.

Before exploring the coast, John bought coffees at a small café that fronted onto the beach and headed for a quiet table with Lola. It was time for a serious talk. The holiday would soon be over, this was to be the last day of their Latin American odyssey.

'So, tonight, Lola, we head for California, at long, long last. You have to be back in Argentina soon, I know. We need to think about how we can keep seeing each other, I don't want to lose you. You've made me a happy man.'

'And I don't want to lose you, Señor John! It's been quite a holiday, definitely the most dangerous one I've ever had, that's for sure. And other things haven't been too bad either, even more exciting than following around after Santos!' she replied with a cheeky smirk all over her face. 'I shall stay with you in California, but only for a few days, I must return to Mendoza, at least for a while, but there are sommelier jobs in places like San Francisco. I can speak English but you, being stupid, can't speak any Spanish.'

She smiled and John laughed.

'I can look for a job in your area, we'll be apart for a while but I'll move as soon as possible. I'll learn Spanish, you can teach me.'

'I'm sure that Tomás will help you. He's a marvellous friend to have and has many contacts in Argentina. We'll work something out but for now, John, let's just enjoy ourselves.'

They drank up their coffee, kissed and proceeded to walk along the seafront arm in arm. Looking like a typical honeymoon couple they strolled past clumps of palm trees whose leafy branches swayed back and forth in the pleasant warmth of the customary onshore breeze. After a short walk on the beach they stopped under a tall Caribbean pine tree, time to enjoy the warm offshore waters again. Lola, in her sexy, cut high on the hips, navy blue swimsuit dashed off across the loose sand towards the sea, John chased after her. After hurling themselves into the breaking waves they splashed about like a couple of excited children on their first day's holiday at the seaside. Eventually they decided to swim out to sea. While their day was all relaxation and frolicking, it would be very different for their companions.

* * * *

It wasn't in the plan but unfortunately for Santos the Andrettis spotted him first. At the time El Bigote was busy calling at houses along a road named *La Pista-La Loma* in the area of Quinn Hill, a high point on the island named after a cotton plantation owner from long ago. Purporting to be a policeman he'd been asking if anyone had seen a gang of American men, who resembled drug dealers, around the place. Santos and Ángel followed in his wake, eager for any snippet of information.

Luca Andretti was delighted when he saw Santos in the distance. The discovery stopped him in his tracks.

'Bruno, look ahead, up the hill, over on the right, that guy in the black gear, that's Santos isn't it? Hell, bro, you know what? We've got the little bastard at long last!'

Bruno stood still by his brother's side, he took off his sunglasses and squinted into the distance. About a hundred and fifty metres further up the road there was a small man dressed all in black. Next to him were two other men: one balding and big with a bushy moustache and the other equally large but younger, probably thirtyish, with a short-cropped hairstyle.

'Hell! You know what, I think you're right, Luca. It looks like Santos, El Bigote's the guy with the stupid moustache. And Ángel da Silva's the younger one. Don't think they've noticed us yet, but if we keep following them they're bound to turn around and clock us.'

All of the Andretti gang were convinced: the three individuals ahead of them, further up the slope, were who they were after but they didn't want a confrontation here, not along a street, too many houses around, there would be witnesses but, to his right, Luca could see patches of forest interspersed with occasional clearings and footpaths that led into the wooded area.

'Bruno, there's six of us, only three of them, who knows where the long-haired guy and the blonde babe have got to. We'll close in on Santos, catch him unawares, take him and his mates into the trees, then we'll kill the fuckers!'

Luca instructed his gang to split up. Two peeled off to the right and headed through the woods, the other couple moved off to the left between the houses and shacks. The plan was to get ahead of the prey, form a pincer movement and cut off their path. Bruno and Luca would follow on behind and observe, taking great care not to be seen. Eventually they'd close in once the gang members had stopped Santos and company in their tracks.

Ángel, with the well-honed instincts of an elite one-time soldier, had a feeling they were being followed. He'd noticed some guys in the distance, further down the hill who didn't look like any of the locals. He mentioned the fact to Santos who told his bodyguard to keep an eye on them, but unperturbed they pressed on uphill, knocking on doors, asking questions.

It was exactly 12.36 when four men, all carrying hand guns, sprang out in front of Santos and his companions. Taken by surprise they were escorted into a nearby field next to the woods. One minute later the Andretti brothers, Luca and Bruno, arrived on the scene. Time for a showdown.

'Luca Andretti, I presume?' said Santos coolly. He knew very well who it was. *Hell, why hadn't he been more careful? Why hadn't he taken Ángel's warning seriously?*

'You presume dead right, you little piece of shit!' screamed Luca, despite being out of breath after the exertion and excitement of rushing up the hill. His eyes bulged as if they were about to burst out of their sockets and his ugly bull neck grew increasingly redder. 'What did you do with my cocaine?' blasted Luca. He shoved the pistol in his right hand under Santos's chin. He looked mad with rage, as if he could pull the trigger at any moment and blow Santos's head to pieces. 'Where the fuck is it?'

Bruno, always the calmer brother who preferred to shy away from such belligerent and unpleasant situations, watched on in silence as the captured trio were disarmed. Santos went on to describe what had happened to the stolen cocaine. He calmly told his captors that it had been hidden in a warehouse and later discovered by someone, the police were informed, they'd impounded it. Neither the Andrettis or Santos would be getting any of it returned, no-one would benefit from its sale, it had probably been destroyed by now. Hoping to extricate himself from the tricky situation he found himself in, Santos said he'd be happy to compensate the Andrettis, half a million dollars was offered, double the worth of the cocaine. Bruno, eager to avoid any violence, said that it sounded like a good deal, it should keep everyone happy as well as alive. But Luca was a man possessed. Expletives and threats gushed out of his mouth like water from a tap turned on to maximum flow.

'You fuckers have pissed me off big time. Now you're all going to die but I'm going to shoot your balls off first. Payback time for what you did to Chico.' He ended the rant before instructing his gang to lead the unfortunate threesome into the forest. Luca would have much preferred his regular killing ground in the remote hills of New York state but Quinn Hill on Great Corn would have to suffice. Eventually they came into a clearing. Luca thought it would be a good place for his victims to die. Their corpses would be left, food for the wildlife. If some of the local kids found the bodies, well just too bad.

'This'll do nicely,' screamed Luca. 'You three, lie down, get on the fucking ground, on your backs, assholes. You're all gonna die slow. By the way, where's the others? ... the guy with the rock star hair do and the blonde bitch?'

* * * *

It was five minutes to six. John and Lola had enjoyed a fantastic day on Arenas beach sunbathing as well as going for a paddle or swim. They were now expecting to be picked up by their companions. Jorge's ancient Ford should be coming into view any time soon. Ten past six came, John was becoming concerned, quarter past the hour arrived, still no battered car. By half past six John was really worried. *Where the hell had they got to? This wasn't like Santos. This wasn't the man who thought of everything, it wasn't like him at all, where was he? Where was Ángel, the world's best bodyguard? And what had happened to El Bigote, he seemed ultra-reliable, a man who knew his way around the block, where'd he got to?*

'They're now half an hour late. I'm getting worried, Lola. Something must have happened. Santos doesn't do late!'

'They've been delayed, I'm sure they're fine, they'll be here soon,' replied Lola confidently, but inwardly she was just as worried as John. This was so unlike Federico.

'We'll give them until quarter to seven. If they're not here by then we'll have to head back. Remember Santos's instructions.'

Fifteen minutes later there was still no sign of their companions. Arenas beach was becoming busier. A game of baseball had started up, the bars were doing better business than earlier, more cars were passing by on the coast road but no rusted-up old Ford with El Bigote at the wheel came into view. It was getting darker, lights were coming on in the surrounding houses. *Where the hell was Santos? Something must have happened.*

* * * *

Earlier that afternoon, in the forest clearing, Luca Andretti had been circling his intended victims. Pleased with his success he mocked them and threatened to blow their fingers off one by one followed by their kneecaps and testicles. Brother Bruno and the four gang members watched on, wondering all the time what exactly their unpredictable boss was actually going to do with them. Luca, the psychopath, was enjoying himself. He walked slowly around his victims lying supine and helpless on the ground. While Luca was waving his pistol about threatening to shoot off various body parts Santos desperately racked his brain for an escape plan but couldn't think of one. He'd tried several times to negotiate and persuade his captor that they could come to a mutually acceptable financial agreement, something to end the feud without any more loss of life but Luca wasn't biting. He just laughed at Santos's ideas. He was revelling in the knowledge that soon he'd kill them after sadistically torturing them first. It was Bruno who interrupted Luca's rantings.

'Quiet, Luca! What the hell's that rustling coming from the forest?'

'What goddam noise? I can't hear anything!'

'Over there.' Bruno pointed to a patch of thick woodland to their left.

'Probably a lousy cat, or maybe some mangy, fucking dog. Hell, Bruno, you're becoming far too edgy. Get a grip for Christ's sake.'

'It might be an animal, but maybe not. Look Luca … we need to find somewhere better than this. We're too far out in the open. There are houses not far away, it's too risky. If anyone reports hearing guns going off the goddam heat will be on us like a rash, remember we've got to get out of here, back home to America, that means the airport, think of all the cops around.'

One of the gang members interrupted the brother's discussion. He said he'd seen a deserted house on his travels through the woodland earlier. It was down near the coast, he suggested they head there, it was well away from any other homes. He thought it a wise move and Bruno strongly agreed with him.

'Right, OK, OK, you're fucking right of course, a quiet house would be better than here, do what I've got to do indoors I suppose,' concluded Luca.

The intended victims, hands tied behind their backs, were told to get up and follow in the footsteps of the guy who'd found the house down by the sea. Luca, Bruno and the other men brought up the rear as they headed through a closely-knit mixture of bushy shrubs and trees following the course of a thin and not very well trodden path that gradually headed downhill to an isolated stretch of the island featuring a rock-strewn shoreline and sandy cove.

The building that eventually appeared in front of them had at one time been an impressive residence. It was typically colonial in design, early twentieth century probably but maybe dating back even further, with a balcony on the upper floor and a veranda that extended outwards at ground level. Its wooden walls had once been a brilliant white but the paintwork was now faded and flaking, the roof was all bright red ceramic tiles, some were missing, maybe from storm damage, the legacy of a hurricane. Such weather events occasionally blighted the area, especially this east-facing coast. Hurricane Joan, in 1988, destroyed most of the island's palm trees and had flattened the flimsier built houses. The balustrades on the balcony and veranda had been painted turquoise but were now bleached and blistered by decades of weathering and neglect. The place could have been a plantation owner's house or a hotel many years ago, it was definitely somewhere that had enjoyed better days. It was clear that no-one was about, the old house was derelict, a shadow of its former glorious self, an icon to a by-gone age.

One of the Andretti gang kicked in the front door before checking the interior. He soon gave the all clear, everyone moved inside. Santos, Ángel and El Bigote were led into what would have been a large living room years ago. There was hardly any furniture, the only piece left was a wooden coffee table covered in dust, on its surface was an old newspaper dating from 1979. The captives were instructed to sit together in the darkest corner of the room well away from the windows.

Luca went back onto the veranda and looked out towards the beach at the head of the bay. What he saw didn't exactly please him, he'd have to wait a little longer before any killings could start. Much to his annoyance four young lads had come out of nowhere and were messing about on the sand kicking a football and fooling around in the sea. The boys, all in their early teens, were enjoying themselves and showed no signs of leaving anytime soon. A frustrated Luca returned inside.

'There's some kids on the beach, we can't do what I've got planned, at least for now. Shit, I don't want any witnesses.'

'What you going to do then? asked a worried looking Bruno fearing for the safety of the boys.

'Wait until they've gone I suppose. We've time enough and can hang around here until dark if we have to.'

'OK, but please leave the kids alone, Luca. We get this job done, soon as possible, then we clear out and get off home?' Bruno didn't fancy hanging around in a sad and deserted house waiting for a bunch of lads to go home for their tea, but he also didn't want them killed.

'We've a plane to catch later this evening, plenty of time yet,' replied Luca. 'I've waited long enough for this moment. I want to see these guys squirm, then I'll enjoy blowing them away to kingdom come.'

After checking his flashy Rolex watch, Luca instructed two of his men to head back to the hotel with instructions to get everyone's belongings together, pay what they owed for their short stay and then go to the airport with everything. They were to wait for Luca and the rest of them, they'd see them later. The plan was to catch an evening flight back to Bluefields, then it would be Miami on the first plane out.

By late afternoon the Andretti gang, together with their captives, were cooped up in the house, waiting with ever increasing impatience for the youngsters to go home. Hopefully they'd clear off soon. Luca could then spring into action. A quarter of an hour later, as the light began to fade, the boys had vacated the beach.

By this time the guys still with Luca and Bruno were gasping for a fag, Luca told them to go outside, he hated cigarette smoke. They walked past the crashed-in wooden door, and once on the veranda headed down some stone steps into what had been a large garden. Untended for years, it was badly overgrown. One of the men produced a box of Marlboros from his pocket and offered a cigarette to his mate. After lighting up they each took a much-needed drag before blowing out the inhaled smoke into the warm and salty air. For the men craving nicotine it felt good, it calmed their frayed nerves. They each took another drag and slowly exhaled. It was the last thing they ever did. A couple of muffled gun shots rang out, both men dropped to the ground, dead before they hit it. *That'll teach 'em to smoke!* thought the person who was standing about twenty metres away from the corpses, a pistol, fitted with silencer, in his right hand.

* * * *

John and Lola eventually decided to catch a taxi to head back to Sally Peachie and El Bigote's home down the shady lane. It didn't take long on such a small island and on arrival they found the house just as they'd left it earlier in the day. There was no sign of the others having returned or evidence to suggest that anyone had been snooping around. They hurriedly packed their belongings into small suitcases checking for passports, visas and money. John, with increasing concern, had been trying to contact Santos for the last few hours but his calls had been ignored. *What did that mean?* The signal wasn't great on the island, sometimes it worked, sometimes it didn't. *Maybe Santos had turned his phone off or maybe he'd lost it?* Both scenarios were highly unlikely, Santos was like a teenager when it came to his mobile, it was like an extension of his body permanently attached to his left hand, his right was reserved for a gun, and he never switched it off even when on charge.

It was getting late, almost nine o'clock. They'd better head for the airport, grab a coffee and look out for Ricky. Hopefully, the others would meet them there. They'd been delayed. *But why?* Both John and Lola knew what Santos had planned. He'd told them that he wanted to find the Andrettis, sort things out, hopefully without any aggravation and bloodshed. *But he'd said they'd rendezvous at six and that hadn't happened.* They now had to follow his instructions: meet Ricky, the plane would leave bang on eleven for California, with or without the others. John and Lola were growing increasingly anxious about the fate of their companions.

* * * *

A few hours earlier, back at the deserted house, it had started to turn dark. Bruno opened up the dusty shutters on the windows to let in some of the fading light from outside. Luca had told his men to take ten minutes off, go for a stroll, have a smoke and then return. *They'd now taken half an hour, where were they?*

'Bruno, keep an eye on things for a moment, they're all tied up, hands and feet, they can't do anything, I'm going to take a quick look to see where the fuck Dave and Chuck have got to.'

'OK, but don't be long over it.'

Luca walked outside, stood still and looked in all directions. He couldn't see his men anywhere. The kids on the beach had long gone, it was now quiet with no-one around, or at least that's what he thought. Thinking that his men would appear soon enough he turned and headed back towards the battered in front door entrance. A sudden, unexpected, unknown voice boomed out from behind him.

'Hold it right there, asshole! Put your hands up, on your head, slowly, do it now!'

A stunned Luca stopped in his tracks and reluctantly obeyed. At first, he didn't know if this person had a gun but after turning his head around he could see someone pointing a powerful hand weapon directly at him. His assailant was wearing a balaclava face mask. *Who the hell was this guy?* Luca was pushed through the doorway with the gun digging into his lower spine. Bruno who'd been by himself for five minutes nervously keeping watch was relieved to see big brother, Luca, at the door, but the feeling didn't last long.

'Put your gun down, or your mate here gets a nasty ache in his back!' ordered the person in disguise. Bruno, shocked by the turn of events, reasoned that he had no choice and dropped his pistol onto the floor of the one-time living room.

Luca was livid and felt full of rage. His prize was being snatched away from him. It was now or never. He always kept a blade up his sleeve for such eventualities. Now standing with his arms down, he let the knife slide slowly along the underside of his forearm, it eventually slipped nicely into his right hand. He waited for the moment to pounce. Silently he counted the seconds down, one, ... two, ... three, ... up to five. Now, ... go for it! Suddenly, Luca sprang off to his right before turning around quickly, intending to cut his assailant across the face. But the guy with the gun wasn't caught by surprise, he stepped back out of reach of Luca, he was someone well trained in close fighting techniques. Luca's wild slash missed its target. The Remington with the silencer went off twice and a couple of bullet holes appeared in Luca's chest. He dropped dead onto the floor. Everyone stared in disbelief at the man in the mask.

'Don't you do anything silly,' he said to Luca's brother.

Bruno, disarmed, stood transfixed. Luca had been shot and was dead. No point in going the same way, hopefully he'd be shown some mercy. He had no idea what had happened to the men who'd gone for a smoke, presumably they'd been shot too. The mystery guy knelt down and picked up Luca's knife. Whilst keeping a careful eye on Bruno, gun trained steadfastly in his direction, the man cut through the ropes that had been used to tie up El Bigote. Then, with a flick of his wrist, he threw the sharp knife into the already dead Luca's chest. Bullseye! ... no problem, he still had the knack. *You never lose it!* he thought. He told Jorge to release the others before slowly taking off his face mask to reveal his identity.

'Joseph! I thought it was you. Man, I've never been so glad to see anyone so much in my life,' shouted El Bigote. Santos and Ángel echoed his sentiments.

'Dat dead, fat dude, he call me an old man, back in *Darrien's*. He was a rude *claffy* (idiot), well I ain't so old I can't sort out a piece of shit like him. Now you, Jorge, you always so good to me, you buy my white lobster, mon. Well, I tell you now, I ain't always been a goddam fisherman. One time I was in dee U.S. of A. army, I knows how to use guns and knives and dis son of a bitch had it coming to him. What you want me do with dee udder fucker, Jorge?'

Santos thought it time to get involved. He didn't want any more bloodshed and he had some respect for Bruno. He seemed like a reasonable man, unlike Luca.

'There's no need for any more killing,' he said. He looked across at a worried Bruno, a man now all by himself and at the mercy of four others. 'Bruno, tell you what I'll do. I'll send you your money, all that you're owed for what went missing, but this feud has to stop. You go home and I do too. Is it a deal?'

'Yeah, yeah, hell yeah! You bet it's a deal!' answered Bruno, his voice full of relief. He'd yearned for a quieter life for years. If these guys were letting him go he'd return to New York, sell up the family business, there'd be plenty of takers. He could use his ill-gotten gains to carve out a new life for himself and his family away from the dangerous world of drug dealing. He'd often thought of retiring, maybe moving south to Florida where the winters were a damn site warmer.

'Me and my friends will be leaving Great Corn soon,' said Santos. 'Don't ever come looking for any of us again. I'll get what's owed to you, it'll be paid to your man in Cordoba, Carlo Pozzo isn't it?'

'Pozzo, that's right. I'll tell him to leave you well alone. It's crazy what we've been doing. Now I've lost my brothers. No big loss though, both were complete and utter assholes, in their different ways.'

'You seem like the clever one, the one that might make it to old age. Tell you what I'm going to do. You'll be left tied up on the beach. Your men will come looking when you don't turn up at the airport. They'll find you. Go back to America, all of you. Tell them you were left alive to tell the story. Don't ever, ever cross my path again!'

Santos, Ángel and El Bigote eventually headed for the airport after Bruno's hands, arms and legs were tied up by ropes, his body was then bound to a large cedar tree at the top of the beach by some cable wire found in an outhouse. Bruno was left facing east onto the waters of the Caribbean, he could maybe watch the sun come up in the morning. Pity he hadn't any shades to wear.

'Enjoy the view!' shouted Santos as he left the last remaining Andretti brother in the dark on the deserted beach. 'Remember what I said and live to be an old man one day. *Adiós, mi amigo!*'

* * * *

John and Lola watched Santos's jet land on the single runway at the island's airport. After greeting Ricky in the Departures area Lola, speaking in Spanish, went through what had happened. Hopefully his boss would turn up before eleven.

They were not to be disappointed. Santos and his companions eventually arrived along with their new best friend, the ex-U.S. army man turned lobster fisherman, Joseph. Santos was looking forward to flying off to the west coast of America. El Bigote, meanwhile, intended to catch a plane to Bluefields, sometime in the next few days, but for now both he and Joseph reckoned on hiding up in Sally Peachie until what remained of the Andretti gang had left the island. Jorge wanted to reward Joseph for his courage and friendship, several free beers and a thousand American dollars were offered and gratefully accepted. Santos trumped that by promising him ten thousand dollars, Joseph thought he'd won the lottery.

Before heading home, El Bigote and Joseph watched Santos's Cessna take off. They'd all escaped from the Andretti mob, safe and relatively unharmed. Santos had suffered a gunshot wound but he'd only been winged, it wasn't serious. Once his plane was cruising at 33,000 feet and heading rapidly north-west, he thanked the others for all their assistance and companionship, it had been an incredible adventure since leaving Mendoza in Tomás's car.

John and Lola decided that the following few hours on the journey to California would be an opportune time to discuss the plight of the Amazon rain forest again and Santos listened attentively to what they had to say. He repeated the pledge he'd made when they were at his Brazilian ranch. He'd do his best to stop further forest clearances in his adopted state of Rondônia. He knew many local and government politicians, he'd use his contacts, pull some strings. Financial support would be given to the conservation movement to protect the existing National Parks and the lands belonging to the remaining indigenous tribes.

Santos seemed in a good mood, he talked about seeing his family in Rio before too long as well as re-opening his legitimate construction business in Mendoza, but he wasn't going into retirement as far as the drugs industry was concerned. That was his most lucrative line of work and he had no moral scruples about it.

Ángel was also keen to get back to Rio, in order to see his girlfriend, Luciana, but that reunion would have to wait for at least another week because he and Santos had things to attend to on the west coast of America. He hoped she hadn't run off with someone during his absence. She was an attractive woman with many admirers and she disapproved of how her lover made his living, even if she was all too happy to accept the high life that Ángel's salary provided.

It was still dark when the plane touched down on the makeshift runway hidden in the quiet, scrub landscape of the Coastal Ranges. As expected, the dependable Ramon Fernandes was there to meet them. After thanking Santos and Ángel for the trip of a lifetime, John and Lola said their goodbyes to the men who'd become their friends. They'd meet again before too long, probably in Argentina.

Ramon, with his passengers huddled together on the back seat, headed for the Napa Valley through mile after mile of remote countryside past silhouetted hillsides and tranquil lakes. It reminded John of his first nocturnal visit to California during the previous fall when on the run from both the English and

Argentinian police. But this time he had a changed identity, a different job and a new woman in his life.

It was approaching sunrise when they turned into the Rodriguez wine estate. Ramon said he'd ring his boss as Tomás wanted to know when they were safely back in California. He dropped John and Lola off at the annexe.

The rural surroundings of the Napa Valley were quiet at this the journey's end. It was far too early for any traffic noise. Only the soothing sounds, experienced by mankind for hundreds of generations, punctured the silence ... the beautiful dawn chorus, birdsong, a pleasure humanity throughout the ages had enjoyed. Although a very different place, listening to the sounds of the natural world outside the annexe reminded John and Lola of their unforgettable experience in the rain forests of Brazil.

The lovers went inside, tired but happy to be safe and together. Hand in hand they headed straight into the shower and then the bedroom, it had been a long day and long night, but not that long, sleep could wait for a little while.

52

It had been over two months since Penny Lester's car accident and she'd recovered enough to return to work. After parking her replacement Ford Puma outside Huntingdon police station, she purposely limped her way through the entrance doors looking around to see if anyone noticed her over-egged, somewhat dramatic entry. She was greeted by a typically jovial PS Bill Conley, regular occupant of a well-worn seat at reception.

'Penny, welcome, pity about the limp though!' he bellowed.

'Great to be back, Bill. I was getting bored stupid doing crosswords and watching daytime TV.'

'The boss will be pleased. George is in his office by the way, he's just returned from Scotland. Some Cambridge academic has been found dead in a remote loch.'

'Sounds interesting, maybe I'll get a trip up there too, but maybe not, Bill. Too bloody cold in the frozen north for me. I'm becoming a soft southerner these days.'

After further small talk Lester headed upstairs to her superior's office. Following more opening pleasantries, mainly about Penny's state of health, they got down to police business. Watling filled his assistant in on all the current cases but especially what he referred to as 'the Scottish incident'. Inevitably, before too long, talk turned to a now closed case and resultant trial.

'Any more on Fen View?' asked Lester.

'You mean about supernatural happenings I suppose, Pen? Thought you might have had enough of that.'

'Too damn right, for obvious reasons, I don't fancy spending another cold night out there that's for sure or seeing any ghosts, but I was wondering, have you done any more research? Have you spoken to Mike and Michel?'

'After what happened to you it's best left alone. We know all we need to and have done everything we can. Hayes is serving time in Birmingham prison, about time too. Ripley, unfortunately, roams free, somewhere in Argentina or America.'

Watling climbed out of his seat and walked towards the window overlooking the back of the police station. He gazed at the trees, now in full leaf, a bright blue sky above all the welcome greenery. Although it was a sunny summer's day his mind went back to being with Penny in his office six months ago, with the rain lashing down outside, on a dark December afternoon. He thought about what they'd both gone through since then: the trip to Argentina, meeting with Ripley and his gangster friend, paranormal happenings, Penny's car accident. The old farm cottage on the Cambridgeshire fens had taken up much of their time over the past seven months throughout the previous autumn, winter and spring. He turned his stare away from outside and looked down at his seated colleague.

'Fen View Cottage, it's been a troubled place for years, Pen. All sorts of stuff has gone on there: tragedy, murder, early deaths, children dying, black magic practices, drug taking, violence, hauntings, illegal burials. You name it, it's probably had it. It's quite a list, the cottage of sins, sadness and the supernatural.'

Watling's desktop phone rang, it was his deputy, Pete Rigsby.

'Hi, George, I've just received a call, all about your favourite spot on the Fens!' he said. 'Something's happened, and you're not going to believe this! Are you sitting down?'

'Surprise me, Pete. Not another body, surely?' replied Watling, eager for information.

He had been standing, but on Rigby's advice, he sat down behind his desk.

'You can relax, no body this time, but the new Fen View, the one the property developer is having built. Well, apparently, it was nearing completion but overnight, get this, George, there's been a fire, one hell of a big fire, all the roof timbers have been burnt, it's caved in, most of the walls have been ruined, the only thing undamaged and intact is the steel frontage and foundations. They're stainless and don't burn apparently. Anyway, I'm off to inspect the damage, along with forensics, to look for any suspicious circumstances, arsonist at work for example. I know you've other things on your plate right now but thought you'd be interested.'

Watling thanked his deputy and asked to be kept informed before discontinuing the call.

'Do you hear that, Pen? The new Fen View, it's only gone and burned down overnight.'

'Unbelievable, boss.'

'That damn cottage, it's cursed, that's what it is!'

Acknowledgements

This follow-up to my first crime thriller novel has been over two years in the making. Started in the spring of 2022, it was eventually completed early in 2025. Writing a novel is an onerous task with all the research and seemingly endless editing process.

Whilst I may be the author, a few other people who help to advise along the road to completion have been invaluable. In particular, I would like to record my thanks to my brilliant assistants/proof readers/editors/travelling companions. Their helpful and constructive comments have been useful in so many ways.

I'd also like to thank Julie and the team at Grosvenor House Publishing for their expertise and Georgina, Max Spielmann Photographers, who turned my digital photograph into a much higher resolution picture for use as the book cover.

EPILOGUE

Much of the book is set in Argentina, a country I visited in the spring (their autumn) of 2024. I travelled from the wine country around Mendoza through the stunning arid landscapes of the Andean Pre-Cordillera to Salta, ending up in Buenos Aires. Essentially a holiday it was also an opportunity to research some of the places mentioned in this book, as well as in 'Sins of the Past'. I drank coffee at the *Essenza* café in Mendoza and toured the extensive grounds of the Parque San Martin. After exploring the city, several *bodegas* (wineries) were visited. Argentina is a place of great contrasts and the daily regime, with afternoon siestas and late nights, is very different to the UK. All the *Argentinos* I met were friendly and helpful. In most cases their English was as restricted as my Spanish but sign language and a limited vocabulary are all you need to get by. I never felt unsafe or threatened. The country's wines and food are both magnificent as is its folk music. The people's zest for life, despite the nation's economic difficulties and social discrepancies, impressed me greatly.

Who believes in ghosts? Most people don't of course. However, I have made use of my own paranormal experience in this novel. It happened a long time ago at an old railway station that had been converted into a private home. One night after going to bed I heard a terrible racket coming from the attic above my bedroom. It sounded as if furniture was being thrown around. I was wide awake, it wasn't a nightmare. Eventually I turned the light on but the noise continued before subsiding, it stopped completely after about a quarter of an hour. I was in the house by myself at the time and decided it would be a good idea to keep the bedroom light on until daybreak! I later found out that the people who'd previously lived in the place had heard strange noises and even seen an apparition. I explored the attic but there was nothing there apart from a few bits of wood. The supernatural is a subject that has fascinated mankind throughout the ages and it will, no doubt, continue to do so, even though we live in a world where increasingly everything has to have an explanation. Maybe some things just defy logic and reason?

AUTHOR PROFILE

I was born in Aldridge, Staffordshire but moved north to the Lake District as a child. After completing my secondary education at Heversham School I went to Durham University (Hatfield College) before moving on to teach at Loughborough Grammar School, specialising in geography as well as the coaching and managing of various sports. In 2007, I founded the Mercian Schools' Football League becoming its chairman and secretary. I enjoyed the busy life of a schoolmaster but, before retiring, I decided to start writing. It had been a simmering ambition ever since my younger days when I considered becoming either a journalist, environmental planner, government diplomat, or maybe even a teacher!

My interests include sport (especially football, cricket and cycling), travel both at home and abroad, social history, the natural world, red wines, walking, gardening, rock music, all things geographical and reading fiction and non-fiction (reference and history in particular), together with writing in different genres. My family and friends keep me busy also.

Back in 2011-13 I researched and wrote a family history (*Meet the Ancestors*) that went back to the C18th. I then started writing and illustrating children's stories (*The Adventures of Green George* and *The Further Adventures of Green George*) from 2014-18. Copies were given to family and friends as well as certain schools and libraries in both Leicestershire and Cumbria. By 2017, I was compiling *The Beynons of Trewern*, a detailed history of the Welsh side of my family. It was sold to family members worldwide with all proceeds going to three different charities. The National Library of Wales, in Aberystwyth, also has a copy. *Born in Birmingham* (2019) traces the English half of my family but morphed into an historical geography of the city as well. I've also compiled a social history about Heversham GS in the sixties and seventies with recollections and reflections on school life back then. My first crime thriller novel was *Sins of the Past* (published at the end of 2022), the follow-up sequel is *The Fugitives (2025)*.

Cover: *Rio de los Patos (River of the Ducks) in Barreal, NW Argentina, looking south-west towards the Andean foothills. (Author's photograph)*